I0543789

ISBN: 978-1-7330665-2-5

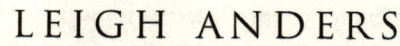

LEIGH ANDERS

RETURN TO MYSTIC HILLS

◆

Dedicated to my amazing family. You are a gift I will love and treasure always.

A special note to my brilliant granddaughter, Zoe—you inspire me in everything you do.

CHAPTER ONE

You can't run from trouble!

Sophie Cameron knew that. But lately, trouble in one form or another glommed onto her like black-bottom mud stuck to the soles of her shoes. No matter how hard she tried to shake it loose, some of it hung on. Sometimes, it spread to other things.

Her ex-husband, Robert, called her "The Fixer," ignoring the fact that she hadn't been able to fix their marriage. But that was a two-person job, and Robert hadn't been inclined to assist with the fix. Robert was right about one thing, though: Sophie never shied away from difficulties or challenges. But recently, she had lost her touch. Some situations were just not fixable. The recent death of her beloved father was one of them. And while there might be a fix for her latest trouble, she didn't even know where to begin or how deep the trouble was.

Frustrated that she couldn't make sense of what she was looking at, Sophie leaned back in her chair and ran her hands through her hair, tossing the auburn strands into a halo of messy curls around her head. She had stared at numbers for so long this morning, her eyesight blurred. But the numbers never changed, so she was starting to think that it might be the financial future of Cameron Stables that was blurred, not her eyesight. And that both surprised and frightened her.

She needed a break, a few minutes away from columns of numbers and business records. A morning ride into the mountains might help her regain perspective. Maybe inspiration would hit and merge her scattered thoughts into one single idea.

Sophie left the house and walked to the barn. She squashed a spark of guilt over leaving unfinished business, but the desk littered with her father's handwritten accounting journals and unpaid bills would be there waiting for her when she returned to the house. This was that sticky-mud kind of trouble you couldn't escape.

Sophie saddled Rose, her sorrel mare, mounted, and rode out of the stable yard.

"Come on, Rose! Let's run!" Sophie urged the mare into a gallop as they passed the gate to the pasture. Rose responded instantly and stretched her long legs into a smooth, rhythmic stride as she raced across the open field. Sophie closed her eyes and raised her face to the brisk wind stirred by Rose's pace.

Exhilarated by the wind in her face and the feeling of power in the pounding hooves beneath her, Sophie urged Rose to run even faster. In a matter of minutes, they reached the far side of the pasture, near the base of the high meadow. Sophie slowed Rose to a walk and relaxed back in the saddle.

The burst of speed had cleared and sharpened Sophie's mind, something the three cups of strong coffee she'd downed this morning had failed to accomplish. A run with Rose was Sophie's magic potion, guaranteed to always make her feel better… at least temporarily.

"Good girl! My sweet Irish Rose." Using the mare's pedigree name, Sophie rubbed Rose's neck affectionately and guided her onto the path leading up to the higher elevation. They soon reached the trail that would take them through the dense woods of Mystic Hills and to its highest peak.

Sophie shivered and pulled her sweater tighter around her as she entered the shady trail. The April air carried a sharp chill, helped along by an umbrella of thick tree branches that overlapped each other and turned the trail into a cool, dark tunnel. She should have chosen a heavier jacket, but in Tampa, where she had lived for the last few years, dressing for cold mornings wasn't something she had to think about. When Sophie decided to take her impromptu ride, she forgot that even the rising sun streaking the pastures with bands of gold wasn't an accurate indicator of the temperature on the mountain.

Rose steadily worked her way up the familiar path with little prompting from Sophie. She paused briefly when they came to a fork in the trail. Sophie guided Rose onto the path to the right, bypassing the left fork, which led into the dense, dark woods—a tract of tall native trees that loomed over piles of damp, rotted stumps, fallen tree limbs, and a tangled mass of underbrush.

While the activities of the nocturnal creatures that lived in the dark woods made it an interesting place at night, it offered little that interested Sophie this morning. More darkness in her life right now was the last thing she needed. No, her destination was the bright sunshine on the peak that overlooked the green meadows and valley. It was the perfect place to temporarily forget all problems, including those that made Sophie flee the office this morning.

The mountainous area through which Sophie rode, with its high, craggy peak, was a local geological phenomenon, a landmass that was a cross between hills and mountains. It wasn't tall enough to be classified as mountains, but with its cliffs, rocky outcrops, and deep ravines, it possessed a more rugged terrain than the surrounding countryside. A quirk of nature had mistakenly plunked the four-hundred-acre formation down in the midst of the rolling meadows and grasslands that were common to this part of central Kentucky.

The planters who migrated to this region from Virginia after the American Revolutionary War grabbed up most of the flat land, leaving this particular acreage unclaimed. The Camerons were horsemen and didn't need large swaths of farmland the same way the tobacco and cotton farmers did. The smaller parcels of flat land adjacent to the hills were adequate as pastures for their horses, so they claimed it for their homestead.

The Cameron Clan, Scots-Irish and proud of it, came from a land where the unexplained was as common as the shamrock and the Irish jig. They firmly believed that only nature's magic could have created this unusual section of land. According to the stories they told, they had seen fairies and possibly even leprechauns in the dark woods.

The Camerons brought their Celtic storytelling traditions with them to America, so the tale fit easily into other family narratives. Still attached to the myths and traditions of their homeland—and to bolster their fairy theory—they named the whole area Mystic Hills and called the dark wooded area Fairy Woods.

"What do you think, Rose? Do fairies live in Fairy Woods? Or was that just a fairytale made up by my prankster-loving ancestors?"

Rose responded with a toss of her head, rattling the rings on her bridle, and a snort.

"Is that a 'No' or an 'I don't know'? Well, I don't know, either. I've never seen one, but if I do, I have a lot of questions for them. I want to find out if there's such a thing as Irish luck and where I can find it."

Sophie left the shadows of the trees at the end of the trail and guided Rose out into the sunshine on the flat crest at the top of Mystic Peak. She pulled Rose to a halt, loosened her hold on the reins, and leaned back in the saddle. Rose began grazing on clumps of grass near her hooves.

The panoramic view of the valley was breathtaking, especially at this time of year—spring. The only thing that could rival it was when the leaves changed and the valley blazed with fall colors. Today, though, the redbud and dogwood trees were in full bloom, contrasting brightly against the dark-green pine, poplar, and sycamore trees. Yet more color came from the meadows, pockmarked with large patches of yellow daisies, wild lilies, and buttercups. Puffy clouds shaped like blobs of whipped cream had pushed away all remnants of fog and left behind a bright blue sky hanging over the valley and meadows. Only the calls of the birds nesting in the trees disturbed the quiet of the morning.

Sophie took a deep breath, filling her lungs with sweet-smelling air as a gentle breeze brushed her cheeks. So peaceful! She'd missed this spot, which her father had introduced her to when she was barely old enough to sit in a saddle. Just like a ride with Rose, the view from the peak always refreshed her perspective on things—both good and bad.

Over the last few years, her move to Tampa after college, her marriage to Robert, and then forming and launching a new marketing agency with him had demanded most of her attention and energy. Sophie now regretted letting those things— even the effort to save her marriage before its eventual failure— completely take over her life. She'd given up one of her favorite things to do—riding to the peak with Rose.

The sound of a helicopter suddenly disrupted the morning quiet. Rose's ears spiked forward at the sound. She pranced sideways, snorted, and tossed her head in disapproval as the intruding sound moved closer.

"Whoa. Easy, Rose. It'll be gone soon." Sophie patted the mare's neck as a helicopter came into view from the east, flying at low altitude, and on track to pass over them. The helicopter's propellors whirled in cadence with the well-tuned engine, and the sound grew louder as it approached. It was close enough for Sophie to read the blue lettering, "Whittaker & Co.," painted on its side. The pilot looked down and gave Sophie a quick wave as he flew by. She returned his wave.

The sharp staccato sound quickly faded to a dull rumble as the helicopter moved on to the west. Sophie shaded her eyes with her hand and followed its route as it banked to the right and then turned northward before dropping out of sight behind a tree-lined hill.

As the sound receded, Sophie shifted in the saddle and immediately forgot the helicopter. She took another deep breath, and her wandering thoughts circled back to the issue she rode up here with the intention of forgetting for a while. And for a brief moment, it *had* slipped her mind, replaced by gentle breezes, thoughts of fairy magic, and the beauty of the countryside.

Mystic Peak *was* a good place to think, so Sophie gave up trying to ignore the issue that had nagged at her for a few days now.

There was nothing she could do to fix the loss of her father, George Cameron, a month ago. Suddenly and without warning, he suffered a massive heart attack while unloading bales of hay in the barnyard. Sophie and her mother were unprepared for the worst event of their lives. Her father's passing left a hole so large, Sophie doubted it could ever be filled. Was the old adage, "Time can heal a broken heart," actually true? Sophie hoped so, but she wasn't counting on it.

While the loss of her father had been the gut punch that knocked the wind right out of her, it was not her only problem.

The second kick life gave her as she mourned her father's death was that the business he had built from scratch was in deep financial trouble. Cameron Stables, an endeavor that had filled him with pride, teetered on the verge of bankruptcy.

On her visits home from Tampa, Sophie had noticed the gradual changes around Cameron Stables. Her father had reduced the number of horses he boarded to only those belonging to his oldest clients and had reduced the staff to only two employees, one full-time and one part-time. He stopped offering riding lessons and horse training, so weeds had taken over the track and training paddock. The rental cabins were boarded up, and tourists no longer came for vacations. Sophie assumed her father was getting ready to retire and was cutting back his workload. Her father, always the optimistic Scots-Irishman, never showed that he was worried about his failing business. Sophie had *assumed* when she should have been *asking* questions.

Her personal drama—her divorce from Robert—had distracted her. She hadn't paid enough attention to the changes at home or questioned the reasons behind the changes. Her father should have asked her for help, but his stubborn pride kept him from doing that. She blamed herself for being too wrapped up in her personal life to realize what was happening at home.

After the funeral, Sophie's mother, Jean, shared what she knew about the state of Cameron Stables' finances: "Business is down because people prefer to visit theme parks rather than come to a horse farm. The local economy is on a downturn, too, so boarding and training horses isn't in demand like it used to be. Financial problems just piled on, and your father didn't know what to do to get the business back on track. I tried to convince him to talk to you, but you know how he thought he could handle everything on his own."

So, Sophie's father had scaled back services, and that had further exacerbated the business's financial slide. The business was drowning in debt. Its revenue wasn't close to keeping up with expenses.

The stack of unpaid bills Sophie found on her first foray into her father's office reinforced the story—and the story was dire. Even Jean didn't realize the full extent of the financial pressures the business was under.

Sophie sold her half of the marketing agency to Robert and moved back home to help her mother try to salvage what was left of her father's business. Or at least get it out of debt. Or do something. She wasn't sure what that "something" was just yet. Sophie needed to come up with a solution soon, or they might lose the property or have to sell part of it to settle their debts. That worst-case scenario was something she didn't want to contemplate. Losing the land that had been in the family for generations would be a black stain on her father's name forever.

Selling her half of the marketing strategy company in Tampa and moving home had not been a hard decision. After more than a year as only business partners, it was becoming clear that she and Robert were no better as business partners than they were as marriage partners. They had differing ideas on just about everything, professionally as well as personally. Sophie would be more useful at home than continuing the tug-of-war she and Robert engaged in every day.

Her divorce from Robert was yesterday's story. They were still friends, and she had placed the marriage in the bin marked "failures to learn from" and tightly locked the lid. Done and over! There were no questions to be asked or answered by her or Robert. Theirs was truly a "no fault" divorce.

A movement below and beyond the fence line separating the Cameron property from their neighbor's caught Sophie's eye. A large bay gelding, its muscular flanks glistening in the sun, topped a rise. The rider guided the horse down the slope, then dismounted on the Thornton side of the railed fence.

Sophie stood in her stirrups, straining for a better look. The man was not Mr. Barnes, the manager of the neighboring property, Thornton Farms. She was certain of that. Who was he then, and what was he doing here? Small game could still be found in the woods on Mystic Hills. Was he a poacher? The distance was too far to see his face, but he didn't appear to be carrying a rifle in his saddle gear. Not a poacher then, but Sophie instinctively knew that he was a stranger. What was he doing on her neighbor's property?

Sophie flicked Rose's reins and urged her across the plateau until she found the path leading down to the meadow and the fence row. The trail was almost perpendicular in spots, but Rose didn't hesitate to step onto the steep path. Sophie leaned back in the saddle as she angled the mare down the slope. Rose picked her way over the loose rocks and gravel until they reached the meadow at the bottom of the trail. Then, Sophie urged Rose into a trot, and they quickly crossed the meadow. As Sophie drew closer to the fence line, the stranger climbed over the railings to the Cameron side and started nailing a poster to a fence post.

The man looked around, alerted to Sophie's presence by Rose's nickered greeting to the gelding and the gelding's snorted response. He tossed the hammer back over the fence, then turned to watch Sophie's approach. Sophie stopped Rose several feet from the stranger but stayed mounted. She could quickly ride away if he turned out to be up to no good or posed a threat to her.

She was right—he was a stranger and new to this area—but something about him nibbled at the back of Sophie's mind. He reminded her of someone. But who? A TV star, a movie actor, or just someone she had met someplace—maybe at an ad cam-

paign launch event? She might recognize him if she could see
his face clearly, but his chin was covered by a stubble beard and
his face was hidden by the brim of a battered Stetson hat pulled
low over shaggy, unruly hair. Dark sunglasses hid his eyes.

The stranger didn't move. His hands rested lightly against
faded denim jeans—jeans that tapered down his legs and ended
over scuffed and worn Western-style boots. The boots were now
planted in a wide, relaxed stance as the man waited patiently for
Sophie to speak. She remained quiet as her eyes moved slowly
over him, still trying to place him. By the slight tilt of his head,
Sophie knew he was inspecting her in the same way and steadily staring—or glaring—back at her.

A sudden burst of memory clarified who he reminded her
of: the "Marlboro Man." Of course! He looked just like the rugged, iconic cowboy of TV commercial fame.

Sophie had learned about the "Marlboro Man" in one of her
college marketing classes. It was a case study in how a manu-
factured image could successfully be used to persuade people
to buy products—even products that were bad for them. But it
was also an example of how public pressure for companies to
be more socially responsible could derail an ad campaign, even
one as popular as the hot "smoking" cowboy in the cigarette
commercials.

Studying the "Marlboro Man" ads in a classroom setting
was one thing, but seeing his likeness in person was a whole
new experience. This man was a creative director's dream. He
was genuine, and nothing about him looked fake or manufac-
tured. Without any enhancements by studio stylists, he could
easily play the role of a tough rough-around-the-edges cowboy,
untamed, free-spirited, and independent—the qualities that had
made the "Marlboro Man" ad campaign so successful.

The stranger pulled open his leather jacket and settled his
hands on his hips, a sign that he was prepared to wait her out.

Sophie didn't look away. Neither spoke.

Rose stamped her feet and swished her tail, slapping it hard against Sophie's thigh and reminding her of why they had raced down to the meadow. Sophie suppressed a smile. Drooling over a stranger, "hot guy" that he was, wasn't the reason.

Sophie had met and worked with handsome men before. They were a common commodity in her industry. But there was something different about this man. Maybe it was in the way he carried himself—confident, self-possessed, and comfortable in who he was.

"You're speechless," the cowboy stated, ending their stare-down and breaking the silence. His voice sounded annoyed by her continued inspection, and his mouth turned up on one side in a knowing smile.

"Yes… no!" Sophie corrected herself, flustered. "No! I'm not," she emphasized. She'd been caught fantasizing about him with what could be loosely described as open-mouthed awe. And he knew it. Heat rose in her cheeks, but she refused to be embarrassed into silence. She still wanted to know who he was and what he was doing here on her land.

The stranger's relaxed stance indicated that he wasn't a threat, so Sophie walked Rose closer to him. She stopped within a few feet, but she still couldn't clearly see his face beneath the hat brim or gage what he was thinking behind his dark glasses. But she *could* see his mouth still curved into a smirk. Ah, so he was familiar with her reaction. Obviously, it was the same one he got from most women he met. She added "conceited and arrogant" to her mental description of him.

"What're you doing here, *cowboy*?" Sophie asked sharply, annoyed by his smugness and the uneasy feeling that he had read her thoughts. "Don't you know that this is private proper-ty?" The question slipped out before she could soften or moder-ate her words. Her emphasis on *cowboy* sounded condescending, even to her, and her question came out as a rude demand. She had high regard for cowboys, but it served him right—payment for his arrogant and satisfied smirk.

The cowboy didn't answer right away. His mouth lost its smirk and tightened into a thin, straight line. She had offended him. Undeterred, Sophie was about to repeat the question when he finally spoke. "Yes, ma'am. Ah… reckon I know that," the cowboy drawled slowly.

Sophie waited impatiently for him to go on. His terse reply matched her earlier "Marlboro Man" characterization—a laconic cowboy and a man of few words.

The cowboy rubbed his stubble-covered chin, pursed his lips, and added, "I'm putting up new signs so *everyone* will know it's private property." He pointed to the "no trespassing" sign he had nailed to the fence post nearby. "I'm checking the fence line, making sure none of the posts are broken. And looking for anything else that's wrong. Boss don't want the horses to get loose or get injured on a broken fence."

Sophie was further annoyed that with his slow drawl, it took him forever to spit out his answer. He slowly and mockingly emphasized each of his reasons for being there, just short of counting them off on his fingers. Judging by his reply, she wasn't the only one annoyed in this encounter.

"The fence is jointly owned, just so you know."

"I do know, ma'am. That doesn't mean I can't fix broken spots without permission." He shrugged his shoulders and added, "It's the law."

"You're Mrs. Thornton's hired hand? She moving back here? I had no idea." Sophie ignored his reminder about fencing laws. She was more curious about Mrs. Thornton moving back to Thornton Farms. "She's been away a long time."

"Whoa there, ma'am." He raised a hand to slow her down. "You can say I work for the owner, but Mrs. Thornton sold the place—to Mr. Whittaker."

"Sold? I don't…"

"Yes, ma'am. I reckon she sold. At least, that's what Whittaker claims. I don't think he's a squatter or is lying." The cowboy moved closer to the fence, grabbed a post, and shook it, checking its sturdiness in the ground.

"New owner? Mrs. Thornton sold?" Sophie repeated. "I can't believe she'd do that. This property has been in the Thornton family for generations."

"As you indicated, I'm just the hired hand, miss." The cowboy shrugged his shoulders, then again rested his hand on his hips. "I don't know the particulars, but I suspect it got mighty expensive to just let the place sit here unoccupied." He added, "Yes ma'am, mighty expensive."

"I'm shocked she would sell." Sophie was having a hard time processing the revelation that the neighboring farm had changed hands. Large farms in this part of Kentucky rarely changed hands and were usually passed down to the next generation.

"She sold, ma'am."

"What's the new owner, Mr. Whittaker, like?" Sophie was curious about the man who would buy the old house and property. Would he force a new imprint on the property or would he respect the history of a house more than 250 years old? Moreover, it was hard to accept that Mrs. Thornton would sell the property at all, since four generations of Thorntons had lived there. "I guess that was his helicopter that flew over earlier, then?"

"Yup! It was his 'copter. But as to your question about Mr. Whittaker, some people like him, some don't. I've got no major complaints about him." He didn't volunteer any additional details.

"Is there a Mrs. Whittaker? I mean… maybe I should pay

her a visit and welcome her to Kingsville."

"No, there's no missus. I'm just guessing here, but Mr. Whittaker might feel he's too old to take on a wife now. Not at his age. But some women still find him attractive. There's no accounting for some people's taste." He smiled as if he enjoyed the gibe at his employer. "By the way, who might you be, miss?"

"I'm Sophie. Sophie Cameron. Our land joins Thornton Farms… or Whittaker Farms… or whatever the new name is." Sophie nodded over her shoulder toward the other side of the meadow.

"Sophie." The stranger tilted his head to one side, studied her for a moment, then nodded in confirmation. "I heard about your father. I'm very sorry for your loss." He added, "If you need anything, Mr. Whittaker will be happy to help out."

"Thank you, and thank Mr. Whittaker. We have everything under control." Sophie's reply was short and formal as she struggled to keep tears from pooling in her eyes at the mention of her father's death.

"As much as I'd like to stand here and chat, I reckon I'd better be on my way. Don't want the boss to dock my pay." The cowboy turned and walked to the fence. Placing a booted foot on one of the rails, he quickly hoisted himself over the fence. Once on the other side, he turned to Sophie. "I've got a long fence row to inspect, and who knows what problems I'll find. See you around, Miss Sophie."

"Let me know what you find. Cameron Stables always pays their share of repairs."

"I doubt that's necessary, but I'll leave that up to you and the boss." He took off his sunglasses and wiped them on his shirt. Sophie caught a brief glimpse of dark-brown eyes that smiled briefly at her before disappearing back behind the glasses.

"Let's go, Big Boy!" the stranger said to his horse as he mounted and picked up the reins. He touched the brim of his hat in goodbye, then turned his horse and galloped northward along the fence row.

Sophie watched him ride away, admiring the way he sat in the saddle. He was an experienced rider, a skill that confirmed Sophie's suspicions that he had actually worked as a cowboy and ranch hand. He paused at the top of the rise, turned in the saddle, and waved his hat at Sophie before riding out of sight on the other side of the hill.

The news of the sale of Thornton Farms had made her forget to ask Cowboy his name or learn much of anything about Mr. Whittaker. The sale wasn't the only thing that had distracted her, though. Her stoic range rider's behavior was hard to figure out. He seemed to be teasing and provoking her for reasons only he knew. Also, did anyone talk *that* folksy these days, even cowboys?

Sophie quickly dismissed the cowboy's behavior and instead mulled over the fact that Thornton Farms had been sold. Seeing the old Thornton Mansion restored would be a good thing for the community. After Mr. Thornton had died in an auto accident, his wife, Muriel, had leased the land to local farmers and turned the house over to caretakers. Muriel, with her teenaged daughter, Lynn, had returned to Lexington, the city of her birth. She rarely returned to Thornton Farms and only made short visits to check on the house and property. Like any house that stood vacant for years, it now needed repairs and renovation.

It was a waste for the property to sit unoccupied, but Sophie disliked the thought of strangers moving in and not appreciating its history and colonial charm. Would Mr. Whittaker recognize the jewel he now owned and restore it to its original splendor? Or would he tear it down and replace it with a modern monstrosity?

Rose suddenly tossed her head and strained against the reins, shaking Sophie from her preoccupation with Thornton

Farms and its new owner.

"Is it breakfast ye be wanting, my Irish Rose?" Sophie asked in a bad imitation of an Irish brogue. "Let's go home, then." Sophie turned Rose around and rode southwest, across the meadow and around the base of Mystic Peak. Breakfast sounded good to her, too.

The encounter and verbal combat with Cowboy had been a short diversion from thinking about what she should be thinking about—what to do to rectify Cameron Stables' bleak financial picture.

As Sophie had hoped when she rode out this morning, she now felt energized by the cool morning ride and more optimistic that there was a way out of their financial hole. But finding that way out was going to take some good old-fashioned Scotsman's grit, along with an Irishman's ingenuity.

CHAPTER TWO

S unlight glinted through the trees and dotted the roof of the spacious and comfortable home as Sophie and Rose neared the main house. Sophie critically examined the exterior, searching for any maintenance issues that might further add to the property's red ink. The house still looked solid and without any noticeable need for repairs. Her father had apparently kept up the maintenance on the house even as his business fell apart. Good! One less thing to worry about.

The house was an unpretentious two-story redbrick in the Georgian architectural style and much smaller than many of its neighbors, but also much newer. The original family home was unsalvageable and so unsafe that when her parents married and came to live there, her father had replaced the old, dilapidated structure with a new, modern house that mimicked some of the features of the original house.

George Cameron's imprint was everywhere in the house and on all corners of the property. It was heartbreaking to know that she would never again hear his voice or his joyful laughter. Sophie couldn't imagine how she would adapt to him not being there, much less how her mother would fare.

The years Sophie had spent growing up in their loving home were so happy, she hadn't been prepared for what life handed her once she left. She had thought all marriages were like her parents.' "Fooled you," life kept saying until she and Robert decided to end their unhappy marriage after only two years. It had barely been a marriage. Toward the end, "cohabitation" would best describe their relationship.

Pete, the man who took care of the horses, came out to meet Sophie when she rode into the stable yard. Sophie turned Rose over to him to unsaddle, rub down, and feed while he fed and watered the other horses. At one time, her father had employed as many as ten men full time and several young men as part-time workers in the stables, plus a couple of women that took care of the rental cabins. Pete and a part-timer, Ben, were all that remained.

Sophie crossed the stable yard and took the winding path shaded by silver maples and black oak trees that led from the barn to the main house. She passed her mother's vegetable garden, which was already showing signs of growth as the seedlings popped up through the rich soil. A rose garden near the back porch was further evidence of her mother's favorite pastime. The rose bushes were starting to bud and would soon be in bloom, providing sweet-smelling roses throughout the house.

Her mother had driven to Paducah yesterday to assist Aunt Rachel, Jean's sister, who was recovering from surgery for a shoulder injury. Aunt Rachel had lost her husband five years ago to cancer, and she and Uncle Joe never had children. She lived alone, so as a retired nurse, Jean was the perfect person to help in her recovery.

Sophie had encouraged her mother to go and spend time

with Aunt Rachel. A change of scenery would be good for Jean and might focus her mind on something other than the painful reminders of the husband she had lost, which she must surely see in every room of the house.

Sophie entered the house through a side door. Patsy, the woman who had cleaned the Cameron house since she started a cleaning service, was working in the kitchen when Sophie walked in.

"Honey! I'm home!" Sophie exclaimed with a laugh.

"Sophie! It's about time! Welcome back!" Patsy, a woman in her mid-thirties, turned from the stove top she was cleaning, crossed the room, and hugged Sophie. "Jean hasn't talked about anything else since she found out you were moving back. She needs you."

"I know, and I'm sorry I haven't come home sooner, like I should have. I wrapped up everything in Tampa last week. This past year has been long and hectic, but I'm home now. Permanently," Sophie replied as she returned Patsy's hug.

"Your mother understands why you didn't come more often. But you're here now and with people who will treat you right— like you should be treated."

"Your flattery is good for my ego, but I was just as much at fault for the marriage falling apart as Robert was. Right now, I need food more than an ego boost." Sophie spotted the coffee pot on the counter. "And I see you made another pot of coffee. You're the best, Patsy!"

Sophie went to the coffee pot, poured herself a cup, and added cream from the pitcher. She took a croissant from the plate on the counter and a jar of grape jelly from the refrigerator, then sat down at the kitchen table in front of a sunny bay window.

"Patsy, did you know that Thornton Farms has been sold? I just found out this morning."

Patsy usually knew everything that went on in the Kingsville area. She never gossiped about her clients, but Sophie's quest for information wasn't about personal details—exactly.

"Yes, I knew," Patsy said as she put the bottle of cleaner under the sink, then pulled a large mixing bowl from the cupboard. Patsy frequently did more than clean at the Cameron house. She often baked bread, pies, and cakes for Sophie's mother when she came to clean the house. Jean had retired from nursing, but she still volunteered at the local hospital, in addition to helping out around Cameron Stables. She didn't have the time to bake, and since Patsy liked baking, it became a Friday ritual for the fifteen years she had worked for Jean.

Patsy went to the pantry and came back with an armful of baking supplies. She started measuring flour into the bowl. "The sale just happened recently. Lynn Thornton called me to ask if I could send a crew over there to clean the place up. Mr. Whittaker wasn't there when I went by to check on my crew, but it sounds like he's giving Lynn the run of the place. She's even hiring the staff. She hired my sister Mattie and her husband Ken to work there." Patsy opened the refrigerator and reached in for a carton of eggs. Her voice was muffled as she asked, "But how did you find out about the sale this morning?"

"I met this macho cowboy while on my ride to Mystic Peak. He's the 'Marlboro Man' in the flesh, right down to the Stetson hat and rancher's jacket." Sophie took a sip of coffee and slathered some jelly on her croissant, then added, "He's a hired hand of Mr. Whittaker's and said he was checking for problems with the fence line between our property and Thornton Farms."

"Ooh, 'Marlboro Man!' I wish I had been with you! I haven't seen a man that good looking since they canceled those TV commercials," Patsy replied. "This cowboy must be something to have made *that* kind of impression on you! This is horse country, you know, and cowboys are common—pretend ones, anyway."

"No, not really. I'm just using 'Marlboro Man' figuratively, as a way to describe how he was dressed. You do know that the men in the commercials were played by multiple men, don't you? And that the images on TV of the rugged, handsome heroes were mostly created in a movie studio? Most of them were pretend cowboys, too."

"Yes, I've heard that. I became a teenager just before they canceled the ads. At that age, though, I thought they were all real hunks. I can see why people wanted to model themselves after him. But you say this cowboy was handsome and sexy and you only noticed how he was dressed? Sure! Like I believe that!" Patsy laughed and wiggled her eyebrows at Sophie.

"I didn't say handsome or sexy. *You* did! Besides, he seemed full of himself, like all the women he meets react the same way I..." Sophie stopped talking and laughed. "Okay, I'll stop digging that hole deeper." Hoping to get the conversation off of Cowboy and back onto the sale of Thornton Farms, she asked, "Does Mom know Thornton Farms was sold? She didn't mention it."

"I doubt she knows. It was very quiet. And she's been so busy, what with grieving the loss of your father, running Cameron Stables, and now helping Rachel. She's barely had time to breathe. It's really good that you came home. She needs you."

"I know. I plan to concentrate on the business. That will relieve her of at least one burden. But back to Lynn Thornton. You said she has the run of the place. Are she and Mr. Whittaker an item?" The cowboy had said that Mr. Whittaker was old and not interested in marriage, but that didn't mean he wouldn't be romantically involved with someone.

"I don't know about them being an item, but Sophie, you know Lynn. As my momma, God rest her soul, would say, Lynn Thornton would chase anything in britches. As for the cowboy, I imagine Mr. Whittaker brought some of his own people with him."

"Yes, I know Lynn, but it's been over fifteen years since I last saw her. We had just finished tenth grade when her father died, and she moved away."

In high school, Lynn could be a little intimidating to the more down-to-earth girls. She had long golden-blonde hair, blue eyes, the latest style of clothes, and was very popular. She demanded to be the center of attention, and she usually got it. Sophie, in her braces and glasses, with brown hair and pale brown eyes, felt geeky and gangly next to Lynn. That all changed some time after Lynn moved away, when Sophie's hair lightened to auburn and her eyes appeared more green than brown once she shed the glasses.

"I never wanted to join Lynn's crowd. Maybe I was a coward and knew I couldn't compete with her. We were friends as children but moved in different circles once we became teenagers. Maybe she's changed now."

"Hmph," Patsy said. "We can hope leopards change their spots. She's living at Thornton Farms at the moment. She runs an interior design company in Lexington. She's helping with the restoration, preserving the original décor and the Thornton family heritage. That's her story at least, but I can't help thinking she has bigger plans."

"That makes sense," Sophie commented. "About the restoration, I mean."

"Yes, but this is Lynn we're talking about. I haven't forgotten how she broke my brother Jimmy's heart when she wasn't yet fifteen. He was seventeen, and I tried to convince him that she was just playing with him. I imagine her entrapment skills are even more honed and sharpened by now." Pasty added a cup of shredded coconut to the cake batter. Her folding action sounded more like beating as she mixed in the coconut. Lynn's treatment of her brother apparently still rankled. And keeping gossip and critical comments about her clients to a minimum didn't include Lynn Thornton.

"When we were that age, we all had a broken heart at least once a month." Sophie smiled at the memory of teenage angst. "When did Thornton Farms sell?"

"Just recently. I'm not sure of the exact date. The property was never listed for sale, so it must have been a private arrangement. The people of Kingsville are happy about it, though. They need jobs." Patsy finished mixing the cake batter and poured it into cake pans, then popped them into the oven and set a timer. "Mattie and Ken were thrilled to be hired. They both lost their jobs when the local racetrack closed down."

"Do you know anything about the new owner, Mr. Whittaker?" Cowboy hadn't divulged many details. Sophie's interest was piqued by the man who was now her neighbor.

"I know only that he's a wealthy businessman. When Mattie met him after Lynn hired her, she asked him where he was born. He said Chicago. You know Mattie. She never meets a stranger. She asked him if that made him a 'damn Yankee,' and he said, 'damned maybe,' but since he moved to the South, he didn't qualify as a 'Yankee.' Appears he has a sense of humor. Mattie and Ken both like him. They don't care where he's from if he can keep them employed and pay them well. I guess he likes Mattie, too, because he asked her to be the head housekeeper."

"I wonder why he moved here. Kingsville isn't exactly a thriving metropolis. What would bring a wealthy businessman from Chicago to central Kentucky? I wonder about his plans for the property."

"He told Mattie that he wants to make Thornton Farms an important part of the community again. 'A landmark,' he called it, 'that should be preserved.'"

"That's encouraging. The Thornton house used to be the

center of social life around Kingsville, didn't it?" Sophie asked. "The horse-racing crowd from Churchill Downs or from Lexington were frequent visitors. My parents attended a couple holiday events there."

"Pretty much," Patsy said. "But none of my folks were invited."

"I only went there for a couple playdates with Lynn. I was very much in awe of the grandeur of the big house. The towering columns in front are enormous, and inside, there's a staircase that goes on forever. It looked very impressive to a five-year-old."

"Mr. Whittaker is fixing the place up and pouring a lot of money into it—at least, according to Mattie." The timer on the oven went off, and Patsy opened the door and pulled the two cake pans from the oven. She stuck a toothpick in to test if it was done, nodded, then set them on the granite countertop. "They've started redoing the ballroom and the downstairs."

"I'm glad he's serious about fixing it up and not tearing it down."

"Me too. I wonder if he'll have parties like the Thorntons did. I can imagine young debutants floating around the ballroom on the arms of handsome men all dressed up in their tuxes." Patsy's face took on a dreamy look. "Young bachelors will be asking you to go with them. Robert will be very jealous."

"Patsy, honey," Sophie laughed, "there aren't any debutants in Kingsville. You've got to stop watching those reality TV dating shows. Our town isn't exactly teeming with handsome bachelors, either. Besides, Robert and I are friends, and he's moved on. Right now, I have more pressing things to worry about than dating and parties."

"Are you saying that you're done with dating? At your age?" Patsy sent Sophie a knowing smile. "Macho Cowboy might be free," she said as she started mixing frosting for the cake.

"Pfft!" Sophie shook her head at Patsy. "You're incorrigible. Speaking of my more important and pressing matters, I'll be in my father's office." Sophie rose from the table, walked to the coffee pot, poured herself another cup of coffee, added cream, and then turned to Patsy. "You can skip that room if you haven't already cleaned it. Knock on the door if you need something."

Sophie left the kitchen and walked down the hall toward her father's office.

CHAPTER THREE

S ophie entered her father's office with dread.

"Suck it up," she told herself. "It's something you have to do." She fervently hoped she wouldn't find more past-due bills, but getting a full and clear picture—even a bad one—of how much debt they carried was the first step in plugging the business's financial hole—a hole that got deeper with each bill she opened.

Sophie had already opened a new bank account for Cameron Stables under her and her mother's names at the local Kingsville Bank. Using her personal funds, Sophie had made a deposit large enough to cover the outstanding bills—or, at least she hoped it would cover all of them.

This morning before she fled to the mountain, she had made at least partial payments to each of the vendors through the bank's website. She would send more later once she felt satisfied that she saw the complete picture—and as long as her money held out.

Her father was a hands-on businessman, a people person who preferred the operational side of his business. He was good at that. He liked working with the horses and getting to know his clients and vacationers personally. Keeping complete and accurate records was never his top priority. His badly kept accounting records took the form of handwritten paper journals.

With the exception of his mobile phone, he didn't own any other digital devices. It was Sophie's laptop that now sat on top of the desk. He probably wouldn't have internet and Wi-Fi in the house if it hadn't come as a package with the cable TV and if her mother hadn't demanded it.

Instead of GAAP—generally accepted accounting principles—her father apparently followed the "out of sight, out of mind" accounting method—bury financial records in with the junk mail and hope they're never seen again. There were stacks of paper in several corners of the room, in addition to the desk drawers, but the largest hoard was in the tall bookcase on one side of the room. Where most people would keep books, her father had devoted the shelves to stacks of magazines, newspaper clippings, old greeting cards, notebooks, and other miscellaneous papers. After a cursory look through the bottom shelves, Sophie decided those could wait for later. She couldn't deal with that mess right now.

The top drawer on the right side of the desk was where she had found the stash of unpaid bills. The desire to search the desk further had dissipated quickly when she opened the second drawer. To say it was disorganized would be putting it kindly. More aptly put, it was one more place where paper clutter went to die.

Sophie now peaked into the second drawer again. Maybe the fairies had straightened it since she last checked. No such luck. It was still a jumbled mess of papers and junk mail her father had saved for reasons only he knew. She quickly pawed through the pile, looking for anything relevant to Cameron Stables' debt crisis. Not seeing anything, she slammed the drawer shut, making the same lackluster promise she'd made to herself about the bookshelves—she'd get back to it later.

That left the drawers on the other side of the desk. Sophie opened the top drawer and found pens, paper clips, a stapler, rubber bands, and an assortment of dust bunnies. She moved onto the larger drawer below. More junk.

"Really, Dad?" she groaned as she pulled out old brochures, instruction booklets that came with the purchase of farm equipment, and flyers promoting events whose dates had long passed. "Why don't *these* belong in the bookcase?"

So far, she hadn't unearthed any more bills. That was encouraging. She reached into the back of the drawer, and her hands hit something solid. Her heart sank when she pulled out a bundle of envelopes held together by a rubber band. A moment later, she took a deep breath, relieved when she saw handwriting on the envelopes rather than the logo of an angry creditor.

"What's this?" she wondered as she removed the rubber band from the bundle and flipped through the stack of letters. They looked like personal letters, and according to the postmarked date, they were arranged chronologically and dated back several years. She opened the first letter, postmarked 2004, and started to read.

Dear Mr. C,

Just wanted to let you know I'm okay. I took your advice and joined the Army. I completed boot camp and am now at Fort Benning, Georgia, in Army Infantry training. These tanks are a little harder to drive than your tractor but easier than learning to ride a bucking bronc. I'm sorry I haven't written sooner but I've been a little busy. :) And I was pissed off at you for telling me that the Army was where I belonged. I took what you said the wrong way.

I realize now your comments weren't criticism but was, as usual, good advice. Sorry I left in the middle of the night and didn't say goodbye. Give my regards to Mrs. C.

    Yours: Wild Bill

Sophie folded the letter and put it back in the envelop. Wild Bill was obviously one of her father's projects. George Cameron had been a sucker for anyone down on their luck, especially kids or a kid who couldn't seem to get a toehold in life. He frequently gave jobs to underprivileged youth during the summers, and sometimes, they remained until they decided on a career or the permanent direction they wanted to take. Her dad had a marshmallow for a heart. Her mother used to tease him that he had more kids than horses around the place. Sophie wondered if she had met this young man or if he had stayed so briefly that he was gone before she had any interaction with him. Apparently, he had left abruptly in the middle of the night after a disagreement with her father.

Sophie opened the next envelope, this one dated 2005.

Dear Mr. C,

I'm in Iraq. Tough place. My sergeant is almost as demanding as you. Came under enemy attack yesterday. Scary. Several injured, and we lost one soldier. Too close. Gotta go. The enemy awaits.

    Yours: Wild Bill

Sophie dropped the letter on the desk and covered her mouth with her hand. She had not expected the young man to be in the midst of such danger. But Wild Bill was in the Army, and there was a war going on at that time. What had it been like to go through what he so briefly described? How did her father feel about having encouraged him to voluntarily place himself in this situation? Sophie didn't know for sure, but as one of her father's protégés, Wild Bill was probably no older than eighteen or nineteen when he wrote this letter. She couldn't help but feel sorry for him. Seeing a buddy die and others injured must have been horrifying.

She opened a third letter, hoping to read that he was now home and uninjured. The postmark was smudged so she couldn't tell the date, but it looked like it was from Georgia. Sophie exhaled with relief, knowing that the young man had made it back from the war zone and returned stateside.

Dear Mr. C,

Successfully dodged Johnny Jihad and made it back in one piece. Back at Ft. Benning grinding along while hoping we won't deploy again anytime soon. As you advised, I'm taking college courses offered on Post. My goal—as many college credits as possible when my commitment is up in '08. The Army has done what you hinted at but didn't say: scared me straight. Put another way: snuffed the cockiness right out of me. :)

Yours: Wild Bill

Sophie sighed again as she folded the letter, relieved that he was well. He hadn't indicated whether he'd sustained any injuries. She'd like to believe he hadn't.

She was now intrigued by the saga of Wild Bill and eager to find out what happened next. She picked up another letter, this one mailed in 2007. From the dates, it appeared that Wild Bill wrote to her father on an annual basis. They were all brief, but kept her father updated on his status. Knowing her father, she was sure that he answered each one of Wild Bill's letters.

Dear Mr. C,

Oh boy! Just got notified that we Tread Heads (Armored Calvary) are heading back to Iraq. Bummer! Not much to say except wish me luck.

Yours: Wild Bill

Sophie looked at the next letter. It was postmarked in 2009. She pawed through the stack to see if she had missed one from 2008. No, the 2009 letter was the next one, but since Wild Bill was still writing, he had once again survived his deployment to the war zone. This letter was a little longer than the previous ones.

Dear Mr. C,

Sorry for not writing sooner. I had a little meeting with an IED, and the IED won. Don't worry. Just a broken leg, a few broken ribs, some bangs and bruises, but I'm all healed now. But I hung up my spurs, so to speak, and left the Army last year. While I was recovering and on desk duty, my CO put me to work in IT. I seem to have a knack for it. I'm now enrolled at the U of Georgia, using the GI Bill. I plan to major in Computer Engineering. If I stay focused, I will graduate in 2010.

Yours: Wild Bill.

PS: Don't worry about Sophie. From what you say, she's a smart kid. She'll see through this Greg fellow and kick him to the curb, just like she did with ole Travis.

Sophie abruptly sat back in her chair, the letter still in her hand. She reread it. They were discussing her, as well as her high school boyfriend, Travis, and her college boyfriend, Greg. She hadn't thought about them in years. It was news to her that her father didn't like either of them. Travis was her first mistake, but she had rectified that quickly. In fact, she had only gone out with him once. She'd been flattered that the senior-class bad boy had noticed the skinny girl with glasses—that some might call a nerd—and wanted to go out with her. Of course, this was before she heard the rumor that Travis had a goal of dating every girl in the eleventh grade before the school year was over.

Pretty soon, the rumor mill took their date further than just going to the movies. Travis bragged that he had added a notch in his belt with Sophie Cameron. The insinuation wasn't true, but the truth didn't matter to the high school crowd. Sophie didn't have a lot of experience with boys, but she wasn't stupid. She dropped Travis before he could spread more lies about her, and she did so publicly in a crowded hallway between classes. Nerd or not, she always stood up for herself.

She had only brought Greg home once during college, but there wasn't a lot to like about him, either. Greg was her first real love—or, more accurately, first real infatuation. At age eighteen, she hadn't yet developed standards for what she was looking for in a boyfriend. She met Greg at Freshman Orientation when she enrolled at the University of Kentucky. Very quickly, it became evident that Greg's goal in life was to play in a rock band, even though he wasn't very good at it. In retrospect, he was more interested in the groupies that hung around the band's performances than in trying to improve his music. Theirs was a short romance, but it lasted a bit longer than her romance with Travis—about three months.

Wild Bill was right: she had come to her senses and broken up with Greg. Sophie could laugh about it now, but since her dad had confided in Wild Bill, he must have taken it more seriously than she had. But following Greg, there was Charlie, who planned to be a stockbroker and whose mood depended on that day's Dow Jones performance. He was followed by James, the English exchange student who couldn't decide anything without first calling his mother in England for advice. Sophie's relationships with all of them sputtered and died quickly.

But then, she went on to make another mistake with Robert. She met Robert when she was recruited out of college to join the marketing firm in Tampa where he worked. They started dating soon after she arrived and later decided to leave the company and start their own marketing company together. That arrangement then led to marriage. They spent so many long hours together building the business that marriage seemed like a natural evolution. Natural, maybe, but their relationship was not strong enough to last.

When she married Robert at age twenty-six, Sophie evidently hadn't wised up in the love department as much as she thought. Their togetherness had simply become a habit that they mistook for love. At least Robert was a nice person and didn't have illusions about being another Mick Jagger. Still, her track record in the romance department had racked up a score of Sophie, zero, and bad judgement, multiple.

Sophie placed the letter back on the stack and picked up another one. Wild Bill had skipped 2010, so this one was postmarked in 2011.

Dear Mr. C,

I keep apologizing for not writing as often as I should, but other things keep getting in the way. I want you to know how much I appreciate all the great advice you've given me over the years. And for not kicking my ass when I pretended to ignore you while I worked for you. I heard everything you said. I'm graduating from college in a few days, and I wouldn't have done it without your encouragement. I'm moving to Texas with one of my college buddies. We're working on some application ideas for the smartphone. You know that newfangled device? If you bought one, we could talk face-to-face. I know how much you hate computers, but you should trade your flip phone in for a smartphone. It doesn't bite. :) Anyway, my friend's father owns a ranch west of Abilene and will hire me to work cattle until I find a job. How hard can working with cows be? They don't talk back. My friend has a cute sister, too, which adds interest. Maybe I'll try for a job in the oil fields and hang out in Texas for a 'spell.'

Yours: Wild Bill

Ah, so that was why her father had suddenly asked her to help him select a new smartphone at the end of 2011! Apparently, Wild Bill was the person who pushed her father into the new digital age of smartphones and apps.

Sophie picked up the last letter. She felt a twinge of sadness that this was the last one. The saga of Wild Bill was an interesting tale, but what was more interesting and heartwarming was how grateful Wild Bill was to her father for his influence on his life. She opened the last letter, postmarked 2012.

Dear Mr. C,

It was great talking to you on video chat, but someone needs some practice using that application, and it isn't me. Ha! Ha! So, I will write until you figure it out. My friend and I developed and sold an app (remember I told you about it?) to a Texas company. Using our herd management app, ranchers can keep track of births, health records, herd movement, and other tools to manage a farm or ranch. Such a simple idea, but we made a fair amount of money from the sale. I also inherited $25K from my parents (I didn't even know they left me that). It became available when I turned 26. They were better doctors than they were businesspeople. I wish they had been as risk-averse with their safety as they were with this safe investment. I think I can turn it into slightly more. The amount is small, but the important thing is that they thought about me and my future.

My buddy and I are moving to California. There's a start-up lithium battery company for electric cars we hope to invest in. If that fails, there are some other tech companies we have our eyes on. Wish me luck. And ask Sophie to help you learn how to use your phone. I imagine she's grown into a beautiful woman over the eight years since I left. Don't take offense at my comment. I know how protective you are of her. I just meant she's probably not the kid she was back when I left.

Yours: Wild Bill

Sophie felt tears burn the back of her eyes. The letter's mention of her father's phone brought back memories. He had indeed asked her to explain the features on his phone—and in particular, how to use the video chat app. As Sophie recalled, he was very interested in the ability to chat with the people he contacted. He never explained why, and she had just assumed

he wanted to see all his callers face-to-face—not just a particular one. Her father was always curious about a wide range of
things, but usually not new technology. Since there were no
more letters from Wild Bill, they must have successfully kept in
touch via the phone after that.

What had Wild Bill meant by his comment about the safety of
his parents? Had his life been touched by tragedy? There was an
untold story here—and probably an interesting one.

Sophie straightened all the letters in their envelops and put
them back in order. She replaced the rubber band, then returned
the stack to its place in the drawer. The letters were like a story that
unfolded over several years. She didn't have her father's replies, but
she knew what he would have written. His letters would have been
filled with concern for the young man as he served in Iraq as well
as encouragement as Wild Bill earned his college degree. There
would have been advice about life in general—lots of advice.

What had happened to Wild Bill? Had he married the sister of
his friend, the Texas girl he mentioned? Did his California dreams
come true? Did he know of her father's passing? Sadly, she'd never
know how his life turned out. A call or chat with Wild Bill would
be nice, if only to let him know about her father's death or find
out where he was and what had happened to him. Unfortunately,
Sophie didn't have the password to her father's phone to access
his contacts. Knowing her father as she did, he probably wrote it
down on paper. But if he had, it was as good as lost, because it was
most likely buried in the mountain of paper somewhere in the
room.

The saga of Wild Bill was interesting and a temporary diversion from Sophie's worry over their financial problems. However,
she needed to get back to work. When she had Cameron Stables'
problems under control, she'd try to locate Wild Bill. Until then,
she didn't have time to do more than just wonder what had happened to him.

CHAPTER FOUR

Sophie forced herself to go back into the office each day that weekend and into the middle of the following week. Every time she entered the office, she felt like a bloodhound following the scent at a crime scene. She kept up the search for clues—in this case, more unpaid bills—in the nooks and crannies around the office. She forced herself to clean out the desk drawers and recycle all the old papers and junk mail. But she refused to touch the mess in the bookcase.

She kept a few papers with her father's scribbled notes, not because what was written was important, but because his handwriting was a connection to him. Of course, she kept the bundle of letters from Wild Bill, another important memento that demonstrated the kind of man George Cameron was.

In the end, the only additional bills she found were recent ones for saddle and other tack repair and for medications from the local veterinarian. They must have come in shortly before her father's death. Finding only those, Sophie breathed a little easier. Maybe, just maybe, she was getting her arms around that part of the problem—or at least getting close to the bottom of the financial hole.

It was probably a good thing that her father didn't have a computer. She hadn't come across his phone's password yet, so any creditors that were set up for paperless billing would be hidden behind another missing password. But setting up auto-mated billing didn't sound like her father. He probably visited the local merchants to chat and pay them in person. Her father's refusal to own a computer just might have saved her an addi-tional headache.

She had already contacted the merchants they owed money to in an effort to mend fences and ask if they would drop the late fees on the account. Most had refused. She didn't press the issue because she understood. In a lot of cases, the fees were substantial. The vendors sympathized with her financial situ-ation, but they were struggling with their own bottom lines. The real surprise was that they hadn't cut off her father's credit before now.

Still, the payments and goodwill contacts with vendors that she'd made wouldn't solve all her problems. New billing state-ments would soon be filling the mailbox again.

Her mother had used part of a small inheritance from her parents to keep the household running. Under Sophie's management, that was going to change. If she couldn't make a profit that would cover all expenses for the property, she would shut down the business altogether and find a job. She hoped it wouldn't come to that, but she had prepared herself for the possibility.

More than once over the last few days, Sophie wished her father had come to her when he found himself drowning in debt. But he was a proud man. Asking his "little girl," as he still thought of her, for help would have been an embarrassment he couldn't face.

On Friday morning, Sophie entered the last of the bills into the bank's payment system. Mission accomplished! Plus, she had almost fifteen thousand dollars of her original deposit left. She couldn't pat herself on the back just yet, though. It would be a few weeks before the pastures greened up, came out of their winter dormancy, and could sustain grazing. Until then, she'd have to buy feed for the horses. And there were also Pete and Ben to pay.

"Dad, what happened?" Sophie asked as she logged out of her computer. She leaned back in her chair and pressed her fingers into her eyeballs. She could almost hear his answer, complete with one of his worn-out jokes: "I was trying to make a dollar out of fifteen cents." She got the joke now.

Sophie's mind was never far from the problems of Cameron Stables. She hadn't been sleeping well, and every time she closed her eyes, all she saw were columns of red ink. Their financial plight had become a living, waking nightmare. She needed to do more than just tread water and use her personal funds. She needed a self-sustaining, long-term plan that would revive the business and increase revenue.

Another ride with Rose up to Mystic Peak might give her inspiration or kick her creative processes into gear. First, though, before leaving the office, she dialed her mother's cell number in Paducah for an update on Aunt Rachel.

"She's doing well," Jean replied to Sophie's inquiry about her aunt. "She's moving her shoulder some. The injury wasn't as bad as first thought. I've convinced her to come stay with us as soon as the doctor gives her the okay. She has to finish a few more visits to the physical therapist before we can come home, though."

"That's fantastic. That way, I'll be able to stay with her when you go back to volunteering at the hospital."

"That won't be necessary. I'm taking extended time off from my volunteer duties. I'm not ready to go back just yet," Jean said, unable to hide the sadness in her voice.

"That's understandable. Having you *and* Aunt Rachel around all the time will be wonderful. I can't wait." Aunt Rachel living with them would provide her mother with company and help stave off the loneliness she must be feeling, even with Sophie living at home.

Sophie hung up the phone, went to the stables, and saddled Rose. She let Rose set the pace and at first, they rode aimlessly across the rolling pastures. Soon, though, Rose ambled toward the path that led up into Mystic Hills.

Before long, they were standing on the peak and gazing out across the valley. The late April sun was warm, and soon, Sophie felt some of the tension leave her body. A kernel of hope sprouted as confidence in her ability to handle the hard task ahead returned. Yes, she could save the business—or at least try. No more second-guessing or stalling.

The fighting spirit of her Scots-Irish ancestors, which the Camerons bragged about at every family reunion, had to mean something. Stubbornness and an unwillingness to give up, mixed with a smart business plan, would return Cameron Stables to a successful business. Sophie had run a business before. The job of saving her father's dream had fallen to her, his only child. She could use her experience, and hopefully, that would be enough to make it happen.

Sophie was suddenly excited by the challenge. The marketing firm she and Robert started together had been a challenge, too, but eventually, it became a very successful marketing company in the Tampa area. Most of their problems as co-owners were self-inflicted wounds because she and Robert frequently disagreed on strategies and techniques. They grudgingly compromised only after everything else had failed.

More than once, Sophie thought about selling her share of the company and striking out on her own. Although Cameron Stables wasn't the business she thought she'd be running, she was anxious to find out how well she could manage a business by herself. Sadly, it was her father's death and the need to rescue his business that was forcing her to test her abilities.

Jean had given Sophie free rein to do what she thought was needed, and she already had a few ideas. But the situation was like a slippery eel. Which end do you pick up first, and how do you keep it from slipping from your grasp? She needed to offer more services to generate money, but she needed money to hire the staff to provide more services.

The banker at the local bank was the father of one of her friends, but she doubted her friendship with Darlene would get her any special treatment. Plus, the unpaid bills had surely ruined the business's credit rating, so what Mr. Taylor could do for her was an open question. He might give her advice, even if he couldn't give her a loan. Stephen, a former high school classmate, was a lawyer and had an office in Kingsville. He was already handling her father's will, so he might be another source of helpful information.

Just as Sophie started to turn Rose onto the trail leading down from the peak, she saw a tall rider on a large bay horse heading in the opposite direction across the former Thornton land. He was far away and his back was turned, but from the way he sat in the saddle, she recognized the rider. It was Cowboy.

What was he doing out here today? Checking the fence row again? Or was he simply out for a morning ride, just like her? He hadn't seen her on the peak and soon disappeared from sight. Good! She didn't feel up to verbally jousting with him today.

Sophie turned Rose over to Pete when she arrived back at

the stable yard and returned to the office. She was mentally formulating a list of questions to ask Mr. Taylor when—or if—she got an appointment with him. But when she sat down behind the desk, the first call she made was to Robert. She wanted to pick his brain about the types of services she should add to Cameron Stables. Robert was good at what he did, stubbornness discounted. He might have new insight into what people were looking for in amenities beyond stabling and training horses. She didn't have to accept everything he suggested.

After they exchanged greetings and she posed her questions, Robert got straight to the point. "First off, you need a website."

"Yes, I know," Sophie replied. "I'm working on it, at least in my head. But if you and one of your girlfriends were renting one of our cabins for a week, what would you expect from the experience?"

"Sophie, I never cheated on you. Cindy and I weren't dating until after our divorce became final," Robert said, sounding hurt.

"I know. I'm sorry if I sounded snarky, like I was accusing you. I wish you and Cindy the best. This business—or lack of business—with the Stables has me in a foul mood. But what would you expect if you visited a place like this?"

"In my opinion, most people—even if they're visiting a place like yours, with horses, trail rides, and so on—like being pampered. They want more than just a place to stay for the night. Or couples do, anyway. Maybe you could turn one of the cabins into a place to gather in the evenings to share a drink or a glass of wine. Offer some catered food or snacks. People like to mingle and share the day's experiences. Sometimes, they remain friends even after they leave the property. Who knows? They might rebook together and return for a reunion!"

"I like that idea, but don't suggest gathering around a campfire for a sing-along. I don't want to turn the place into a dude ranch," Sophie replied.

"Why not?" Robert chuckled then added, "Right! I remember now. You can't sing. Well, then make it more romantic than a dude ranch. Add hot tubs and heart-shaped beds to all the cabins."

"Now you sound ridiculous. No surprise there, but at least you're thinking romantically for a change."

"I'm sorry if I ever made you feel as if you were just another coworker during our marriage," Robert said. "Too much togetherness, I guess."

"Not just coworkers—co-owners, remember? And each with a different idea of how to run a marketing business." Sophie paused, then said, "That's all water under the bridge. And thank you for the suggestions. You've given me something to think about. Of course, all my plans hinge on whether I can get financing for such an operation."

Sophie said goodbye to Robert, then called the bank. She made an appointment with Mr. Taylor for the Friday morning of the following week.

Sophie spent the rest of the day working on a website. She discarded the first version and started over. She wished Wild Bill, the techie her father's encouragement had helped create, was around to give her a hand. She kept tweaking until she was finally satisfied. The design looked professional and user-friendly. A company logo and catchy tagline were still missing, but she would come up with those later once inspiration hit. She would also decide on pricing once she researched the current rates charged at similar properties.

The next morning, Sophie started to draft a business plan, then decided to first take inventory of what was currently on the property. She grabbed her digital tablet, left the house, and walked toward the barn.

As she walked, she paused frequently to make notes on the

tablet as ideas came to her. Her father still owned ten horses, plus Rose. Thankfully, he hadn't sold them. The cost of finding and purchasing good riding horses was not something she wanted to deal with, even if she wasn't operating on a shoe-string budget. She would use the horses they owned for group trail rides or riding lessons for locals when rentals were slow. Rose could be used in a pinch when they had more requests than horses. In addition to the horses they owned, they currently boarded five horses. She estimated that the pastures were large enough to support boarding another eight.

The barn was a large structure, which fit well with her plans. Sophie entered the barn and browsed through the stalls, assessing their condition. A good cleaning and some paint in the office was about all that seemed to be needed.

Satisfied that everything was in order inside the barn, Sophie walked around the outside, checking for loose or rotted boards or anything else that needed repairing. That done, she stepped away from the barn to get a better look at the roof. The roof, along with the interior of the barn, were solid. No major repairs were needed at this time.

She next walked to the cabins, which were located in a large stand of trees and a good distance from the main house for privacy. Built on a slight hill, they offered a view of the rolling pastures and Mystic Hills. A road ran in front of all the units, with a short driveway leading up to the front of each cabin. Tall hedges separated the cabins, giving the occupants additional privacy from their neighbors.

Built in the late 1990s, there were ten cabins, each with a maximum capacity of five people. Two of the cabins were duplexes while the rest were either one- or two-bedroom stand-alone units. All had finished lofts with bunk beds, sleeper sofas in the living room, and a galley kitchen. The interior of each cabin was finished with golden pine paneling, which appeared

to have held up well. All the cabins looked structurally solid.
Sophie would have the water and plumbing checked once she
could hire a maintenance person.

The major problem with the cabins was the décor. It was
very much outdated, unless one like the 1990s' "chintz and
frills" style. Sophie made a note to replace the décor as well as
purchase new bedding, including mattresses, pots, pans, and
dishes. In addition, each cabin would need one important item:
a TV. Her father had never thought it necessary to install cable
TV, internet, or Wi-Fi in the cabins, but those services were
something most people now required, even when on vacation.
She added digital services to the list of improvements needed to
make the cabins ready for visitors.

Once Sophie had finished inventorying the last cabin, she
sat down on a wooden bench on the back patio to rest and fine-
tune her plans. All the cabins had front porches and concrete
patios in the back. There was porch furniture stored in the barn
for each cabin.

What else was needed to modernize the property? She added firepits to her list of improvements. Installed in the yard just
off the patio of each cabin, they would offer a place for families
to roast marshmallows and tell ghost stories or for couples to
cuddle and share a glass of wine in the cool evenings. Guests
could rest and watch the fireflies light up the trees on Mystic
Hills and in the meadows on warm summer nights—a nice way
to wind down after a day of hiking and trail riding.

Sophie left the cabin area and started to walk back toward
the barn and main house. As she reached a flat terraced portion
of land located between the cabins and the gate to the property,
she paused and looked around.

Sophie slowly turned in a circle as she inspected the area.
A new idea occurred to her. Instead of using one of the cabins
for get-togethers in the evenings, as Robert suggested, why not

build a covered pavilion—an open-air clubhouse or entertainment area?

She'd install canvas curtains that could be lowered during periods of rain or when chilly weather arrived. Adding see-through magnetic screens would keep mosquitoes and bugs at bay but not block the view during pleasant weather. A structure like this would be more economical to build than an enclosed facility. Plus, during nice weather, it would bring the feeling of the outdoors inside.

Suddenly on a roll, another idea struck Sophie. She pulled out her phone and called her mother in Paducah.

"Mom," she said as soon as Jean answered, "how would you like to design a rose and flower garden?"

"We already have a rose and flower garden," Jean responded.

"Not that one. I mean one for our guests to stroll through. You know the flat spot between the cabins and the front gate? The west end has both sunlight and shade trees—the perfect place for a garden. Flowers would attract butterflies and hummingbirds, which is always a nice touch. It would be a place for couples to wander along the garden paths, holding hands or exchanging kisses in the moonlight."

"My goodness! You've put some thought into this." Jean laughed. "That does sound romantic."

"We could add a couple of benches beneath the trees, providing a place for guests to sit quietly together before they return to their cabins. They could watch the moon rise over Mystic Hills."

"Well, I'm up for it, but I won't be back for a couple weeks yet."

"I'll send you a picture of the area. You can draw up the plans on your tablet and send them to the landscape architect—once I hire one."

"I guess that would work. I'll start thinking about it."

"It'll be located not far from an entertainment pavilion site I'm going to have built."

"What? We're going to entertain, too? You have been busy!"

"Lots of ideas. Very little money," Sophie said with a laugh. "But I'm working on that, too."

Sophie ended the call, pleased that her mother seemed as excited as she was. This was a project Jean would enjoy. She knew more about growing and caring for plants than anyone Sophie knew.

Sophie added other amenities they could offer to her list. Safari tents set up on the high meadow would appeal to people who wanted to sleep out under the stars but not exactly rough it. Sophie had once run an ad campaign for a company that sold safari tents. These "glamping" tents, complete with comfortable beds, living spaces, and bathrooms, were all the rage now. They would hardly qualify as the rustic experience some might prefer, so maybe one safari tent and one regular tent would be the way to go, appealing to a cross section of people. She could add more if demand was there.

If guests were the athletic type, they might like to take a guided nighttime ride into the Fairy Woods to see firsthand the mysterious place the original Camerons thought was inhabited by fairies. Sophie quickly discarded that idea. It was a special place, a unique ecological feature. A large group trooping through the area might damage the site. But she *could* offer a lottery drawing for those who were interested. That way, she could keep the numbers low and manageable by selecting no more than two couples for the ride.

Some of Sophie's ideas for a romantic evening came from her marriage to Robert. A fun evening for him was watching football or some other sporting event on TV, while she wanted to dress up and go out for dinner and dancing. At first, she tried to add some spice to their marriage, but Robert was never interested in that, and eventually, she gave up on that, too. Neither tried to accommodate the other's wishes, so they each pursued their separate interests.

Thinking of Robert and his love of sports made her think of another feature she could add: a sports area that included a volleyball court, basketball hoop, horseshoe pit, cornhole site, and some pieces of playground equipment for children. Maybe not theme-park level, but it would be old-fashioned fun. Later, as the financial picture improved, she could add a tennis court and a spa center with massages.

Cameron Stables certainly had the space for the expansion she envisioned. Of course, if space was money, she wouldn't be needing a loan. Setting aside the idea of a tennis court and spa for another day, Sophie decided to include her other ideas in the business plan she would present to Mr. Taylor on Friday.

She returned to the office, excited by her plans. She reached for the phone to call Robert again to get his opinion on what she was planning but briefly hesitated. She didn't want to call him again, but this was important. Besides, they were both used to being annoyed by each other, so a little more wouldn't matter. Cindy, on the other hand, might not be pleased that Robert's ex was in frequent contact with him. Cindy could rest easy, though. Sophie wanted Robert's marketing skills and expertise, nothing more.

"What do you think of the tagline, 'Cameron Stables, Rustic Redefined'?" she asked after describing the improvements she had in mind.

"I like it," Robert replied. "It accurately fits what you describe. Sounds like you're on the right track."

"Yes. It's a combination of trail rides, nature hikes, and a game area, but also with chef-prepared dining, music, dancing, wine tastings, and so on."

"I think it's a good plan," Robert said. He added with a

chuckle, "I'm disappointed that you eliminated the campfire singing and heart-shaped beds, though. Still, let me know if I can help in any way."

"Not a dude ranch, Dude," Sophie reminded him. "But thanks. I appreciate your feedback."

Sophie spent the rest of the week polishing her business plan and readying it for her Friday-morning appointment with Mr. Taylor. She was armed with cost projections for renovations, a rough estimate of labor costs for staffing needs, monthly recurring expenses, a separate budget for emergencies, and projected income. She would handle all the advertising herself, with a little help from Robert and her former company. She would *not* put up the land for collateral under any circumstances. They owned it outright, and that was how it would remain until her mother decided to sell.

Sophie was warmly welcomed by Mr. Taylor. Once seated and after Sophie accepted Mr. Taylor's condolences for the loss of her father, she presented her business plan. He listened attentively, but Sophie could tell before he even opened his mouth that the answer wouldn't be what she wanted to hear.

"I'm sorry. I really am. Your father asked for a loan awhile back, but his credit was in such terrible shape that the bank managers wouldn't approve a loan. It was hard for me to deny him, but I know it was even harder for him to hear the bank's rejection. I don't want to get your hopes up and put you through that when I know the same thing will happen again."

"But this is a whole new plan, and it's me asking." Sophie wouldn't give in at the first 'no.'

"I know, Sophie, but you're still borrowing under the Cameron Stables name. I'm confident that the loan application will be rejected," Mr. Taylor said. "I'm sorry. I really am."

What Mr. Taylor said was true, and Sophie had expected it. But she wasn't done yet. She had prepared herself for rejection, so she had one last idea to throw out. She had hoped that by some miracle, she wouldn't have to do it this way, but this was the only alternative she had come up with.

"I have another idea that maybe you'll approve. What if I move all my savings from my bank in Tampa and deposit it in your bank? Could I get a loan using a portion of my savings as collateral?"

"I... ah, yes, I think we could do that. But are you sure you want to put your savings at risk? What if your plans for the business don't work out? You would lose it all."

"I believe I have a solid plan. I'm going to do everything I can to make it work," Sophie replied. "I would make payments on the loan but still maintain my savings balance, even though it would be held by your bank. But I'll be smart. I won't do anything foolish or extravagant. And by doing it this way, I'm protecting my savings by not spending it, instead using it as collateral."

"You're sure about this?" Mr. Taylor asked.

"Yes. I won't default on the loan. I promise. I'll pay it off one way or another. This business was my father's dream. He was successful at one time, but times changed, and keeping up was tough for him. His dream never changed, though. I'm just updating and modernizing to match the times." Sophie crossed her fingers in her lap. Brave words were easy to say. Making it happen was another thing. But she really did believe she could turn the business around.

"Okay. You've convinced me. Your passion for the project is persuasive," Mr. Taylor said with a smile. "I expect you'll make it work. And you know I'm rooting for you."

Mr. Taylor gave Sophie the paperwork that would transfer her savings account balance from Tampa to his bank. She then completed the application for the collateral loan. With a promise that he would process it as soon as the transfer was complete and let her know, Sophie left his office. As she walked through the automatic door at the front of the bank, she heard someone call her name. She turned and spotted Mr. Taylor's daughter, Darlene, coming toward her.

"Darlene! How are you?" Sophie hugged her. They had been close friends in high school but hadn't seen each other for a couple of years. "What are you doing here?"

"I'm bringing lunch to my Dad." Darlene held up a white box. "I run the Cherry Blossom Restaurant over on Cross Street, and bringing Dad his lunch has become a Friday ritual. Now, he expects it. But how are you doing?"

"I'm doing well. Just here on business," Sophie replied.

"I'm sorry about your father," Darlene said. "I can only imagine how hard it must be for you and your mother."

"Thank you," Sophie said. "We're okay. Just trying to adjust."

"I need to drop this off to Dad before it gets cold, but why don't we meet tonight to catch up? Just like old times."

"I… uh, I better not. I still have some things I need to take care of at the house…" Sophie's voice trailed off. Did she *really* want to spend another night alone with marketing plans, spreadsheets, and income and loss projections while cooped up in her father's office? No. She was tired of thinking about business. A break sounded nice.

"Come on! Let's get together. There's a great new place called The Feed Bag on Center Street. It's half-priced margarita night. I'll meet you on the patio at seven. What do you say?"

"Okay. You've convinced me. I could use a break. Mom has gone to stay with Aunt Rachel, so the house is spooky-quiet. I'll meet you on the patio of The Feed Bag at seven tonight."

Sophie finished her errands in town, which included a quick stop at the supermarket to pick up some premade dinners and then a stop by the local internet provider for an estimate on installing internet and cable TV throughout the property. The estimate was joltingly expensive, but the service was essential for a modern business. She left with a promise to call and set up an appointment when the property was ready for the installation.

By the time she returned home, Patsy had finished her Friday cleaning and left the house. Two loaves of freshly baked bread sat on the counter. Sophie pinched off a piece and popped it in her mouth. She wasn't much of a cook herself, as evidenced by her purchases at the grocery store, but she wouldn't starve completely as long as Patsy did her Friday baking.

Sophie refused to enter her father's office and get sucked into reviewing financial documents or sorting through the papers in the bookcase or the credenza. She hadn't yet started either pile. She pulled the office door closed so it wouldn't taunt her and, with a glass of sweet tea, went outside to the back patio. She sat down in a rocker shaded by birch trees, put her feet up on a small table, and relaxed. She closed her eyes.

Relatively speaking, she'd had a successful day.

Sophie fell asleep and woke up from her short nap feeling refreshed. She dressed for her evening out, then drove into town. As she parked in the back lot next to The Feed Bag's patio dining area, she spotted Darlene standing by a table and waving to her. The patio was crowded with Friday-night diners. The sound of laughter and conversation greeted Sophie as she walked across the parking lot.

A waiter arrived to take their orders as soon as Sophie sat down at the table with Darlene. They ordered their food, along with the house specialty—margaritas. Sophie and Darlene then began to catch up on the years that had passed since they last saw each other.

The waiter had just delivered their food when Darlene said, "Don't look now, but I think you have an admirer. He's been glancing this way, and I'm sure it's not me he's looking at."

"How can you be sure?" Sophie asked. "You know more people here than I do."

"I don't know this guy. And he didn't start looking this way until you arrived. I think he knows you or wants to know you. He's to your right, at the table in the corner under the awning."

Sophie slowly turned her head to the right. She tried to be nonchalant, but that was impossible since she had to turn much of her body to see the person in question. Sure enough, someone beneath the awning near the wall was looking her way. He smiled and raised two fingers to his forehead in greeting when she looked in his direction.

"Cowboy," Sophie said quietly. It was the rider she had met in the meadow near Mystic Hill. He sat with two other men and a blonde woman. One man wore a business suit. Cowboy had replaced his "Marlboro Man" attire with khakis and a polo shirt.

"Who? Cowboy? You know him?" Darlene asked.

"No, not really. I met him when I was out riding the other day. He works for Mr. Whittaker, the new owner of Thornton Farms." Sophie surmised that the man in the suit was Mr. Whittaker and that the other man at their table, dressed similarly to Cowboy, was another employee Whittaker had brought with him. "Is that by any chance Lynn Thornton with them?"

"That's her. I'd know that profile anywhere," Darlene replied. "Remember how she lorded her wealth over us? And how she'd say, 'I'm a Thornton,' as if that made her better than the rest of us?" Darlene mimicked a snooty, female voice, even more snooty than Sophie remembered Lynn actually using.

"I don't think she was that bad," Sophie said with a laugh. "Maybe she was just as insecure as we were back then. According to Patsy Martin, Lynn is redecorating the Thornton Mansion. She looks rather cozy with Mr. Whittaker."

"She does. But if I were in her shoes, I'd turn my attention to Cowboy or to the other guy. Maybe they don't have as much money as Suit Man. Lynn always goes where the money is. Cats always land on their feet, don't they?"

"Maybe we're the ones being catty, not Lynn." Sophie smiled at Darlene, then snuck another glance at Cowboy. He took a sip of his drink, then lifted the glass and nodded another salute in her direction. Sophie quickly turned back to her plate, choosing to ignore him.

"It's hard being available again, isn't it?" Darlene asked as she looked across the table at Sophie. "When Clark and I broke up, it was funny how men seemed to sense I was single again. I think they have radar that can spot single women."

"Cowboy is not making a pass, if that's what you're hinting at," Sophie protested. "And some men make passes and flirt whether a woman is single or not. It's in their DNA. My guess is that he's one of those." Or maybe it was plain arrogance that made Cowboy think he could flirt even from across the room. On the other hand, it was just a greeting, so maybe flirting wasn't what he was doing. She'd been out of the dating scene so long, she might not recognize flirting. "I've been divorced for a year and haven't met anyone or had anyone try to romance me. Sorry to destroy your theory. And now, I'm completely focused on business."

"It was also funny," Darlene continued reminiscing, ignoring Sophie's comment, "how I vowed to never get involved with anyone again. Now, I'm dating Ted. You remember Ted Langley from the class just ahead of us, right? It's nice having someone special in my life again."

"I do remember Ted, and I'm happy for you both," Sophie said, still not agreeing with Darlene's premise that Cowboy was flirting with her. "I just don't think love is for me. Otherwise, I'd have found it before now." Love hadn't turned out to be as she'd once imagined it would—that all-consuming feeling for each other where both partners are equally invested. In her experience, love had been more like running a grueling marathon you didn't want to run. The first mile started out hopeful, but by the second mile, you wanted to quit and go home. Maybe her idea of love and romance was just a fantasy she'd built up in her mind, and in reality, it was never as she'd imagined it.

"You just haven't met the right person yet. Take Cowboy's pass as a compliment," Darlene advised. "And get used to it. Since you're not tied to that marketing agency with your ex, you're finally free to explore—and enjoy."

"Hmph! It wasn't a pass," Sophie repeated. "And I don't like being watched by someone skulking in the shadows." Okay, maybe she was wrong to refer to Cowboy's look as "skulking." His smile was warm, even from across the patio, so it might qualify as a pass. It was something to consider, but she wouldn't admit that fact to Darlene. Cowboy was probably just indulging in the folksy, friendly manner of the West. Even more likely, he was teasing her again for reasons only he knew.

Sophie again casually looked toward the corner where he sat, but he and his party had left.

CHAPTER FIVE

Sophie quietly eased open the door and peeked into the bedroom next to hers. Jamie lay curled on her side, her angelic face relaxed in sleep, and her feet tangled in the bedcovers. Sophie tiptoed to the bed and gently straightened the blanket over the sleeping child. Then, she left the room and walked down the hall to the bathroom for her morning shower.

Sophie was babysitting for Pete and his wife Jenny while they spent the weekend in Nashville. Sophie had volunteered to—or rather, insisted on—keeping Jamie while they enjoyed some much-needed time together.

In truth, Sophie had encouraged Jenny and Pete to take a weekend off and spend it together. Life was about to get hectic around Cameron Stables—providing, of course, that her business plan worked out as she hoped. Ben was filling in for Pete while he was in Nashville. Sophie had recently offered Ben a full-time position, and he eagerly accepted.

With a carload of baby necessities, a favorite blanket and toys, and many instructions from Jenny, Sophie had picked

Jamie up yesterday and brought her home with her. Jamie was all cuteness and had a sweet disposition, so keeping her for the weekend was all pleasure. She was easily entertained and had been enthralled by her visit with the farm animals yesterday afternoon. Jamie had giggled and played with the new litter of barn kittens after they visited with the horses in the paddock. One of the kitties would be going home with Jamie, but Jenny and Pete didn't know that yet.

Sophie stopped to look out her bedroom window on the way to the bathroom. Over the past week—and once she got the bank loan—the property's expansion had gained traction. She spotted Ian, the landscape architect, staking out the design Jean had sketched out and sent to him from Paducah. They worked well together, even with her mother directing the design from two hundred miles away. It would be a few more days before Jean and Rachel returned home so Jean could supervise in person.

More evidence that Sophie's vision for Cameron Stables was taking shape were the scars in the ground on the high meadow. The construction crew from a camping equipment company had leveled the ground in preparation of installing the tents next week. Another construction crew would also begin building the covered entertainment pavilion in the coming week.

Sophie left the window and made her way to the bathroom. As the warm water from the shower flowed over her, she thought about all the things she had accomplished thus far.

Patsy was sending a crew next week to clean and scrub all the cabins and repaint the porch furniture. Sophie had made a trip to a discount warehouse in Lexington and purchased new bedding, linens, rugs, décor pieces, TVs, and a few other items for the cabins. The total bill was jaw dropping, but everything she purchased was needed. The items would be delivered as soon as Sophie was ready for them.

The local internet provider would wire the cabins for internet service, Wi-Fi, and TV once all the construction and excavations were done. Pete and Ben had volunteered to set up the volleyball court, horseshoe pit, and playground equipment.

Her original plan had been to open by the end of May when tourist season began, but as was her usual way, that proved to be overly optimistic. She hadn't even finished her part of the work—designing and launching the website. Robert had agreed to use his company's platforms and resources to help her with advertising and marketing, so that was one less thing to worry about.

There were many things left to accomplish, though, and one of the largest items on her to-do list loomed large—hiring staff. She needed to start the search now and begin interviewing. Where to start the search was the problem. Her father had been like the Pied Piper with how he collected young men who were willing to work entry-level jobs as stable hands and learn under his tutelage. She didn't have his knack for that.

Sophie stepped out of the shower, dried off, and dressed in faded jeans and an old college T-shirt. As she wrapped a towel around her freshly shampooed hair, she heard movement in the guest bedroom. When Sophie opened the bedroom door, Jamie was awake and sitting up in bed, rubbing her eyes with her fists.

"Good morning, Jamie Love," Sophie said as she bent and picked her up. "You are my Jamie Love, aren't you?"

Jamie nodded, then yawned. "Mommy! Where's Mommy?"

"Your mommy and daddy will be back soon. You're staying with Auntie Sophie." Sophie gave her a hug. "Let's go take a nice bubble bath. Would you like that?"

Jamie nodded again.

Sophie filled the bathtub with bubble bath, and Jamie splashed and played for several minutes, giggling as she chased the bubbles around the tub. She soon tired of the game, though, and reached toward Sophie to pull her from the water. Sophie dried her off, brushed her soft blonde curls, and dressed her in shorts and a T-shirt.

"Want to go get breakfast?" At Jamie's nod, Sophie planted a kiss on top of the girl's head, picked her up, and started down the stairs. When they were midway down the stairs, the front doorbell rang.

"Ooh, we have company, Jamie! Want to see who it is?" Sophie settled Jamie on her hip, walked down the rest of the steps, and opened the door.

A stranger stood on her porch. Well, he wasn't exactly a stranger. It was Cowboy. Except for the leather jacket, he was dressed much like he had been at their first meeting. Today, he was clean-shaven and his hair had been trimmed, but he still had that rugged appeal she'd noticed at their first meeting. He wasn't wearing sunglasses, and his dark-brown eyes smiled at her as he removed his Stetson hat. His eyes softened as they moved to Jamie. He started to say something.

"Cowboy," Sophie said in surprise, interrupting whatever he was going to say. "What are you doing here? Mr. Whittaker sent his hired hand to check the fence posts in our front yard?" she gently teased.

"Mornin', ma'am," Cowboy said, ignoring her question.

"Cowboy. Daddy," Jamie said, reaching toward the man.

"That's not Daddy, sweetie," Sophie said. She explained to the man, "This is Jamie. She just means that you dress like her daddy. He wears a hat similar to yours."

"Glad to meet you, Jamie. I'm Zach."

"Cowboy Zach," Jamie said as she reached for him again.

Zach reached out as Jamie pulled away from Sophie and fell into his arms. He settled Jamie in the crook of his elbow, then placed his hat on her head. It slipped down over her eyes. Jamie giggled and pushed the hat back on her head.

"Huh! I guess she's not afraid of strangers. Or maybe she just likes cowboys. My feelings could get hurt. I was on my way to the kitchen to feed Jamie. Since she prefers you, Cowboy Zach, over me, why don't you come in and have a cup of coffee?" Sophie opened the door wider.

"Thank you, ma'am. Don't mind if I do," Zach replied as he stepped into the house.

Sophie looked at him for a few seconds, then turned and walked toward the kitchen. She wondered again if his folksy speech was only for her benefit or if it was his natural way of speaking.

Zach followed her into the kitchen, and Sophie pointed to a chair at the kitchen table. Zach sat down and settled Jamie on his lap. He took his hat off Jamie's head and placed it on a nearby chair.

"Did you enjoy your dinner at The Feed Bag?" Zach asked. "I would have come by your table to say hello, but you and your friend looked deep in conversation."

"I did enjoy it. That was Darlene, a friend from high school. We were catching up on our lives during the years I lived out of state. Do you want coffee?" At Zach's nod, Sophie poured a cup of coffee for him and another for herself. She placed the cream and sugar on the table along with a plate of scones from Patsy's Friday baking. Zach entertained Jamie by bouncing her on his knee as Sophie fixed a pot of oatmeal for Jamie's breakfast. She ladled some into a bowl, then cooled it.

"Jamie Love, you need to get into your highchair for your breakfast. I have oatmeal. You love oatmeal," Sophie cajoled.

"No," Jamie protested. "Eat with Cowboy." Jamie turned and gabbed Zach by the front of his shirt. She shook her head. "No. I want Cowboy Zach."

"It's okay. She can sit with me while she eats." Zach pushed his chair closer to the table, giving Jamie easier access to the table.

"She's messy," Sophie cautioned. "You want oatmeal in your hair?"

"I've had far worse in my hair, Miss Sophie," Zach said, smiling broadly. "It'll be alright."

"Don't say I didn't warn you," Sophie cautioned again as she placed the bowl of oatmeal and a cup of milk on the table in front of Zach and Jamie. "To catch the overflow," she explained as she spread a dish towel over the back of Jamie's shoulders, covering Zach's shirt.

Sophie sat down across from them. As she drank her coffee, she watched Jamie eat her breakfast with a minimum of assistance from Zach. She was just waiting for a spoonful of oatmeal to go flying through the air and land atop Zach's head, leaving streaks of oatmeal running down his face. Jamie handled her spoon very well, though, and wasn't as messy as she usually was when sitting in her highchair.

Zach and Jamie—the large man gently holding the tiny girl as she eats oatmeal could be a Norman Rockwell painting, Sophie thought as she watched them together. Maybe her initial impression of Cowboy as conceited and full of himself was wrong. His natural and unaffected gentleness with Jamie appeared normal behavior for him. Jamie contently sat in his lap and silently ate her breakfast. Sophie's prediction hadn't come true, and it left her a little miffed that Zach wasn't covered in oatmeal.

"A two-year-old child eating calmly! Wow! Tell me, Cowboy Zach, do you have this calming effect on all females?" Sophie's question came out peeved.

"With some I do. Others, I don't," Zach replied shortly. He added with a teasing grin, "Most females are like horses, Miss Sophie. If you treat them gently and with respect, most usually come around."

"Pfft," Sophie snorted. "Comparing women to horses! With

comments like that, no wonder women don't, as you put it, 'come around.'"

"I said 'most' do. There's always a few exceptions." Zach pushed Jamie's empty bowl back from the edge of the table, then held her cup of milk close to her mouth so she could drink.

Sophie rose, went to the sink, wet a cloth, and returned to wipe Jamie's face. As she bent toward Jamie, she was only inches away from Zach's face. Their eyes met and held before Sophie pulled back abruptly. The towel wrapped around her head came unwound, fell forward, and slipped onto Zach's shoulder. Sophie's wet hair tumbled over her face.

"I'm sorry! I forgot about the towel on my head! I'd just showered..." Sophie's voice trailed off as she grabbed the towel and tried to rewind it around her head.

"Leave it off. It's fine," Zach said slowly. With a mischievous glint in his eyes, he added, "There's nothing sweeter than a filly after she's had a bath and been rubbed down."

Sophie's hands froze in the middle of her attempt to rewind the towel around her head. Frustrated, she pulled the towel off completely. Her first urge was to throw it at Zach. She decided to not assault her guest and tossed the towel on a nearby chair instead.

Was Zach's remark about women in general or was it flirtatiously aimed at her specifically? Or was it just a roundabout attempt to put her at ease over her hair that looked like a bird's nest sitting atop her head? No, the glint in his eyes meant it was just another attempt to tease and provoke her. Should she be offended? She settled on pretending that his words had nothing to do with her.

"Oh my goodness! The horse analogies again! Your problems with women are becoming clearer by the minute."

"I don't recall saying I had a problem... ma'am," Zach replied. "I manage."

I just bet you do, Sophie thought as she met his teasing brown eyes with her own.

"Down," Jamie said as she began to squirm on Zach's lap, diverting his attention from Sophie. He had another comment ready, she felt certain. "Get down," Jamie repeated.

"She can get down." Sophie took Jamie from Zach, then sat her on a play rug at the edge of the room. Jamie picked a large puzzle from her pile of toys and began playing with the pieces.

Sophie returned to the table to finish her coffee. She picked up a scone, took a bite, and pushed the plate toward Zach.

Zach waved off the pastries. "I notice some grading and stakes being laid out on the knoll below the high meadow." He nodded in the direction the landscape architect was working. "Are you building something?" He was serious now, and his voice had lost some of its folksy twang.

"It's part of my attempt to revive Cameron Stables. I want to open up the cabin rentals again and hopefully save my father's business. The stakes are for a flower and rose garden—a place for guest to wander about, relax, and have a glass of wine in the evening after a day of trail riding or hiking or whatever they choose to do."

"I see," Zach replied. "Rebuilding a business is a big goal. What other plans are in the works?"

Over the next several minutes, Sophie briefly shared her plans, what she had already accomplished, and how much was left to be done.

"You've obviously thought this through," Zach commented. "You know, if you get swamped with guests and have the need, you can always borrow horses from Thornton Farms. We currently have five, plus my bay."

"Loaning horses would be very kind of Mr. Whittaker, but I doubt we'll need them. 'Swamped' will likely happen only in my dreams," Sophie said with a laugh. "I'm going slow and not doing anything crazy. I'll expand more when there's a need. My biggest chore right now is finding staff. Renovating and adding amenities might be the easiest part."

"Oh! Speaking of renovations… I got sidetracked. You know, by horses and women, two of my favorite things," Zach said with a smile. "The reason I came by was to invite you to the grand opening of the renovated Thornton Farms next Saturday night."

"Mr. Whittaker has it finished?"

"Yes. Well, the bottom floor is finished, anyway. The house didn't need major changes. The upstairs still needs redecorating and some refurbishing, but the guests won't be going up there. And even that area should be finished in another month or two." Zach pulled an invitation from his shirt pocket and passed it to Sophie. "Seven p.m. Saturday night. Will your mother be able to come?"

"No, she's in Paducah with my aunt who's recovering from surgery. She hopes to be home within a couple of weeks—as soon as my Aunt Rachel is able to come with her."

Zach nodded. "About hiring staff… I might have an idea that could help you out—with stable hands, at least. I'll see what I can come up with and let you know at the grand opening."

"Thank you. All ideas are welcome," Sophie replied. "Mr. Whittaker doesn't mind that his employee is spending time solving his neighbor's problems?"

"Nah. As head honcho at Thornton Farms, I do a lot of the decision-making."

"Well, thank him for me. And for the invitation. Maybe he'd be willing to give me tips on how to turn a failing business into a successful one."

"I'm sure he'll be willing to help in any way he can." Zach rose from the table. "I should be going. I have managerial duties to attend to." He walked over to Jamie and picked her up.

"Goodbye, Jamie. Cowboy Zach was very happy to meet you."
He gave her a hug, then sat her back down on the play rug

"Cowboy Zach! Cowboy Zach!" Jamie repeated as Sophie
and Zach walked toward the front door.

"And goodbye to you, too, Miss Sophie," Zach said as he
stopped at the front door and turned toward Sophie.

"Thanks for stopping by, Cowboy."

"I'll probably see you Saturday night," Zach said. "Mr.
Whittaker usually lets the hired help attend his social func-
tions." Zach stepped outside and settled his hat on his head. He
touched the brim in his usual goodbye salute. "See you, Miss
Sophie."

As Sophie closed the door, she considered her guest. Cowboy Zach was an intriguing man—friendly, polite, and admit-
tedly extremely good looking. But what was his story? Had Mr.
Whittaker brought him to Kentucky, as Patsy said? Were there
cowboys in Chicago?

He hadn't shared any personal details about himself during
their conversations. No, he'd been too busy throwing out
oblique remarks that she could interpret however she wanted
to. What was that about, other than annoying her and enjoying
every minute of it? But he had offered to help her find staff. If he
followed through on that, Cowboy Zach could tease her to his
heart's content.

CHAPTER SIX

W here've you been?" Eli, Zach's longtime friend, looked up from where he sat behind the desk as Zach walked through the door. His laptop was open, and a stack of papers was spread out in front of him. "You need to use the desk?" He indicated the chair he was sitting in.

"Nah." Zach tossed his hat onto a sofa on the other side of the room and waved away the offer. He sat down in one of the chairs facing the desk. He picked up a baseball from the corner of the desk and began tossing it back and forth from hand to hand. "I went over to invite the Camerons to the grand opening on Saturday."

"I thought Jack was delivering the invitations," Eli said. "Oh… I get it! You wanted to personally deliver the one to the Camerons—and to Sophie in particular."

"Well… I thought it was the thing to do since we're next-door neighbors." Zach paused, then added, "Sophie doesn't re-member me at all." He kept up his juggling act with the baseball.

"Of course she doesn't! It's been, what, sixteen, seventeen

years since you last saw her? You've changed from the skinny kid you were back then. Heck, your butt didn't fill out your jeans when I met you in college."

"That's mostly because the Army had worked it off of me. But I've bulked up some since, don't you think?" Zach folded his arms and flexed his biceps. But he didn't smile. His mind was still on his visit with Sophie.

"You've definitely put on a few pounds. But didn't you tell me that Mr. Cameron made you boys keep your distance where his daughter was concerned? She probably never got a good look at you."

"I saddled her horse for her once or twice before her father shooed me away. He acted as if I was going to maul her or something. I just wanted to talk. But mostly, I just curried the horses after she and her friends came back from riding."

"So, the conversations you had were with her horse?" Eli smiled at his friend. "That's probably not the best way to get to know someone."

"You're right. I guess we never actually had a conversation. As I recall, she was pretty shy. Plus, there was her eagle-eyed father breathing down my shirt collar."

"She was a teenager then, right? Maybe she didn't find you attractive or want to hang out with you." Eli dodged the baseball Zach tossed toward him, then picked it up and replaced it on the corner of the desk.

"You're right... again. She was a kid and more interested in spending time with her friends than with the hired help."

"Well, did you have a nice visit with her today?"

"Mostly. I—"

"Did you introduce yourself? Oh no! You didn't use that fake Western accent on her, did you?" Eli interrupted. "That works on college chicks, but not on a mature woman." Eli shook his head at Zach. "Haven't I taught you anything where women are concerned?"

"It just happened that day we met on Mystic Hills. I couldn't stop myself after she insulted me and called me 'cowboy.' The way she said 'cowboy' and just assumed I was a hired hand kinda stung."

"I thought you'd shed that thin skin of yours."

"I have, but I don't like it when people judge me by assumptions or their perceptions. Maybe you're right and I'm still a little touchy." Sophie hadn't actually sneered, but she'd sounded as if she had him figured out. "And there's something about her that makes me want to rile her up."

"First, as a *real* cowboy from Texas, I'm offended that you were offended by being called a cowboy. It's not an insult. Secondly, I figure you had a *log*, not a chip, on your shoulder when you worked for her dad. Thirdly, this school-boy teasing might get you burned. That fiery hair should give you warning."

"How do you know the color of her hair?"

"I've seen her before."

"You have? Where?"

"Down, Romeo! I haven't actually met her, but she was standing on the butte the morning I flew back from Richmond. You'd have to be blind to miss that hair, even from the air. And I saw her on the patio at The Feed Bag when we were there. I also noticed that you saw her, too. Your ears spiked forward when she walked in, just like my stallion does when he spots a mare."

"Ha! Now, you're exaggerating. Let's just say she's not that gangly teenager anymore." Zach didn't fully understand what made him put on the cowboy act when he was around Sophie. Sure, she had labeled him as such at their first meeting, but discussing it now with Eli made it seem more immature than when he was in the moment.

"I get it. She's beautiful. All fire and ice! And definitely not a kid!" Eli grinned, expecting a reaction, but Zach was momentarily lost in his memories.

"It's funny how things work out sometimes," Zach said. "I wouldn't have worked for her father or met her at all if I hadn't been tired and overslept that morning. I'd hitchhiked for miles the day before. I was exhausted."

"Mr. Cameron walked into the barn and found you asleep in the loft, right?" Eli asked. "I remember you telling me that story."

"Yes. I planned to be up and headed further south before daylight. Looking back, George didn't actually threaten me, but it sure seemed like he did at the time. According to him, I had to work that day to pay for my night's lodging… and the hot breakfast he forced on me. I ended up staying there all summer. He let me and another guy share the apartment over the carriage house and paid me a salary."

"Sounds like he was a nice guy."

"Yes, George was a great person," Zach agreed. "He showed an interest in me, and boy, could he give advice! More advice than any seventeen-year-old kid wanted or thought he needed. Not that I didn't need it. I was a lost young man when I arrived at Cameron Stables."

Luckily, George Cameron and the US Army had straightened him out. Neither coddled him. With time, he began to believe he could make something of his life. No more just accepting what life threw at him and barely squeaking by in the process.

"You've put all that behind you now. But Sophie's going to be really pissed when she finds out you're just messing with her."

"Maybe. That thought had crossed my mind, but I've been having too much fun playing the part she expects of me." Sophie's response would not be pretty when she found out that Cowboy was just an act.

"Isn't Sophie married?"

"Divorced, according to George the last time we talked. She has a cute kid, though, about two years old. But I don't remember George saying anything about having a granddaughter. Jamie likes me, though, even if her mother doesn't. I fed her breakfast."

"What? You fed breakfast to a kid? A two-year old?" Eli laughed as he pictured his friend feeding a toddler.

"Well, I held her while she ate. But I like kids. I dated a girl at Fort Benning who had a two-year-old and a four-year-old. I got along better with them than with her. Kids are amazing. Their needs are very basic. They accept life as it comes... at least until they become teenagers."

"The teen years can be rough," Eli agreed.

"So, why were you looking for me?" Zach ask Eli, pushing away the memories of his own teen years. "You need something?"

"I inspected the new building this morning. The crew is finishing the inside now. They should be done in a week or so."

"The bunkhouse? That's good. It's going up faster than expected. Lynn is supposed to furnish and decorate it."

"The *bunkhouse*? Is that what we're calling it? Eight bedrooms with a shared bathroom between the bedrooms, a communal kitchen, and a living area. It looks very nice." Eli handed Zach his phone with some pictures he'd taken of the construction.

"Looks good. Exactly like the plans," Zach said as he reviewed the pictures. "The contractor has done a nice job, don't you think?" He handed the phone back to Eli.

"I've never seen a bunkhouse like this before. If we'd had one like this on our ranch, I'd have moved out of the main house into the bunkhouse. I wouldn't have had to share a bathroom with my sister... and you."

"I don't believe for one second that you'd give up your mom's cooking. That woman knows how to cook!"

"You make a good point. I bet my sister is a good cook, too," Eli said pointedly.

"I know what you're hinting at," Zach replied. "As I've said before, your sister and I are friends, nothing more, and we've never been more than friends. Besides, she's in love with that Air Force captain from the base near your ranch. At least, that's what she told me the last time we talked." Eli looked up from the papers he was reading in surprise. "You didn't know that? I guess I'm the big brother she never had."

"That's not funny," Eli insisted.

"You're so busy keeping tabs on my life, your sister fell in love, and you missed it. Lighten up! Lisa knows what she's doing. I think this guy is the right one for her."

"Huh!" Eli replied, sounding unconvinced. "Lisa's coming to Louisville in a few days for a horse auction. I'll find out what's going on with this captain I've never heard of."

"Leave your sister alone, Sherlock. It won't end well for you," Zach advised. "Is your father still laid up with his broken leg?"

"Yeah. He can't travel yet, but I think he's also tired of traveling. If you've seen one horse auction, you've seen them all. Since I'm not interested in taking over the ranch, he's giving more and more responsibility to Lisa. He's finally accepted the fact that I'm not a rancher and is hopefully over his disappointment that I chose to attend the University of Georgia and study computer science and not Texas A&M, his alma mater."

"Lisa's captain is from a ranching family. And he's a Texas Aggie graduate. Score one for the captain," Zach teased. "Your father likes him, and your sister loves him." Lisa was only two years younger than Eli, but he often acted like she was still sixteen. "Poor Eli, everyone's happy but him."

"I'm happy if she's happy," Eli replied. "But never mind my sister. My mom wants you to come back with me when I stop to visit on my return to California at the end of the summer."

"I'll visit soon, but I have more work to do here before I can leave. You can go home sooner if you want. I know you miss Abby, and she might even miss you a little."

"Very funny!" Eli responded. "Abby and I are going to meet up—possibly in New York—when she has an extended layover after a return flight from Europe. But I plan to stay here until the first of September, as promised."

"Well, if you change your mind, feel free to go home early. Sophie is trying to breathe life back into Cameron Stables— her father's business. I want to quietly help her if I can. At least offer any advice that she'll accept. George took me in, so I'd like to help his daughter."

"By quietly, you mean without her knowing?"

"No, not exactly. I don't want to see Cameron Stables— George's dream—or any other business around Kingsville go under. I want to help but be subtle about it and not appear to be interfering. She'll want to do this on her on—for her father. If she thought for a minute that I was drifting into her lane, she'd shred me alive."

"Uh-huh!" Eli said with a smile. "I doubt George Cameron's dream—or jobs for Kingsville—has anything to do with you acting like an infatuated lovesick schoolboy."

"In my experience, a one-way infatuation always ends poorly."

"I've known you a long time, pardner, and the one-way infatuations you mention are always directed at you, not from you. I'm beginning to understand why."

"You're not right *all* the time, pardner." Zach picked up the baseball again and good-naturedly tossed it at Eli. Eli successfully dodged the baseball a second time.

◆

Sophie emptied the shopping bags onto her bed. She had just returned from Kingsville's sole evening wear boutique, where she had purchased a dress for the Grand Opening of the Thornton Farms Mansion. The invitation had indicated that the dress code was semiformal.

Sophie stood before the full-length mirror and held the black cocktail dress in front of her. The dress had a classic design with clean tailored lines. A band of crisp white fabric ran diagonally across the bodice, and the A-line skirt stopped just above her knee. The color contrasted well with her auburn hair. Her Grandmother Cameron's black star sapphire necklace would nestle perfectly in the dropped V neckline.

As she hung the dress in her closet, Sophie wondered who else would be attending the open house. The movers and shakers of Kingsville, no doubt, but would Cowboy be there? Would he add a bolo tie to his denim shirt and call it Western formal wear? He'd said that Mr. Whittaker usually invited his employees to such events, and odds were, if Cowboy was invited, he'd attend, not wanting to miss a chance to poke fun at her with his folksy insinuations and try to rattle her.

Sophie heard the roar of a car's engine and looked out the upstairs window. A yellow Porsche was racing up the driveway. She recognized the car. It belonged to her attorney, Stephen Hampton. He was bringing some additional papers that would complete the transfer of Cameron Stables solely to her and her mother's possession.

Sophie smiled at the incongruity of the man behind the wheel. Stephen was a conservative attorney from an ultraconservative family. At least, until he climbed behind the wheel of the latest flashy car he owned. His need for speed led him to occasionally race in minor heats at an auto track near Louisville. Sophie suspected that he mostly did it to horrify his straight-laced blue blood family, especially his mother.

Sophie had known Stephen since they were in high school. They had even dated a few times after the humiliation of the Travis incident. Their relationship had never been more than friends, even though her parents highly approved of him. He was a refreshing change from Travis. They were each other's backup dates when both were without partners for a school dance or other school function. Sophie was a pro at cementing long-lasting male friendships, but not so much with romantic ones.

Sophie opened the front door and welcomed Stephen into the house. After she signed the papers he'd brought, she gave him a tour of the property and showed him the features she'd added. They stopped at the fence around the training area to watch Pete work with one of the horses.

"You're training horses, too?" Stephen asked as they leaned on the fence.

"We've had a couple of inquiries from owners with young and untrained horses. I don't think we'll make this a major part of the services we offer, but since we're boarding these already, training them will bring in additional revenue until we get established. Pete has volunteered to take on that job. He's experienced and is a good trainer. This horse has been broken to saddle, but Pete's trying to smooth him out and get him to accept commands from the rider."

"Pete looks like he knows what he's doing," Stephen stated.

"Pete will have him behaving and accepting directions from whomever is in the saddle within a couple more sessions. Most of our boarders require minimal attention, but an occasional demonstration like what Pete's doing now might entertain some guests. Most people aren't familiar with how an untrained horse becomes a safe riding mount."

They left the training area and walked around to view the other construction sites. The entertainment shelter was almost done, as was the rose and flower garden. Sophie pointed out the location where the tents would be installed in the meadow east of the cabins. The disturbed earth where the water and electric lines had been installed could be seen from where they stood.

"I think you're on the right track here," Stephen commented.

"You think so? My latest target date to open is around the middle of June—that is, if all the changes go as expected. I've had to be patient and flexible because I can't completely control the pace of construction. Whether my plans are successful and will make money is a completely different story—one with a happy ending, I hope."

They walked back toward the house and stopped by Stephen's car parked in the driveway.

"I wanted to ask if you'd like to go to the Grand Opening at the Thornton Farms Mansion with me on Saturday. It'll be just like old times," Stephen said before getting into his car.

"I appreciate the invitation, but I'm going with someone else." Since Patsy had said she'd never been invited to a formal party at the Thornton Mansion, Sophie had asked her to be her plus-one.

"Okay. I'm sure I'll see you there," Stephen said. "It'll be nice to see what Whittaker has done to the place. I hear he has the resources to redo it in any way he chooses."

"I'm sure it will be nice. I'm looking forward to seeing the restoration, too." She was looking forward to spending an evening all dressed up and partying with the good citizens of Kingsville. And Cowboy had promised to provide her with a source for finding staff.

CHAPTER SEVEN

Patsy arrived at Cameron Stables on Saturday night with her blue eyes filled with excitement.

"You look gorgeous," Sophie complimented Patsy as they climbed into Sophie's car for the ride to Thornton Farms. "The burgundy color of your dress compliments your blonde hair perfectly."

"Thanks. You look great, too. Let's face it. We're both lookers." Patsy laughed as she climbed into the passenger seat and fastened her seat belt. "Let's go break some hearts."

"You got it," Sophie replied as she started the car. She drove through the gate and pulled out onto the gravel road that ran along the front of the Cameron property. Sophie followed the gravel road until they came to an intersection with a two-lane road. She made a left turn and pulled onto the paved road.

The two-lane road, scenic in normal times, was a colorful and beautiful route at this time of year. Blooming redbud, crab apple, and dogwood trees lined both sides of the road.

Farmland sprawled out as far as the eye could see. Interspersed among fields of hay, soybeans, and sorghum were rolling pastures where sleek horses roamed freely and grazed on the green grass.

Patsy, excited about an evening out, talked nonstop as they sped along the two-lane road that led to Thornton Farms. "Thanks for inviting me. Since James and I separated, my social life has been pretty blah and almost nonexistent," Patsy said. "Any time I leave the house, it's for work or errands."

"You're welcome. My social life isn't exactly on fire, either." Sophie laughed. "But I have too many other things to think about now. A social life would only complicate things. In my experience, relationships take more time than they're worth."

"Do you really mean that? I hate to think you're that cynical!"

"I'm sorry," Sophie said with a laugh. "People who bad-mouth relationships are those who don't have a relationship to brag about. And that's me."

"Yeah, I know. I've been there. James says that he wants to reconcile, but I'm getting used to living by myself. Not having someone make demands on my time can be very appealing." Patsy sighed in exasperation. "But the funny thing is, I miss him. I even miss our arguments."

"I remember James as a nice man. Living alone has its disadvantages, for sure, but a person needs someone they can count on, someone with whom they have common likes and interests." Sophie's words were based on experience. "It shouldn't be one-sided or feel like an unpaid job."

"Does arguing all the time count as a common interest? Though, it wasn't that way at first." Patsy's voice was filled with sadness and longing.

"Everyone argues sometimes, and I don't think all arguments are bad, but you need a special deep-down connection, whatever that might be," Sophie said. "I've yet to feel that. But that's *my* idea of a marriage, anyway."

"Listen to you! Sophie, the marriage counselor."

"Sophie, the divorced struggling businesswoman, you mean. My best advice is don't take advice from me on matters of the heart. My idea of what makes a marriage work may not even exist. I hope you two work it out and find the magic you once had." Sophie decided that it was time to change the subject and divert Patsy's thoughts away from James. This night was supposed to be celebratory and happy. "Have you been to the Thornton Mansion since the renovation?"

"I stopped by briefly after my crew had finished cleaning the place, so it'll be good to see it now, after they've finished with the decorating. They finished it quickly. It took me three years to redo my kitchen. James and I fought over every decision, but nothing we argued over seems important now. James hired on with the construction crew that's working for Mr. Whittaker, too."

Sophie's effort to change the subject hadn't worked. Patsy was still in love with James. Otherwise, she wouldn't bring him up so often.

"They did finish quickly. Having plenty of money makes it easier, I'm sure. Plus, having a live-in decorator like Lynn doesn't hurt," Sophie said, making another stab at directing Patsy's thoughts away from James and their failing marriage. Mentioning Lynn should do it.

"Lynn was there when I stopped by—ordering my people around like she was the lady of the manor or something," Patsy fumed. "She hasn't changed—still lording it over everyone. But from all accounts, she's good at her profession."

"I've not heard otherwise," Sophie agreed.

The Thornton Mansion was about five miles by car from Cameron Stables, and just like Cameron Stables, a gravel road led off the paved road toward the property. Before long, they had entered the gates of Thornton Farms. Clouds of pink petals from the flowering plum trees that lined the long driveway blew across the front of Sophie's car as they approached the mansion.

"Looks like we're here," Sophie said as she pulled into the next available slot in a long line of cars parked in front of the mansion.

The house, built in the late seventeen hundreds, was a behemoth by local standards. The brick exterior had faded over time to a soft red, but the house retained its original footprint of a three-story structure in the center with one-story wings branching off on three sides. Over the years, various members of the Thornton family had modernized the interior by adding central air conditioning, heating, and plumbing. At one time, an owner had reconfigured one of the downstairs rooms and turned it into a kitchen. The original kitchen, located in a separate building outside the main house, had been turned into a caretaker's cottage.

As Sophie and Patsy exited the car and walked across the front driveway, Sophie noted that the house's exterior looked exactly as she remembered it. Mr. Whittaker had not made any changes there.

A man Sophie didn't know dressed in a fitted butler's jacket and black bow tie met them as they crossed the Greek-styled portico and approached the door. He smiled in welcome as he opened the door for them.

"Good evening. Welcome. The party is this way," he said as he led them across the entryway and down a hallway toward the ballroom. Music and laughter could be heard as they got closer to the opened double doors of the ballroom. The butler bowed slightly and said, "Enjoy your evening." Then, he turned and walked back toward the front entrance.

Sophie and Patsy walked through the doorway and into a

room filled with guests. Small groups of people milled around talking, laughing, and visiting. Some guests stood at bar-height tables while others sat in chairs at traditional tables. The chandelier in the center of the room had been restored and showered diamond crystals of light over the crowded room. The refinished handrails and newel posts on the sweeping spiral staircase and the carved moldings around the ceiling gleamed golden in the light.

"It's beautiful," Patsy breathed, then sighed in awe. "Just like in a fairy tale."

"Yes. It's very close to the original, as I remember it," Sophie agreed. "I see our host." Sophie nodded toward the man she had seen with Cowboy at the restaurant when she met Darlene for dinner. "He's over there with Lynn. We need to say hello and introduce ourselves."

Sophie started to cross the room to speak to the man engrossed in a conversation with Lynn, but someone stepped in front of her and blocked her way.

"Cowboy," Sophie said in greeting as she looked up into Zach's smiling face. He was dressed in a dark suit and tie—not a bolo tie, either. "Looking good. I see you left your Stetson at home," she added as her eyes roved over him. "Don't you feel like something's missing without it?"

"Evening, Miss Sophie. You look beautiful tonight. You too, ma'am," Zach said, nodding at Patsy. "Actually, I miss my horse even more than my hat or my boots," he added in a slow drawl as he returned her smile. "Sometimes, you have to bend to the rules of etiquette and get all spiffed up to meet the neighbors, regardless of the inconvenience." He shrugged his shoulders against the confinement of his suit jacket and pulled at the tie around his throat. "I'm just a lowly cowboy at heart, Miss Sophie. Not used to all this finery."

"Very true. Society demands that from all of us at times.

This is Patsy. Patsy, this is Cowboy—I mean Zach." Sophie introduced them. "We were on our way to say hello to our host and to Lynn."

Patsy started to say something, but Sophie's attention was on the dark eyes that twinkled at her in amusement. Zach always smiled that way when she was around him. His teasing smile was getting just a little bit annoying.

"First, let's get you something to drink." Zach signaled to one of the waiters that circled the room carrying trays of champagne. The waiter was at his elbow immediately. Zach took two glasses of champagne off the tray and handed one to Sophie and one to Patsy. He then took one for himself. He tipped his glass toward them before taking a sip. The waiter stood patiently at Zach's side.

"Can I get you anything else, Mr. Whittaker?" the waiter asked.

"No." Zach shook his head. "Thank you, Johnny. That's all for now."

"Yes, sir, Mr. Whittaker. Just signal if you want something." The waiter gave a slight bow to them before moving on to another group of guests nearby.

Sophie gulped, almost choking on her champagne as the waiter's words sank in. She quickly placed her hand over her mouth, stopping herself from spewing her drink all over Zach and Patsy. Zach stood calmly in front of her, his eyes sparkling with a teasing smile. He shrugged in a half-hearted apology.

"What? *You're* Whittaker? But the man…with Lynn…" Sophie stammered.

"Things aren't always the way some people perceive them to be. They jump to conclusions," Zach stated, the Western twang gone from his voice. "Zach Whittaker. Welcome to my home, both of you." He shook Patsy's hand, then turned back to Sophie. "The man you're referring to is Cal Dixon, my attorney. He and Lynn are coordinating the house renovations. Or at least, that's the excuse they give for spending so much time together. I wonder, though. They look pretty cozy, don't you think?" He nodded toward Cal and Lynn who stood close together, still in conversation.

"Don't try to distract me! You lied to me." Sophie frowned, blushing as she heatedly accused him. "Why would you do that—not tell me who you are?"

"Hold up! I never lied to you. If you recall, it was you who decided who I was. You never got beyond 'Cowboy, the hired hand,'" Zach reminded her, then smiled. "You didn't ask for my name. As I recall, you were distracted the day we met and all on your own."

Sophie was certain she hadn't called him "Cowboy" with the same disdain he now put into the word, but she had been a bit abrupt. And yes, she had been distracted. She was embarrassed that he had recognized the cause of her distraction.

Out of the corner of her eye, Sophie saw Patsy edge away from the conversation and move toward a table nearby to sit with her sister Mattie and Mattie's husband Ken—Zach's employees. Patsy had escaped, not wanting to be a part of their squabble. While she applauded Zach's nice gesture of inviting his employees to the party, it didn't lessen her anger. The fact remained that he had played her for a fool—twice. She now understood why she always felt like she was the butt of a secret joke when he was around.

As Sophie absorbed the shock of finding out Cowboy Zach's true identity—owner of Whitaker & Co. and this beautiful mansion—fairness prodded her to grudgingly admit that he was right. She had jumped to conclusions about him based entirely on his looks—completely wrong conclusions.

"You're right. I apologize," Sophie said with reluctance. "I didn't mean to insult you. In fact, I love cowboys." Sophie's cheeks warmed under his stare. Zach quirked an eyebrow at her, and his eyes twinkled as Sophie tried to explain her meaning. "I mean, I admire the work they do. It's a tough job."

"Apology accepted—even a reluctant one." Zach smiled, then waved away her apology. "And no hard feelings. I've been wrong a time or two myself."

"A time or two? It must be nice to be nearly perfect," Sophie retorted.

"I wouldn't know about perfect. Truce?" Zach stuck out his hand to Sophie. "I didn't correct your mistake, either, or introduce myself."

Sophie shook his hand and nodded, accepting his overture of friendship.

"How's Jamie?" Zach asked. "You have a cute kid, there, by the way."

"Thanks. She *is* a beautiful, sweet child," Sophie returned. "She's at home and should be in bed soon." Now, who was assuming? He hadn't asked if Jamie was hers when he stopped by, and in the process of feeding Jamie, she hadn't explained that she was babysitting for Jenny and Pete. She didn't correct him now. It was her own secret joke—a small one, but the best she had at the moment as payback for him keeping his real identity secret. "I sincerely apologize for my assumptions about you. It wasn't my intent to insult you," Sophie repeated so it was clear that she could admit when she was wrong.

"Assumptions? Who?" The third man Sophie remembered from their group at The Feed Bag, a tall, slender man with sandy brown hair, walked up beside them and addressed Sophie. "Surely, 'Mr. Assume the Worst and Expect the Worst' here isn't assuming something?" He hooked a thumb toward Zach. "I *assume* you must be Sophie."

"Sophie Cameron," Zach said as he introduced her to the man. "Eli Reardon, my business partner and the man who never misses an opportunity to interrupt me when I'm talking to a beautiful woman."

"Someone has to keep you on track." Eli punched Zach good-naturedly on the arm. "But I'll leave you to charm the lady. Remember my fatherly advice, though: avoid all trite, worn-out pickup lines. Get some new material. It was good to meet you, Sophie." Eli gave Zach a thumbs-up sign of encouragement as he turned and walked away.

"Pay no attention to Eli." Zach shook his head and smiled at Eli's back as he joined a group of men at the bar on the other end of the room. "He's good at company business, but he also enjoys involving himself in my personal life."

"This room looks amazing," Sophie said, diverting the conversation back to the purpose of the party. "I'd love to see more of the restoration."

"I'd love to show it to you," Zach replied. He held out his arm to Sophie.

"Lead the way." She laced her hand through his elbow and let him lead her out through the ballroom door into the hallway.

Zach's tour first took Sophie through the living areas located across the hall from the ballroom. There were two living rooms, one for large gatherings and a smaller reception room for entertaining smaller, less formal groups. They continued through a large dining room and into a second, smaller dining room for more intimate dinners.

Adjacent to the dining areas were the kitchen and butler's pantry. At the moment, it was filled with catering staff preparing the meal that would be served shortly. The caterers looked up and nodded to Sophie and Zach, then went back to their dinner preparations. The kitchen was large, and new appliances had recently been added.

"It's beautiful. The whole house is just beautiful," Sophie said as she looked around the kitchen.

"This is where I eat unless I have guests," Zach said as he pointed to a kitchen table in a nook nearby. It sat next to double windows that framed an outside terrace and pool area.

"So much space for one man… uh… unless you have family living with you."

"No family, but I have to agree with you. It's a lot of space."

After they left the kitchen area, Zach showed her a large office located next to a library fully stocked with books. They then moved on to the more private areas of the house. First, there was a media room with a large-screen TV and comfortable seating. Located next to the media room was a space that contained a pool table and a variety of video games—the "boy toys" that the original builder could never have dreamed would ever exist. Despite the modern-day updates, the original architecture had been preserved in every room.

Zach led her back to the hallway and on past the ballroom to a door at the end of the hall. On the way, they passed other groups of guests touring the home. Zach paused before the door to the wing that branched out to the north side of the property.

"This wing isn't open or ready for visitors," Zach said, nodding toward a "do not enter" sign on the door. "It's my private quarters, with another office off the master bedroom and also a small gym. There are empty rooms that were once bedrooms, but I haven't decided on a purpose for them just yet. I'll make some upgrades, but as with the rest of the house, all the original woodwork and ceiling moldings and any salvageable furniture will be saved. My goal is for the house to look as it did when Lynn's family lived here, only better, once it's all refurbished. Who knows? I might donate it to the Historical Conservation Committee."

"You would do that?" Sophie asked, incredulous. "That would be an impressive gift."

"I would," Zach replied without further explanation. He looked at her and smiled. "What? You don't think a cowboy can be philanthropic?"

"You need to get over that," Sophie replied. "Trust me, calling you 'Cowboy' wasn't an insult." *Not in the least*, she silently added, recalling how easily she had spun a romantic profile for him based entirely on his looks, then shoehorned him into her idea of a handsome, rugged, independent cowboy, all based on nothing more than an old TV commercial. No wonder she forgot to ask his name. The man standing before her still easily fit her original imagined profile, even though he was now dressed in a suit and tie.

"I accept your word." Zach placed his hand on the small of her back and guided her down the hallway toward the ballroom. He stopped just outside the entrance. "The buffet dinner will be served soon, but afterward, why don't you meet me on the terrace where it's quiet, and we can talk. I have an idea about filling some of your staffing needs at Cameron Stables."

"Great! I'll be there. I'm open to all suggestions." Sophie nodded, then stepped into the ballroom. Zach followed close behind.

"Sophie!" Stephen called out as he approached and hugged her. "Would you join me for dinner? I have a table over there." He pointed to a table where several people were already seated. Sophie stalled before answering. Abruptly walking away from Zach seemed rude, and she had come to the party with Patsy. She didn't want to abandon either of them.

Sophie quickly glanced around the room to find Patsy. She hadn't seen her since Zach had joined them. Patsy was still sitting with Mattie and Ken. And wasn't that James sitting with her now? It was obvious that Patsy wouldn't miss her.

"You two enjoy your dinner," Zach said. "I need to introduce myself to all my neighbors. I'll see you later." He touched Sophie's arm, then turned and walked away.

Sophie's eyes followed Zach as he walked to the raised plat-form where the band had just taken a break. She and Stephen turned toward the stage as Zach approached the microphone.

"Hello, Kingsville citizens!" Zach began. "Welcome to the open house for the renovated Thornton Farms Mansion. I'm the new owner, Zach Whittaker. No, make that *caretaker* of this magnificent house. I don't know what you've heard about me, but disregard any derogatory remarks and accept as gospel all compliments."

There was a ripple of laughter around the room.

"I hope you like what we've done to the mansion." Applause broke out from the crowd. When it died down, Zach continued, "Of course, I have to thank Lynn Thornton for her excellent taste in decorating, for keeping us on schedule, and for sticking to the original period design. I promise you, I will continue to keep that in mind as we finish up any remaining renovations. Enjoy your dinner and please join in the dancing afterward." Zach stepped down from the dais and joined Eli across the room.

Stephen guided Sophie to the buffet that was laid out on wide antique sideboards and serving tables. They appeared to either be part of the house's original furnishings or new acqui-sitions from that period. Sophie filled her plate, then followed Stephen to his table. The other occupants were his friends and colleagues. Sophie had a vague knowledge of who they were, but she was not personal friends with any of them. They all wel-comed her and included her in conversation as they ate dinner. Once Stephen mentioned that Sophie was reopening Cameron Stables, several asked her to share her plans for the property. Sophie happily went into detail about the enhancements and new amenities she envisioned. Some of her listeners might be future guests, so she needed to spread the word every chance she got.

Once dinner was over, the ballroom lights dimmed, and the band took their places on the raised platform again. They began playing a current dance tune, and Stephen invited Sophie to join him in a dance as other guests filed onto the dance floor.

When the music ended after the first song, Sophie excused herself to go the ladies' room to freshen up. She looked for Stephen when she returned, but he was dancing with a woman from his office. They appeared to be having fun chatting and laughing. Stephan was never one to be without someone to talk to, and she doubted he would miss her if she left to meet Zach on the terrace.

Sophie skirted around the dance floor, then went through the double doors that stood open to the terrace to let in the cool nighttime breeze. She crossed the terrace and leaned against the railing to wait for Zach.

The terrace stretched out to the edge of an oval-shaped swimming pool—the one she had seen earlier through the kitchen windows. Pots of blooming plants and lighted tiki torches decorated the perimeter of the pool. Fireflies blinked across the lawn that gently sloped away from the house and pool. It was a beautiful night, a beautiful house, and a peaceful, tranquil setting.

Sophie drew in a deep breath, seemingly the first relaxing breath she'd taken in a while. Most of her waking hours since she'd discovered Cameron Stables' bleak financial position had been spent thinking about and planning the business's reorganization. Only in recent days had she started to think that the daunting task might be manageable—and successful.

The music from the ballroom floated out to the terrace and up into the star-filled night sky. Sophie shook back her hair as a gentle breeze blew across the terrace. It was heavenly cool and refreshing against her skin. She felt a presence next to her.

Zach's elbow brushed her hand as he leaned against the railing beside her.

"The stars are big and bright deep in the heart of Kentucky," Sophie said as she acknowledged his presence, then looked back up at the starry night.

"I think you might have the location wrong, Little Lady," Zach drawled in his fake accent. He smiled at her. "You need to let this cowboy show you a star-filled Texas night out on the open prairie—no city lights, and the only sound is the beating heart of your lover beside you. You'll realize how wrong you are."

For a moment, Sophie let herself visualize the romantic picture painted by Zach's words. If that was a trite, worn-out pickup line, she'd probably swoon at his feet over an original one. But Sophie smiled and cautioned, "And you need to remember what your friend Eli said about using worn-out pickup lines."

"You mean it's not working?"

"Hardly. Surely, you can do better."

"I'll work on it. I guess I'm out of practice."

"Now that, I believe! But tell me, Zach—I'm curious—what is the *real* Zach all about? Who are you when you aren't playing cowboy?" Sophie asked as she waved her hand toward the open land in front of them. "What brought you here, to this two-hundred-year-old house with all this farmland? Is this the beginning of a Whittaker agricultural empire, or is it just an addition to an already flourishing empire?"

"'Empire' is too grand a title for my businesses. And no, no agricultural empire in the making. I've been successful, but on what I'd call a normal scale. It's not a mystery. I like to think that hard work got me here—along with a few lucky breaks along the way. I'm involved in a lot of things—too many, I sometimes think—but I might settle here or use it as a retreat when things get crazy." Zach's eyes became serious and darkened as he looked at her. "Not everyone gets a straight shot at their goal. Sometimes, it's a complicated route. Then, when they do reach success, they often need the peace and solitude of a place like Kingsville. Sometimes, they long for things they still don't have."

"Really?" Sophie wasn't buying it. "You just threw a dart at a map, and it landed on Kingsville? Were you looking for a place to move your business?"

"No. As the boss, I can work from anywhere. And no darts were involved." Zach laughed as his somber tone was replaced by teasing. "I found out that this farm was for sale from Cal, my attorney, who lives in Lexington. I looked into it and made an offer. Not too bad for a range rider, huh?"

"A successful builder of an 'almost' empire—that I heard was from Chicago, by the way—chooses to live in tiny Kingsville, Kentucky? I find that story hard to accept." Sophie wasn't letting up. "What complicated road led you here?"

Zach was quiet for a moment. "Remind me another time, and I'll tell you the complicated, though unexciting, story of Zach Whittaker, businessman and cowboy extraordinaire. The night's too beautiful to get bogged down in the boring details of my life."

"I'd like to hear it," Sophie said. "'Lowly cowpunch-er-turned-businessman' would make a good plot for a TV drama." Sophie hoped to make him laugh and pull him back from the somber note she'd detected in his remarks. The teasing tone fit him better.

"I have never punched a cow in my life," Zach replied with a laugh. "But we're getting away from what I wanted to talk to you about." His voice was light again. "Remember? About hiring staff for your business?"

"I'm listening."

"I don't know all your property's needs, but I imagine you need help with the horses, around the barn, and with other chores that pop up. My idea is for you to hire youngsters who are looking for their first job, most likely with little or no experience, but willing to work and learn."

"That sounds great, but where do we find such people?"

"I was thinking young men who have aged out of foster care and don't have any other place to go. Give them a fresh start by giving them a job and a chance to make a life for themselves."

"Foster care?" This was a different approach than she'd expected and a source of labor Sophie would never have thought of on her own.

"Yes. I'd like to hire a couple to work for Thornton Farms, too. I'm building quarters that could house about eight young men. Your employees could live there, too. I, or my manager, would get them to your place each day. They'd need an experienced adult to supervise and train them—or ride herd, since you like cowboy-speak."

"You've thought this through, I see," Sophie stated, ignoring his comment about cowboys. "I would pay their rent, of course, if this plan works out."

"No rent needed." Zach waved away her offer. "The bunkhouse is built and just standing there, empty."

"My father used to give jobs to young men who were just starting out, but his effort was definitely not this organized. He mostly hired kids who were down on their luck for one reason or another—even some that just wandered onto our property. Others were recommended by a friend. He gave jobs to them all."

"I've heard that about your father. But I think we should do this right, by first talking to a professional, someone who can give us a sense of the young men's past and find out any specific problems they've had to overcome. I'd like to know their bios before meeting with them and keep the process from being like a traditional interview."

"That makes sense. Knowing their histories would make it easier to help them."

"Yes, but I don't want to search them out and give them hope of landing a job, then reject them because they need the kind of help we're not qualified to give. Rejection would just pile more disappointment on top of the disappointment they've already experienced. Personally, I don't think *minor* behavioral problems in their pasts should disqualify them, but mainly, they need to have a desire to improve their current situation."

"I like your idea. Saving my dad's dream is what's behind my efforts to save the business. He would certainly approve of giving these young men a helping hand. But why are you doing it?"

"What, a cowboy can't be a philanthropist?" Zach repeated his earlier teasing comment.

"Eli was right. You need to give up the cowboy act. You might dress the part at times, but I bet you know nothing about cows."

"Yes, I do. They produce great steaks—and, of course, milk. Doesn't that qualify me as an expert?" Zach laughed, then sobered. "But back to the plan. I have an appointment Monday in Frankfort with the Department for Community-Based Services, the agency that handles services for foster kids. Would you like to go with me?"

"Don't they have a local office we could contact?" Sophie asked.

"They have a regional office that serves the counties in the Bluegrass region, but I want to go to the department head. Actually, my appointment is with his assistant. We don't need their approval, since the kids will be eighteen and will have left foster care, but I'd like to let the department know what we're doing. There are people who take advantage of vulnerable youth for cheap labor. I don't want to be accused—or have you accused—of doing such a thing."

"That's a good idea. Get the approval of the authorities first." Sophie nodded in agreement.

"And they should be able to direct us to potential candidates—or at least their last known addresses. Without their help, it might take us weeks to find them."

"Another good point. I don't have weeks to waste if I hope to open soon. I'm guessing you got this appointment because you know the assistant to the department head?"

"No, but I know someone who knows the assistant—Cal, again."

"I figured you had some kind of connection," Sophie said. "Yes, I'd like to go with you."

"I'll pick you up, say, around eight a.m. on Monday. Will that work?"

"Sure. I'll be ready," Sophie responded.

"Good! Now, are you ready to go back to the party?" Zach pushed himself away from the terrace railing and turned toward her. "Hold still." He stepped closer, then reached out and placed one hand on the back of her head, holding it still. He pulled something from the top of her hair with his other hand. "Firefly. Caught in your hair," he said. He opened his palm, and a firefly took flight and blinked away into the darkness. Zach's other hand lingered on the back of Sophie's head.

"Thanks," Sophie said softly. The pressure of his hand pulled her head slightly toward him. He stopped abruptly but didn't remove his hand from her head. He stood close enough that Sophie could see tawny glints of the moon's reflection in his eyes. She felt the urge to lean closer to him, but her better judgement stopped her. She barely knew him, and what she thought she knew had been completely wrong.

"Zach. There you are!" Lynn spoke from behind them, just outside the ballroom door. "I've been looking for you. Your guests are leaving and asking for you."

"Okay, thanks. I'll be there in a minute," Zach replied. He slowly let his hand slide down the back of Sophie's head in a brief caress, then pulled it away. His eyes lingered on Sophie's face for a moment.

"We'd better go," Sophie said quietly, though she didn't step away. Had Zach been about to kiss her? Was she disappointed that he hadn't followed through? *Yes, disappointment is exactly what I'm feeling.* Apparently, her anger at him for not telling her who he was had dissipated as quicky as that firefly had blinked its way across the lawn.

"You're right. I need to say goodbye to my guests."

Sophie turned from the terrace railing and began to walk across the terrace toward the door where Lynn stood. Zach followed close behind her.

"Monday at eight," Zach reminded her as they entered the ballroom. With a touch on her shoulder, he left her, crossed the room, and went down the hallway that led toward the front door.

Sophie looked around for Patsy. She spotted her still sitting at her sister's table—with James. Sophie approached the pair and bent down to quietly ask, "Patsy, are you ready to leave?"

"James is going to drive me home—or at least to your place to pick up my car. We're going home to have a long talk," Patsy whispered back.

"Okay. No problem," Sophie replied.

"You don't mind driving back by yourself?"

"No, of course not. Good luck," Sophie replied quietly, patting Patsy on the arm. She made her way to the hallway and toward the front door. Zach was saying goodnight to his guests as they streamed out the door. Lynn stood by his side.

"I've been ditched by my date," Sophie said lightly when it was her turn to say goodnight. At Zach's questioning look, she added, "Patsy. My plus-one. She found a better offer in James."

"Oh. I see. I can drive you home," Zach offered.

"No, but thanks. That's not necessary. I drove my car, and it's not that far. Thanks for a lovely evening." Sophie turned to Lynn. "The house looks beautiful. You should be very proud of what you've done here. What does your mother think of the restoration?"

"I'm so glad you came, Sophie. Mom didn't come tonight. She said she'd wait for a private tour when everything is complete and she can browse at her leisure. I think she's afraid of digging up painful memories from when we lost my father."

"I can understand that," Sophie sympathized. "I hope she does come see it, though. It's as magnificent as I remember it."

"I'm sorry we didn't get a chance to talk tonight and catch up on old times," Lynn said. "My hostess duties kept me busy, and my cohost got tied up elsewhere. I think he was out enjoying the moonlight on the terrace." Lynn cut her eyes toward Zach, then back at Sophie. "Mom used to say there was magic on the terrace—a perfect view of the stars while standing in the Kentucky moonlight. According to her, romance literally floats in the air out there, wafting in on the sweet smell of gardenias and roses from the garden." Lynn turned to Zach and needled him, "Did you feel the magic, Zach?"

Was Lynn jealous that she had found Zach and Sophie together on the terrace? And was she now goading him with a reminder that his place as host was by her side?

Sophie looked at Zach for his reaction. If he had a reaction at all, it didn't show. He was calm and unperturbed by Lynn's comments. Zach didn't answer Lynn's question, but he gave Sophie a slight smile along with a quick wink, then turned to shake hands with another departing guest.

"Old times are overrated," Sophie said to Lynn, ignoring the other woman's comment about romance on the terrace.

"Maybe so, but it would be nice to catch up. Maybe we can

get together soon," Lynn suggested as she turned back to Sophie.

"Sure. Give me a call sometime," Sophie replied noncommittally. With a wave, she stepped through the door and out into the night. She crossed the portico, then made her way to her car.

As Sophie started her car and backed out of her parking spot, she thought about her conversation with Lynn. Getting together to talk? About the old days? What was that about?

The "old days" with Lynn were not something Sophie missed or longed to relive. She had left childish rivalries behind a long time ago. She did wonder, though, about the relationship between Lynn and Zach. The Lynn she knew from years ago wouldn't pass up the opportunity to go after someone with Zach's apparent wealth, good looks, and stature.

And as Sophie recalled from the past, no one had ever been able to resist Lynn's charms, either.

CHAPTER EIGHT

S ophie spent Sunday morning reviewing the design of the website for Cameron Stables. She was ready to go live as soon as the new construction was complete and she could add photos that would show site browsers the restful, inviting beauty of the property.

As she worked, Sophie's thoughts turned to the party last night at the Thornton Mansion. She was still a little shocked that Cowboy Zach turned out to be Zach Whittaker, new owner of Thornton Farms. She had frequently wondered why he always seemed amused about something when they were together. His secretive smile as he joked and teased her made sense now. She had created her own idea of who he was, and it never occurred to her that she could be wrong. He could have corrected her, but apparently, he was having too much fun at her expense.

Sophie closed the draft of the website and began looking over her plans for advertising. She had researched other competing properties, and with her refined approach, she felt confident that she would be offering additional amenities not found in most vacation horse farms—or at least among those in the nearby region.

Advertising was the least of her worries, though. That was her niche. She had set a budget but was prepared to go above that—within reason, of course—if it was required to smartly and effectively persuade people to come and spend time at beautiful Cameron Stables. The old adage in business was still true—it took money to make money. Getting the word out was the core of success. She would not skimp on advertising.

A presence on all the high-profile social media platforms was a must to reach a wide audience. She planned to use email lists from her former company, which Robert had sent her. Digital ads and strategically placed content keywords on internet search engines that would direct traffic to the website rounded out her online efforts at this point. There were a couple of print equestrian magazines still in business in Lexington where she would place print ads for people who didn't live in the digital world.

The grand opening date was set for some time in June around Father's Day—the perfect holiday for a family getaway. By then, vacation season would be in full swing. June would also be an ideal time to promote romance and attract couples who were celebrating anniversaries or engagements or who just wanted to shake off the winter doldrums and spend time alone and away from the madness of their daily lives. This plan had then inspired another idea: Cameron Stables as a wedding venue, where guests filled the cabins in the days before, during, and after the wedding day.

Sophie had added a wine-tasting night to the list of activities offered. A local wine distributer had agreed to host the event. It would appeal to a variety of guests and add a touch of class, in keeping with her "rustic redefined" theme.

The list of amenities available appeared comprehensive for a property like Cameron Stables and was workable in theory, but they would require lots of behind-the-scenes coordination. And to provide that coordination, she would need to hire staff for several positions, including a manager.

Sophie pulled a pad of paper toward her and began listing the positions she needed to fill. First, she wrote down "stable hands," but left the number needed open. She was counting on her trip with Zach tomorrow to help her fill those positions. The number depended on how many suitable contacts the agency gave them.

Next on her list was a customer service representative. After a thorough cleaning and new paint job, a small building near the property's entrance would serve as a welcome center. Internet service would be added soon. Arriving guests would check in and get a map of the property, directions to their cabins, and a schedule of events there. By the time they arrived, they should have already signed up for guided hikes, trail rides, riding lessons, and any other event either on the website or by phone.

Another critical position that needed filling was a twenty-four-hour security detail. The apartment over the carriage house had been cleaned and updated and was ready for occupancy by live-in security personnel. Sophie's ideal candidates for that job would be a married couple with backgrounds in security or law enforcement. She just needed to find such a couple.

Rounding out the list of job openings were an operations manager and a maintenance person. Everyone she listed would be critical to the success of the business.

Sophie pushed the list away and drummed her pen on the desk. She was finished with her administrative chores for the day. Now what?

Feeling restless and missing her mother, Sophie decided to

get out of the house, take the golf cart to the high meadow, and check out the tents. The camping company had installed the tents yesterday.

Sophie buzzed up the newly cut path and soon reached the tent area on the high meadow near the tree line. She parked the golf cart and began her inspection of the tents and their installation.

The regular tent didn't have the finery of the safari tent, but it would be perfect for anyone who wanted a more rustic and traditional camping experience. Trees provided shade and privacy for both tents, but still afforded guests a view of the rolling pastures and sprawling property. Outdoor grills and firepits had been installed on a patio in front of each tent.

Wow! This is amazing! Sophie thought as she stepped up on the platform and entered the safari tent. It was a large and spacious two-room enclosure. A folding privacy screen separated the sleeping area from the living room. Over the bed was a removable flap that covered a skylight in the ceiling, which offered a romantic view of the starry night sky if the couple desired. The bathroom was bigger and better appointed than the one in Sophie's first apartment at college. An air conditioning unit sat quietly in one corner. *When this is fully furnished, I could live up here.*

Except for the bedroom furniture, the safari tent was ready for occupancy. The bedroom furniture, other soft furnishings, and lighting would be delivered closer to the opening date.

Sophie left the tent area and drove back down the hill toward the rose and flower garden. She parked the golf cart, then followed the winding crushed gravel path through the newly planted roses and other flower beds. Many of the plants were beginning to bloom, and drops of dew sparkled on the blossoms and leaves. The smell of fresh mulch sweetened the air.

Sophie sat down on one of the benches in the shade of a

maple tree. The beauty of the garden and the freshness of the morning made her miss her mother even more and prompted Sophie to call her mother—the person responsible for this beautiful spot. Jean would want an update on the garden's status.

"It's going well," Sophie answered her mother's question after they exchanged greetings. "I can't wait for you to see everything. The garden is absolutely beautiful and so peaceful. But how is Aunt Rachel?"

"Rachel is doing great," Jean replied. "Her shoulder gets stronger every day. We'll know more after her doctor's appointment tomorrow."

"When do you think you'll be home?" Sophie was anxious for her mother to see all the changes she'd made to the property. She needed Jean's approval as well as validation that she was on the right track with her approach. Fresh eyes would spot any missed details.

"We'll be there as soon as the doctor releases Rachel to travel. There's no reason to think it won't be tomorrow."

"I'm anxious for you to get home—and to get your blessing on what I've done."

"I'm anxious to see it, too. I've seen the garden digitally, but I want to see it up close," Jean said. "But I know everything you've done is perfect."

"I really hope you're right," Sophie replied as she hung up the call.

◆

Sophie was ready for their trip to Frankfort the next morning when Zach knocked on her door at eight. He was wearing a business suit, but his tie hung loosely around his neck.

"Do you want to come in?" Sophie asked after she opened the door.

"I think we need to get started," Zach replied. "You never know what delays we might run into."

"You're right." Sophie picked up her purse from the table in the entryway. "Traffic can be unpredictable.

"Yeah, traffic is often a problem," Zach agreed, "but I've got a shortcut."

"Let's hope it's not one of those shortcuts that take longer," Sophie replied as Zach led her to his pickup and helped her in.

"Ha! You have so little confidence in me, Miss Sophie!" Zach laughed, then climbed into the driver's side. He turned around in the driveway and pulled out onto the gravel road.

They talked companionably as he drove.

"I notice you've done a lot around your place since I was there last," Zach remarked.

"I have," Sophie replied. She gave him a rundown of what was finished and what was left to do. Trusting Zach to know the route, she didn't pay much attention to their direction. However, when Zach turned onto a newly cut road into Thornton Farms, Sophie sat up straight and looked around. "Aren't we going to Frankfort? This isn't the route."

"Don't worry. You'll see," Zach assured her as he drove through some trees and out into an open field. A helicopter sat on a pad in the middle of the field. "Whittaker & Co." was painted on its side. "My shortcut, which you so quickly dismissed." Zach stopped the truck and exited. Sophie slid out of the passenger seat and met Zach at the front the pickup.

"Of course. A helicopter. Doesn't everyone have one?" Sophie asked sarcastically.

"Another perk of being the boss." Zach led Sophie to the side of the helicopter and showed her the footplates to assist her climb into the helicopter's cockpit.

Sophie accepted Zach's assistance as she climbed into the helicopter. She'd thought they were driving to Frankfort, so she had worn a dress appropriate for a business meeting. She'd had no idea she'd have to climb a helicopter's narrow metal steps. She settled into her seat and pulled at and straightened her skirt. She looked down at Zach, who was waiting on the ground for her to get settled before shutting the door. "Where's the pilot?" she asked.

"You're looking at him," Zach replied. He closed the door, then walked around the front and opened the pilot's door. He took off his suit jacket and tie, placed them on the back seat, then climbed up into the pilot's seat.

"You're an air jockey as well as a range rider? A man with many talents!"

"You have no idea," Zach said as he wagged his eyebrows at her.

"But I saw this helicopter fly over the day I met you at Mystic Peak," Sophie said, ignoring his suggestive comment. "Don't tell me it was flying itself."

"That was Eli. He was coming back from picking up something Lynn had ordered for the mansion's restoration. We have a pilot and a small plane that we use for some flights, but the 'copter works best for short, local flights."

"Of course! Everyone has a helicopter, a pilot's license, *and* a private plane," Sophie said with a nervous laugh.

"Don't worry. Relax. I'm a very safe and experienced pilot. Today's weather is perfect, and I've filed a flight plan. I always follow all safety rules. I won't be buzzing anyone on the ground," Zach loudly assured her as he started the engines and readied the helicopter for flight. The rotors whined and started spinning as they prepared for liftoff. "Come on. Let's ride this horse to Frankfort. It's a short flight, only about thirty minutes. I'll keep you safe. I promise." He handed Sophie a set of headphones.

Sophie was unconvinced about the safety of the helicopter but nodded as she placed the headphones over her ears.

"Trust me, ma'am. This horse doesn't buck." Zach's twangy voice came through loud and clear.

Sophie shook her head, exasperated that he would kid regarding such a serious topic, but she couldn't keep from returning his smile. "Roger that, Cowboy. I'm holding you to that promise," Sophie replied as she anxiously eyed him across the cockpit.

They lifted off and were soon high above the countryside. The city of Kingsville spread out before them in the distance. Directly beneath the helicopter was Thornton Farms, with the mansion centered in acres of grassy pastures, trees, and sprawling farmland.

After a few minutes, Zach touched her arm and pointed downward. They were now flying over Cameron Stables. The main house, the cabins, the barn, and the rest of the property was clearly visible in the morning sun.

Sophie's attention was focused on the morning activity on the ground. Pete was in the pasture pumping water into the troughs. Some of the horses grazed on the greening grass while others moved toward the watering troughs. The landscape company was re-sodding the grass in the high meadow, covering the scars left when the water and sewer lines were laid. The construction crew had arrived as scheduled and were hanging the canvas curtains and magnetic screens on the entertainment pavilion.

Zach changed direction, and they were immediately centered over Mystic Hills and the rocky peak where Sophie had first spotted Zach checking the fence row down below. She was mesmerized by the aerial view. The mountainous area and surrounding lands were beautiful even on the ground, but seeing it all from the air was breathtaking.

"Relax," Zach said again. Sophie hadn't been aware that she was clutching the side of her seat until Zach reached over and pulled the clenched fingers of her left hand into his. He continued to hold her hand. Sophie, reassured by his touch, threaded her fingers through his. "Are you afraid of flying?" he asked.

Sophie shook her head. "Not really. Or, at least, I didn't think I was. But I've never flown in a helicopter before. There's so little protection around the sides."

"You won't fall out." Zach smiled and squeezed her hand. "I got you! See?" He raised his hand that firmly held hers. "I won't make any sudden dips or turns. Trust me?"

Sophie nodded and forced her body to relax.

Zach left Mystic Hills behind and picked up their route, which followed Interstate 75. Before long, a small airport on the outskirts of Frankfort came into view. He released Sophie's hand to focus his full attention on landing the helicopter. He maneuvered it around a row of small planes parked on the tarmac, then hovered over a helipad. In a matter of seconds, the helicopter set down smoothly on the hard surface. Zach shut off the engine, and the rotors slowly came to a stop. Quiet returned to the cabin.

"That wasn't so bad, was it?" Zach asked as he took off his headphones and looked at Sophie.

"The only way to go." Sophie laughed but breathed an obvious sigh of relief.

"You don't need to apologize for being nervous. The first time I went up and the pilot banked to the right, I thought the machine was turning over."

Someone knocked on the helicopter door next to the Zach. He opened the door and instructed the person outside, "Help the lady out of the passenger side, will you, Wesley?"

Sophie's door opened a moment later, and a man dressed

in a black suit reached up to assist her down. As soon as she touched the ground, the man led her toward a limousine parked on the grass several feet away from the helipad. He opened the door of the backseat and motioned for her to climb in. A chauffer, too? Despite Zach's protestations that he didn't own an empire—which was becoming suspect—he certainly traveled in style.

"Good morning, Mr. Whittaker," the driver said as Zach appeared on the other side of the car. The driver walked around the limousine and opened the door for Zach. Zach shrugged into his suit jacket, straightened it, then climbed in beside Sophie.

"This is about what I expected after a private helicopter flight," Sophie said as she leaned back into the limo's plush seats. She tried to insert a sarcastic tone, but in truth, it was exactly what she expected. As she spent more time with Zach, it was becoming clearer just how badly off-target her initial impression had been. Zach Whittaker was definitely more business mogul than range-riding cowboy.

"This is more like what my personal assistant wanted," Zach said as he began to tie his necktie. "She said, 'You're going to the capitol. Politicians pay more attention to you if you flaunt wealth… even if you don't have any.' I frequently threaten to fire her, but my threats don't change the way she thinks or what she does."

The limo hit a bump as it turned onto the paved roadway. Sophie was tossed against Zach's side of the limo, practically landing in his lap. Zach threw his hands up in frustration as the bouncing car made the tie slip from his fingers. "Wesley, you need to turn back. I think you missed a pothole back there!"

"Sorry, sir," Wesley apologized, but Sophie saw his eyes in the rearview mirror crinkle in a smile. Did Wesley the chauffer also moonlight as a matchmaker on the side?

"Here, let me tie that." Sophie picked up both ends of the necktie and began forming the knot before Wesley could find another minefield of potholes. "So, I assume your PA is blonde, around thirty, and thinks Zach Whittaker rules the world?"

"Hmph! Maybe she was thirty about thirty years ago. And that blonde hair would now be called gray. Apparently, she thinks *she* rules the world, not me." Zach grinned as Sophie pretended to pull both ends of the necktie tightly around his neck. "Didn't we have a previous discussion about your wild assumptions?"

"Shush! And be still so I can tie this properly."

Sophie finished the necktie, patted his chest, and started to move back to her side of the car. Zach tightened his arms around her, keeping her close and facing him. His eyes locked with hers and filled with a look Sophie couldn't quite interpret. Then, he loosened his hold, and the look quickly passed. Sophie's pulse settled back to normal. Whatever Zach had been thinking left his eyes so quickly, Sophie wasn't sure if it had been real or if she'd imagined it.

"Thanks," Zach said softly, then settled back into his seat.

"Mr. Whittaker," the driver called back. "We'll soon be at Main Street, where the State Office Building is located. I'll drop you at the door. When your meeting is over, just text me. I'll pick you up within five-to-ten minutes."

"Thanks, Wesley," Zach replied as the car turned onto Main Street. Soon after, they pulled into a parking slot in front of the building. Wesley shut off the engine, got out of the car, and opened Zach's door before coming around the car to open Sophie's as well.

"Have a good meeting, sir," Wesley said as Zach took Sophie's elbow and guided her toward the door to the office building.

Inside, they walked to the bank of elevators and entered when one of the doors opened. Zach punched the button for the third floor.

"We're looking for the office of Olivia Williamson. Our appointment is at nine-thirty." He looked at his watch. "We're right on time. She said to just walk in," Zach added as they exited the elevator and walked down the hallway and past a reception area without stopping. "Ah. Here it is." Zach knock softly on the door, then opened it.

Sophie entered, and Zach followed her into the room. A woman in her mid-forties rose from behind a desk.

"Mr. Whittaker. Welcome. So nice to meet you," Ms. Williamson said as she came from behind the desk to shake hands with Zach.

"Thanks for seeing us. This is Sophie Cameron," Zach introduced Sophie.

"Welcome Miss. Cameron." Ms. Williamson shook Sophie's hand, motioned for them to take a seat, then returned to her chair behind the desk. "After we talked on the phone, I gathered some information for you. But first, please describe your plans for me again."

Zach went over the plans he and Sophie had discussed concerning the hiring of a few young men who had left foster care, offering them entry-level positions at Cameron Stables and Thornton Farms.

"We're not looking for cheap labor," Zach said. "I want to make that clear. These young men will be paid competitive wages, with a chance for raises and to advance into other jobs as they open up."

Sophie nodded in agreement. "I need to staff my business," she added, "but I will encourage them to aspire for a better future through college, a trade school, an apprenticeship, or whatever. The drive to find careers better than what I can offer them at this time is one of the qualities I'm looking for." Sophie thought of the letters Wild Bill had written to her father.

What Wild Bill had described was her model for what she now planned. "I will encourage them and mentor them, but of course, it will be up to them what they choose to do."

Zach then told Ms. Williamson about the quarters he had built at Thornton Farms. He handed his phone to her to show her photographs of the bunkhouse.

"Very impressive! Maybe I'll send *my* kids to live with you," Ms. Williamson said with a chuckle. She nodded toward a photograph of two dark-haired boys around ages twelve and fourteen sitting on the corner of her desk.

"These are your boys?" Zach asked as he picked up the picture for a closer look. "I can see some mischief in the eyes of the younger one. They look like happy kids. You must be very proud."

"Very perceptive," Ms. Williamson said. "That's Noah and Tyler. I have to keep a constant eye on Tyler, the younger one. But yes, I think they're happy boys."

"You can tell that just by looking at them. Happy kids have a sparkle and glow about them." Zach looked over at Sophie. "Jamie has that same sparkle."

"She does." Sophie nodded her agreement as Zach returned the photograph to its place on the desk.

Zach's voice and manner were devoid of any pandering. He hadn't complimented Ms. Williamson's children to sway her or get her cooperation. He believed what he said about the Williamson boys. He was a very observant person, and as Sophie had noticed during his interaction with Jamie, his interest in children was genuine.

Despite Zach's teasing and his ability to find humor in most situations—at least where she was concerned—Sophie had noticed a shadow of sadness in his eyes on the terrace Saturday night. She suspected that behind his jovial manner, Zach had been seasoned by adversity, maybe even touched by tragedy.

"As for your request," Ms. Williamson said as she got back to the official reason for their meeting. "I have six boys in your region that have turned eighteen or will turn eighteen soon. I've compiled a packet of information with a short bio on each one, including the latest addresses I have for them. It's not part of my job or your responsibility, but if you don't mind, I'd like an update periodically on how they're doing. I'm interested in how this experiment turns out."

After thanking Ms. Williamson and assuring her that they would keep her updated on the boys' progress, Zach and Sophie left her office. Wesley picked them up in the limo shortly after he received Zach's text. It didn't take them long to get back to the airfield and lift off the helipad for the flight back to Kingsville.

Sophie wasn't as nervous on the return trip. The aerial view of the scenery below kept her occupied, and she now had confidence in Zach's abilities as a pilot. She was disappointed when, within thirty minutes, they touched down at Thornton Farms.

"It's lunchtime. Do you want to go somewhere in town and have lunch?" Zach asked as he drove onto the blacktopped road that would take them to Cameron Stables.

"That sounds good," Sophie replied. "Let's go to the Cherry Blossom on Cross Street. I want to speak to Darlene, the owner."

As they drove into town, Zach returned to the reason for their meeting with Ms. Williamson. "I know you're busy with finding the other staff you need, so if you like, I can check out the list Ms. Williamson gave us. I'll go over all my findings with you before making any offers to the boys."

"If you're sure you can take time away from your business," Sophie replied. "That would help me a lot."

"I have time. I'm the boss, remember?" Zach said with a smile. "Eli knows the business as well as I do. He'll let me know if anything comes up that needs my attention."

"Ms. Williamson only had six names. How does that fill both our needs?" Sophie asked.

"They may not all work out. Your needs are the most immediate, so we'll fill your positions first. The boys may have friends or know others who are in similar situations. They probably have a network and might recommend additional candidates."

"Okay. You know, if he were still with us, my father would be very happy with what we're doing for these kids."

"We can call it 'Operation George,'" Zach said. "In honor of the help he so freely gave kids in need."

"I like that." Sophie swallowed the lump in her throat at the mention of her father. She pointed to a restaurant as they turned onto Cross Street. "There's the Cherry Blossom."

Zach found a parking spot in the lot behind the restaurant. They walked around the building and entered the front door. Darlene widened her eyes at Sophie when she saw them come through the door together. The restaurant was busy, but she pointed to an empty booth near a window on the street side that the busboy had just cleaned. Sophie and Zach slid into the booth and faced each other across the table. A waitress appeared quickly.

"I'll have a glass of sweet tea while I look at the menu," Sophie told the waitress. Zach nodded in concurrence.

Sophie opened her menu. The restaurant served mostly country favorites, as well as burgers, sandwiches, fries, and a variety of desserts. Darlene had trained at a well-known culinary school in Lexington, so she could do more than the country favorites on the menu. But to be a successful restauranteur, she had to offer what the good citizens of Kingsville wanted to eat. Sophie ordered a grilled chicken sandwich and fries while Zach ordered smothered steak with mashed potatoes and steamed green beans.

"What?" Zach responded to Sophie's amused expression

when the waitress set his heaping plate in front of him. "I don't often get food like this."

"You need to get out more," Darlene said as she stepped up to their table. "But whatever you're eating, it isn't hurting you." She looked over Zach's muscular frame, then laughed. "Compliments come with the meal. How're you both doing?"

"Doing great," Sophie replied before introducing Darlene to Zach.

"I remember you—from The Feed Bag." Zach stood and shook Darlene's hand.

"Do you have time to sit down for a few minutes?" Sophie asked. "I've got something I want to talk to you about."

"I can take a break." Darlene signaled to another woman behind the counter that she was taking a break to visit with Sophie and Zach. Then, she looked from Sophie to Zach and back at Sophie again. "So, what are you up to today, Soph? Getting acquainted with your new neighbor?" She gave Sophie a knowing look and rolled her eyes toward Zach. "But how can I help?"

"Have you ever thought about adding catering to your business?" Sophie asked, ignoring Darlene's comments. She scooted over to let Darlene sit down next to her in the booth.

"I did at one point, but Kingsville isn't exactly brimming with social events that need catering. The local clientele doesn't do a lot of entertaining."

"Lynn had to hire a caterer from Lexington for the open house," Zach said. "I'm sure she'd rather have had one closer."

"I'm not sure that's true… with Lynn," Darlene said hesitantly. "She was… never mind."

"Ah… I see. There's history here." Zach looked from Sophie to Darlene.

"You wouldn't understand," Sophie said. "You were never an awkward teenage girl thrown in amongst the she-wolves in high school."

"You're right about that. Just bullies and jocks at my high school," Zach replied. "But Darlene, I'd hire you for any function we have at Thornton Farms. Lynn will be finished with her job soon and leave. I'll need someone I can call on."

"How do you know I'm any good as a caterer?" Darlene challenged. "You should *not* buy a 'pig in a poke,' as we say here in Kentucky."

"I'm not completely sure what a 'poke' is, but from the connotation, I've probably bought several 'pigs in pokes' in my lifetime. Some turned out to be hickory smoked hams, while others were no more than the squeal. But anyone who can make a smothered steak like this is a chef in my book. And I trust Sophie's judgement, although she does assume a lot." Zach smiled at Sophie across the table.

Sophie ignored Zach's teasing. After the day they'd spent together, an easy camaraderie had grown between them. His teasing, even when he slipped into his fake Western accent, didn't bother her anymore. And right now, she had a business proposition to present to Darlene.

"Back to my catering needs." Sophie turned toward Darlene, ready to get the conversation back on topic. "I'd need a variety of dishes. Smothered steak might be alright for some people, but I want food that's more elegant for specials occasions. You know, for lovers who want a romantic weekend getaway or are celebrating an anniversary. Or for weddings. Your desserts are always elegant and are already famous around here. I'll need an expert's advice because I'm just feeling my way here—completely in the dark. I need a menu that's flexible depending on who my guests are or what the occasion is."

"Lovers, huh?" Zach interrupted. "That's a great idea. I might be interested in that special."

"Ignore him," Sophie advised Darlene. "He just wants attention." Sophie's smile took the rudeness out of her words. "What do you say?"

"I'm in," Darlene said. "I've been itching to diversify and ramp up my cooking skills. I'll work up a list of suggestions and a price sheet. I'll invite you both to come by one night and do a taste test."

Zach started to say something, but Sophie playfully held up one finger to stop him. He reached across the table, clasped her finger, and pulled it down. He continued to hold her hand down on the table.

Sophie looked at Darlene and said, "Just let me know when. I know Cowboy here will come at the mere mention of food of any kind."

"I wasn't going to say anything about taste testing," Zach objected, "but I'm in, too. I was going to ask if you have a place to set up the food at your place, Sophie."

"I have plans to install a small kitchen area on one side of the entertainment pavilion. I'll check with you, Darlene, before I purchase the equipment we'll need."

"Send me a list of what you think is needed and fits your budget, and I'll let you know if its adequate," Darlene said as she rose from the table. "I'll call you, and we can talk more. Right now, I'd better get back to the kitchen."

Sophie and Zach finished their lunches, paid their bill, and left the café. They were soon speeding back toward Cameron Stables. As they drove through the gates, the carriage house came into view. Jean's car was parked next to Sophie's in the garage beneath the apartment.

"My mother's home!" Sophie opened the door as soon as Zach stopped the truck in the driveway. She rushed toward the house, leaving Zach to tag along behind her.

"Mom! Aunt Rachel!" Sophie called out as she rushed through the front door.

"In the kitchen, having a snack!" Jean yelled back.

Sophie practically ran into the kitchen and hugged her mother as she rose to meet her. "I missed you." She moved on and hugged her aunt. "Aunt Rachel, I'm so glad you came."

As Sophie stepped back from her hugs, she noticed Zach leaning against the kitchen doorway, watching them. "Mom, this is Zach Whittaker, the new owner of Thornton Farms. Zach, this is my mother and my Aunt Rachel."

"Oh my goodness! Is it you?" Jean asked in wonder. She stood up and clasped both hands over her heart. "Wild Bill! Is it really you?" She quickly crossed the room and embraced Zach in a tight hug. She pulled back, looked him over, and gently squeezed his arms. She looked up and gently touched the side of his face. "My oh my! Wild Bill! You certainly grew into a handsome man. And that skinny body of yours filled out well. But I'd recognize those eyes and that smile anywhere. I can't believe you're here!"

"Hello, Mrs. Cameron," Zach said as he smiled widely and hugged Jean. "It really is me. And despite the efforts of some people to kill me, I managed to grow up."

"I heard that someone had bought the Thornton place, but I never heard who. I had no idea it was you. I'm floored that you're here. Wild Bill, imagine that!" Jean clasped Zach's hand in both of hers.

"I wish I had come sooner and spent some time with Mr. C. I'm very sorry for your loss."

"I know," Jean replied in a shaky voice. "You stayed in touch, and that meant a lot to him."

"Wild Bill? *You're* Wild Bill?" Sophie choked out. She stood frozen in place, her mouth hanging open and her eyes wide with shock. Zach was constantly surprising her. Just when she thought she knew him, the story kept changing. So many different facets to the same man.

"Yes," Jean said. "That's the nickname your dad gave him.

But I haven't seen him since…" Jean paused as she tried to recall the year.

"2004," Sophie said. Zach and Jean turned to stare at her in surprise, and she explained, "Dad kept your letters. I found them and read them. I had no idea you were the writer."

"Yes, that's right. 2004. But Zach, come join us," Jean invited. She returned to the table and pointed to an empty seat next to her. "Rachel and I are having a little snack. We left Paducah right after her appointment. We were anxious to get home and didn't even stop to eat. Can I get you a glass of tea?"

"Thanks, but Sophie and I just ate." Zach pulled out the chair and sat down. He pulled out the chair beside him as Sophie approached. Zach looked around the room, then at Sophie. "By the way, where's Jamie?"

"Jamie? She's with her parents. I was babysitting the day you stopped by," Sophie replied. As the confusion cleared from Zach's face, she added, "Didn't we have a discussion about *assuming*?"

"I do believe we did," Zach replied with a laugh. "Guilty as charged."

"How did Dad come up with the nickname of 'Wild Bill'?" Sophie asked her mother as she sat down beside Zach. Her shock was wearing off, and her brain had shifted back into gear. Wild Bill and Zach were one and the same! How extraordinary was that? The insecure young man in the letters had turned into the confident—sometimes over-confident—and self-assured man sitting beside her.

"When Zach arrived here, he didn't know one end of a horse from the other." Jean chuckled as she remembered the pugnacious kid who had fallen asleep in their barn. "What he lacked in skills, he made up for in bravado. And perseverance, I might add."

"In my defense, I only knew what I'd seen in movies," Zach

said. "Riding looked easy. You just held on and galloped as fast as the horse could go."

"He'd go riding helter-skelter across the pasture, bouncing up and down, slipping and sliding in the saddle. Your dad and I both worried that he'd slide off one day and break something. George started calling him 'Wild Bill'—affectionately, of course. But Zach stuck to it, and pretty soon, he figured it all out. By the end of his time here, he had become an excellent rider."

"He did," Sophie affirmed with a smile. "He rides like a cowboy."

"Aw shucks, ma'am. You're too kind," Zach said as he returned Sophie's smile.

"We were both very worried when you were injured in Iraq," Jean said. "I hope you're fully recovered without any lingering problems."

"I am. A broken leg and a hip contusion were the worst of it. I had a few other bangs here and there, but luckily, I healed completely. Some of my buddies weren't so lucky," Zach said, clearly uncomfortable with talking about his injuries and the memory of his fellow soldiers. "But it made me reflect on what I wanted from life. Being an angry person and being mad at the world all the time had worn thin, even to me."

"How did you end up working for my father?" Sophie was curious about this part of his story. And why, according to one of his letters, he left suddenly without saying goodbye.

"There's not much to say—not much that's pretty, anyway. I ran away from foster care as soon as I graduated from high school. I didn't want to hang around and force my foster parents to ask me to leave." Zach drummed his fingers on the table in front of him. This was another topic he was uncomfortable discussing.

"Oh! Foster care!" The reason for their trip to Frankfort was now clear. "Now I understand why you're interested in helping foster kids." Sophie reached over and covered Zach's hands with hers. He laced his fingers with hers. She felt him relax as she gently rubbed the back of his hand. "You don't have to tell us if it's too painful to talk about."

"It was a long time ago. At age seventeen, almost eighteen, I was penniless and an orphan. I guess I didn't want to be a burden to anyone. My reasons weren't as clear to me then as they are now."

Zach, still holding Sophie's hand, began his story. He was hesitant at first, but then sped up his narrative, as if rushing to get through that period of his life.

Zach had entered the "system" when his parents were killed in private airplane crash. They were both doctors, and his father, the pilot, was flying them home from a medical conference in Las Vegas when the plane went down. The National Transportation Safety Board ruled that the crash was due to pilot error while flying during bad weather conditions. His father ignored the foggy skies, dooming their lives to get back home to their son. Or that's how Zach interpreted the crash. Guilt over being the reason for his father's risky flight just added to his grief.

Without any close relatives willing to take Zach in, he became a ward of the state. No strangers stepped forward for one reason or another to adopt him. A sullen and angry thirteen-year-old boy mad at the world over his shattered life was more than anyone wanted to deal with. He left his last foster home in the middle of the night and hitchhiked south, with no final destination in mind.

"Didn't your parents have an estate that could have helped you once you reached majority?" Sophie asked.

"My parents had a few assets—mostly, their medical practice and their home. I'm not sure about savings accounts, but the family of another passenger on the plane sued my parents' estate for wrongful death since the accident was officially ruled my father's fault. That's a long process. I think it was still unsettled and in court when I left," Zach said. "I didn't have any fight left in me or the desire to stick around. Luck hadn't been with me thus far, so in the infinite wisdom of a seventeen-year-old, I believed that I already knew the outcome of that suit. It would be another loss in the end. I was sure of it. Worldly possessions didn't mean anything to me, either, because they wouldn't put my life back together."

"I'm so sorry," Sophie said. "How did the lawsuit turn out? Do you know?"

"Not really. I did my best to hide because I didn't want to deal with it. I assume that they ruled in favor of the family. A bank eventually found me, and I received a few bucks from the estate that was saved under my name. I was in the army by then. It's mostly all just a bad memory now," Zach assured her.

"How does my father figure into all this?"

"During my hitchhike south, I wandered off the main road into Kingsville. I came by this place, spotted the barn, and spent the night there. George found me the next morning. When I woke up and saw George scowling down at me, I tried to bluster my way out, but he scared the bejesus out of me. After a dressing down, he gave me a job and a place to stay. But in what had become my normal pattern, I ran away, again without saying goodbye. Jean, I'm sorry for that."

"George was very proud of you and how you overcame your difficult start. The highlight of his day was receiving a letter or having a chat with you."

"George was a great friend and mentor." Zach looked at his watch and gave Sophie's hand a squeeze. Then, he abruptly pushed back his chair from the table and stood. Apparently, as far as he was concerned, this story was over, and he didn't want to discuss it anymore. "I wish I could stay longer, but I need to get home and welcome a visitor to Thornton Farms," Zach said, addressing the three of them. "She'll be arriving shortly. Mrs. C, we need to get together again, soon."

"We do," Jean agreed. "Anytime you want to come by. You know you're always welcome."

"I'll walk you out," Sophie said.

Zach said goodbye to Jean and Rachel, then turned and walked toward the door. Sophie followed him.

"I'll let you know what I find after I look over our list of recruits," Zach said as he opened the door, then turned toward Sophie. "Thanks for not having a full-fledged panic attack on the flight."

"I'd like to say that I don't panic, but I really thought it might happen at first," Sophie replied with a laugh. "The trip was pleasant once I got over feeling like I was going to fall out the door. Also, thanks for your help with my staffing needs."

"Sure. What are neighbors for?" Zach shuffled his feet, a nervous gesture that contrasted with his usual self-assured demeanor. "Uh… I don't remember all that I wrote to your father, but parts of my letters might have been gibberish."

"No, not gibberish. The letters were important to my father. He kept them all." Zach was embarrassed, Sophie realized. He couldn't remember what he might have said as a young man who was struggling to find his way in life, and he was nervous that she had read his thoughts from that time. "But just so you know, I only went out with Travis once."

"Ah. I do remember that. Old Travis got kicked to the curb. Good! You deserved better."

"Did you fall in love with the sister of your college friend in Texas?" Sophie asked.

"The sister?" Zach asked with a frown. "Oh, I did bare my soul in those letters, didn't I? Lisa became very important to me, but soon after I arrived in Texas, I became totally focused on

building an information technology business while also working as a ranch hand. Romancing my best friend's sister would
have taken up too much time. And I guess I was still stuck on
another girl from my past. But that's another story. Maybe I'll
tell you that one another time."

"Hmmm... a lost love! I'd love to hear it. Wild Bill, you've led
a very complicated life."

"The simple life of a cowboy is never complicated unless he
makes it that way, ma'am. Wild Bill has a knack for that." Zach
smiled, then reached out, hugged her briefly, and said, "I'll
keep you updated on Ms. Williamson's list. Call me if you need
anything."

Zach's words on the terrace the other night, "Not everyone
gets a straight shot at their goal. Sometimes, it's a complicated
route," now made sense. Losing his parents and being forced
into foster care was not the road she had expected. The past that
Zach had overcome made all her problems seem simple.

Wild Bill's letters were a diary of sorts that contained the
highlights of the long and bumpy road Zach had traveled to
reach his current status as a successful businessman. Even after
reading Wild Bill's personal letters to her father, Sophie was
certain she didn't know all the twists and turns Zach's life had
taken. The "other girl" he mentioned might have been a part of
that crooked road.

Although Zach's teasing could become annoying at times,
especially when she wanted to be serious, she'd had a good time
with him today. He was funny, entertaining, and an interesting
man. Sophie didn't remember him from the time he'd worked
for her father, but her father always employed several young
men at a time, and they came and went quickly. She was probably too deep in her own teenage drama at the time to notice the
young stable hand.

Then again, maybe it wasn't only the "Marlboro Man" that

Zach reminded her of when she first met him in the meadow. An image of him from when he worked for her father might have lingered, stored somewhere in the back of her mind. A younger version of Zach would have possessed many of the same mannerisms as grown-up Zach.

Her mother was right. Zach wasn't a skinny kid anymore. He filled out his suit trousers as well as his jeans. Sophie smiled at her rude thoughts about Zach's backside as she watched him walk to his truck.

Rugged "Marlboro Man" and skinny Wild Bill rolled into one complete package—handsome Zach, a tall man with dark laughing eyes and a kind smile. If she were looking for a romance, he would top her list of candidates.

Down, girl! Remember your Grandmother Cameron's advice when you first started dating: "The moth dies quietly, while the flame burns on."

It took a few breakups before she understood that advice. Sophie didn't want to be that moth. The flame of wealthy, sophisticated Zach would surely burn on, regardless of how many of his romances died. He'd never be lacking for a relationship with a woman—or with many women. And he hadn't said it was over between him and the "other girl" he mentioned. For all Sophie knew, the important female visitor coming to Thornton Farms tonight might be that "other girl" or the latest "new girl."

Your previous relationships proved that you're not cut out for romance. All were complete failures, Sophie reminded herself. *Nor do you have time to develop a relationship, even if Zach were free and interested in you. And standing here lustfully eying your neighbor's backside is not where your thoughts ought to be. Your plate is already overflowing.*

Fantasizing about romance and her neighbor from a safe position in her doorway was just that—a fantasy. Her musings about love and romance were just hypothetical. Her fear of

becoming a dying moth, the element of time, and most importantly, the lack of a suitable and willing partner made her odds
of falling in love anytime soon slim to none.

Sophie sighed heavily as the taillights of Zach's truck disappeared into the fading light. She left the entryway and walked
back toward the kitchen. Her mother and Aunt Rachel were
waiting for her to update them on the progress of saving their
business. That was one thing she had control over—well, mostly
had control over.

CHAPTER NINE

As soon as Zach got home after leaving the Cameron house, he changed from his business suit into jeans, boots, and a T-shirt and went into his office. He settled behind his desk and opened the folder Ms. Williamson had given him and Sophie. He began reading the bios of the young men.

Their stories were depressing. He tried not to get side-tracked by the details—unfit parents due to drug addiction, neglect, verbal and physical abuse. It was an old and recurring story for foster kids.

As he read the heartbreaking stories of the children who had been removed from the people who were supposed to care for them, Zach thought—and not for the first time—that people should have to pass a psychological exam before they could have children. But since that wasn't going to happen, he had to look past what had been and concentrate on what he could do to help some of them now.

Zach ran his hands through his hair in frustration as the

words on the pages brought back memories of his own pain and confusion and the helplessness he felt after his parents died. Sharing some of the details with Sophie, her mother, and her aunt this evening should have made him feel better, but it hadn't. Talking about the most horrible time in his life always left him feeling vulnerable and exposed. He managed better when he closed himself off and kept the sad details inside, even though he knew that wasn't always the best way to handle the situation.

Eli knew some sketchy details about the loss of his parents, and Jean knew the basics of his early life. If asked, he never hid his past or denied what happened. He just didn't talk about the details or how the tragedy had affected him personally. Ignoring the past and concentrating on the present had worked for him thus far. He didn't want sympathy or pity from anyone—especially not from Sophie now that she knew his story, too.

Zach rose from his desk and walked to the window to stare out at the terrace and the darkening landscape beyond the pool. The rising moon had just become a glimmer on the horizon. Twilight was falling fast and bringing the fireflies out en masse. They blinked across the lawn in a seemingly endless quest to reach some unknown destination. In his teen years, he had felt much like the fireflies. He was aimlessly going somewhere, but not at all sure of his destination.

An accident had taken his parents, put him in foster care, and filled him with grief and anger over the injustice of it all. Why him? Why, out of all the people in the world, had life chosen him and destroyed his family one foggy night? As a young boy, he wanted to strike out at something, but ended up holding it all inside. At that age, he didn't have the skills to process what had happened to him, and he didn't have a target for his anger—just bad luck and fickle fate. And neither of those things cared that his world had crashed and burned. The powerlessness he felt against those unseen forces was what had angered him the most about his situation.

Zach never acted out his anger or became a problem for anyone who took him in. Instead, he learned to hide his resentment and bottle up his anger. Inside, he felt hollow. On the outside, he was quiet and sullen. Although his foster parents tried, none of them could totally break through his seeming disinterest in everything around him.

George Cameron, in his bossy way, had poked and prodded Zach toward taking control of his life, losing his sullen attitude, and thinking about finding a purpose. George had bluntly pointed out that it was up to Zach whether he let his past control his future. No one else could do it for him. Miraculously, George's advice penetrated his thick skull, but it penetrated only after he ran away from Cameron Stables.

He had moved on from his anger over what had happened to him so long ago. His past was just that—in the past. But he couldn't erase the memories of how difficult it had been to reach this point. Reading the bios of these foster kids now brought his own struggles back to the surface.

Zach took several deep breaths and forced his attention to the job at hand. He turned away from the window and returned to his desk, ready to finish reading the information in the folder. He'd let himself temporarily get sucked into the sadness found in the pages in the file.

"Focus, Whittaker! Your purpose is to help these kids," Zach ordered himself. But having lived through foster care himself didn't give him the professional insight needed to help all of them. Some of their problems were too severe. He could, though, model his interactions with some of these young men on the time he spent with George Cameron. Would that be enough? Saving the few he could personally reach didn't sound like much of a strategy for a problem as large as the foster care system, but it was a start and all he could do at the moment.

Zach leaned back in his chair and put his booted feet up on the desk. He pushed his personal experiences aside and concentrated on the young men's bios and what they needed from him. A lesson he'd learned from George was that they didn't need pity or coddling. They needed assistance in getting a foothold on a path toward a stable future. The young men probably hadn't learned this yet, but they needed goals to feel useful and productive. He could help them find those goals.

If Ms. Williamson's information was up-to-date, the boys on his list all lived within a forty-mile radius of Kingsville. The best way to judge what foster care had done to them or for them was to visit each of them.

"My oh my! Lord Whittaker, busy working in his castle!" a female voice said from the office doorway. A pretty blonde woman stepped into the room.

"Lisa!" Zach exclaimed as he removed his feet from the desk, rose, and hurried across the room to hug her. Eli was behind her. "It's great to see you! How was your flight?"

"Nothing exciting. It's really good to see you and Eli both, even if I did have to fly halfway across the country to find you." Lisa looked around the room, then out at the terrace and pool framed by the large windows. "This isn't your average ranch house, is it?"

"Not exactly," Zach replied as he motioned for her to take a seat. "But we're trying to make it homey while respecting its past history." Lisa sat down, and Eli took the chair beside her. Zach settled against the edge of the desk. "We grow more crops than horses—or, at least the farmers who lease the land do. But we have a few horses, so we can pretend to be ranchers."

"Pretending won't use this beautiful property to its full advantage. You should come with me to the auction tomorrow. Maybe pick up a stallion and a couple mares for breeding. This is Kentucky, after all. According to the auction brochure, there's some good buys."

"I have some other business to attend to tomorrow, but Eli can go. That would give you more time to visit with each other before you fly back to Texas. And he's better at assessing horse-flesh than I am. But I'm not interested in breeding. We could, however, use a couple more riding horses."

"We could?" Eli asked. "Oh! This wouldn't have anything to do with your offer to loan horses to a certain woman and close neighbor, would it?"

"A woman and Zach? Did I feel the earth shake? The ladies of California will be heartbroken," Lisa asked, her eyes wide with curiosity. "That was fast! You just moved here, so she must be something. Tell me more."

"Don't listen to your brother. Remember that time he was thrown off his horse and landed on his head? He still suffers from that concussion," Zach replied, scowling at Eli.

"Auburn hair. Green eyes. A real looker." Eli looked at Lisa and nodded. "Yup! I think he's smitten."

"Smitten? You really should get your head looked at, Eli," Zach said again. "I've known Sophie for years."

"You didn't actually know Sophie back then," Eli asserted. "Even you said so. But now, you do."

"Excuse me, Mr. Whittaker," Mattie interrupted from the doorway. "Cook wants to know if you want the dining room set up for your guests. Dinner will be ready in about fifteen minutes."

"Just the kitchen table is fine. Lynn and Cal went out somewhere for dinner, so it's just the three of us. And thanks, Mattie," Zach replied. "We'll be there in a few minutes."

"A mansion? A cook? A housekeeper? Where has our ranching buddy Zach gone?" Lisa looked at Eli, and they both laughed. "Should we bow and curtsy?"

"I'm glad you're having a good time. It's a big house, and I need help running it. I still fix my own breakfast. You remember those tasty Western omelets I used to fix, don't you?"

"Yes. And I miss them," Lisa replied with a pout. "You started making them shortly after Eli brought you to Texas to live with us. And remember when you and I would sneak downstairs after everyone had gone to bed and have a beer or a glass of wine? I miss those long talks we had."

"You did what?" Eli sat up straight and looked accusingly from Lisa to Zach.

"You didn't know? Don't worry. We just talked," Lisa replied. "We couldn't do more, since Dad was always roaming around at night, looking for a second piece of pie. We went to the bunkhouse when we did more than talk."

Lisa and Zach exchanged smiles. Zach counted the seconds in his head as he waited for Eli to explode.

"You did what?" Eli repeated loudly. "Where was I?" He scowled at his sister, then gave Zach a hostile look. "I told you that Lisa was off-limits when I invited you to come home with me."

"Once a dork, always a dork." Lisa shook her head in dismay at her brother. "I agree with Zach. You need to get your head examined. You were probably upstairs stuck deep in your computer—where we usually found you. It would serve you right if we had done the dirty deed, but there was nothing but friendship between me and Zach. I don't know why Abby puts up with you, big brother."

"She's a flight attendant, and she travels a lot," Zach said. "It's the only way."

"Well… I'm sorry. I…" Eli smiled sheepishly as he started to apologize. He quickly shifted to defending himself. "Someone needed to be an adult back then. You two weren't."

"At some point, you appointed yourself my protector," Lisa

said. "It's annoying, but it's fun to see how far into the weeds you'll wander. Teasing you is a blast, so I can't stay mad at you very long. Besides, no one ever listens to you anyway."

"Eli dishes it out, but he can't take it," Zach said as he grinned at his friend and business partner. He rose from the edge of the desk. "Let's go see what's for dinner."

After they finished the meal the cook had prepared, they sat around the table, reminiscing about their time working together on the Double R, the Reardons' Texas ranch. Eli and Lisa good-naturedly teased Zach about his inexperience as a ranch hand when he first arrived. He had worked around horses for George Cameron, but that in no way prepared him for cattle roundups or branding and tagging cattle as the hot, dry Texas sun beat down on him. It didn't take Zach long to give up his fantasy about the romantic life of a working cowboy and get serious about a different career—information technology—the one he had studied for at the University of Georgia.

Eventually, they finished retelling their stories, some true and some exaggerated, and decided to call it a night.

"Here's the keys to my truck." Zach handed a set of keys to Eli as they said goodnight at the foot of the staircase. "Take the horse trailer, and if you find a couple of good riding horses, buy them."

"I'll do that," Eli replied with a laugh. "Two horses for one green-eyed lady."

CHAPTER TEN

Z ach said goodbye to Lisa in the driveway the next morning as she and Eli prepared to drive to Louisville. She would catch a flight back to Texas later that evening from Louisville.

"Don't be a stranger, as your dad always said," Zach said as he hugged Lisa goodbye.

"I won't. I wish I had time to meet the green-eyed, auburn-haired beauty who has finally punctured that hard heart of yours, but I have to get home. I plan to return for the wedding, though." Lisa laughed as she returned his hug.

"Hmph! You've been listening to Eli again," Zach replied with a snort. He laughed, then retorted, "You'll probably be tied down with a passel of kids before that happens, ma'am."

"Don't joke. You deserve someone who makes you happy. You've flown solo far too long," Lisa insisted.

"Go! And be happy with Captain Dave. Don't worry about me," Zach said. Putting on his Western twang, he added, "I'm like them tumbleweeds that blow from hither to yonder, remember? And always alone."

"You're impossible! Eli created a monster when he brought the city boy to our ranch. But just to remind you, 'them tumbleweeds' often get tangled up in a fence row—or, in this case, love—and tumble no more." Lisa gave him one last hug and climbed into the truck beside Eli.

Zach waved goodbye to Lisa and Eli, then returned to his office for the packet of information on the foster kids that Ms. Williamson had given him.

He stopped by the bunkhouse to quickly check on its progress before climbing into his SUV and backing out of the garage. He stopped and double-checked the GPS directions to his first destination—Dinkman, Kentucky, located about twenty miles outside of Kingsville.

Less than thirty minutes later, he entered the town that was really more of a crossroads than a proper town. Rows of small, dilapidated wood-framed houses lined both sides of the street. A small mom-and-pop grocery store and a convenience store with a filling station were the only businesses he passed before he reached the address he was looking for—613 Easy Street, a duplex. Whoever named the street must have had an ironic sense of humor, because Zach was certain that living on this street was anything but easy.

He parked in front of a tiny house. As he got out of the car, dogs began barking from several directions. None of the dogs appeared to be running loose, so he continued his walk up to the front door. He knocked and heard movement inside. A young man with curly black hair and matching the picture Ms. Williamson had given him answered the door.

Beau Benson had turned eighteen two months ago. He had been abandoned on a street corner by his parents when he was twelve years old. A policeman spotted him sitting on the curb and had taken him to a local social services agency for children.

Beau had bounced around from home to home before leaving foster care and ending up in Dinkman. Dinkman was not a thriving metropolis, but rent was cheap, a good sign that he had realistic expectations.

"Beau Benson?" Zach asked.

"We're not buying anything," Beau replied firmly. "Don't you see the sign, 'No solicitors'?" He nodded to the sign by the door.

"I see it, but I'm not selling anything," Zach said. "I'm Zach Whittaker. Can I talk with you about a possible job opportunity?"

"Are you a perv? Looking for recruits? I've been warned about people like that. I don't do that stuff."

"I'm not a pervert," Zach assured him. Beau's distrust was normal, and Zach understood. Beau's world had been built on one disappointment after another, so why should he believe anyone who said they had his best interests at heart?

"I'm not convinced, but come in." Beau didn't smile, but he stepped back and held the door open.

Zach entered a small living room with an adjoining kitchen area. The room was cluttered but not dirty. Dishes had been washed and placed on a drain board by the sink. A good sign. Beau was trying to make the best of his difficult situation.

"Do you live here alone?" Zach asked. He sat down in a straight-backed chair that Beau pushed toward him.

"No, my brother lives here. He's a big, tough guy, so you better not try anything. He'll be back soon."

Zach almost smiled at Beau's nervousness and his hollow bravado. Zach recalled trying to act the tough guy the morning Mr. Cameron had found him asleep in his barn. Beau's defensive manner reminded Zach of himself many years ago. Beau, like young Zach, didn't realize that others saw right through his tough act.

"I'm not here to try anything. I was hoping to offer you a job working with horses on a farm. Do you think you'd be interested in that?"

Zach heard a noise at the back of the house. The back door opened, and another young man, hot and sweaty from the hot and humid day, entered the house. He called out to Beau, "Guess what? I got twenty dollars for your graphic novels. The man wanted to give me ten, but I held out. This'll help with the rent." He stopped at the edge of the living room when he saw Zach. "Who are you?"

"I'm Zach. I was just talking with Beau about a job opportunity."

"What kind of a job? We're not into any funny or illegal stuff," Beau's brother said.

"I'm not into funny or illegal stuff, either," Zach replied. Was there something about him that made them think he was running a male prostitution ring or was in the drug business? They had seen things a child should not see, but Zach doubted either one would recognize an actual pervert. "What's your name?"

"I'm Chandler. So, what kind of job? There's a chance I can get Beau a job at the convenience store where I work part-time."

"Working in the stables at a horse farm. It's hard work— cleaning stables, moving bales of hay around, exercising horses. But you get a chance to learn how to ride and how to take care of horses. Once you've proven yourself, you might get to do other jobs." Zach recognized empty bluster when he saw it. Chandler worked part-time, but his boss would hire Beau, also? Not likely.

"You only fill in when Mr. Watson has to leave and go somewhere." Beau had spotted the falseness of Chandler's statement, too. "You don't have a real job. Mr. Watson isn't going to hire me, Chandler." Beau looked back at Zach. "I'm not going anywhere without Chandler. Can you hire him, too?"

Zach turned the question over in his mind. He didn't have

any information on Chandler, but he guessed he was only about a year older than Beau. Chandler had been scraping by, if that, according to the evidence around them. But he had taken in his younger brother and shared his meager earnings with him. Zach's instincts told him that Chandler was doing all he could to care for himself and his brother. That showed good character, and a trait like that would never appear in a written bio, even if he had one on Chandler.

"I need to talk with my partner before making any final decisions," Zach said as he stood up. "But I think we might have a place for you both. I'll be in touch no later than Friday."

"Pardon me if I don't believe you," Chandler said with sarcasm. "What's the catch?"

"You can believe me. The catch is that you have to be willing to work hard, be dependable, and learn. You'll be paid a salary, plus room and board." Zach handed each of them a business card. "Do either of you have a phone?"

"Here's Mr. Watson's number. You can call his store. He'll let me know you called, and I'll call you back." Chandler wrote a number on a piece of paper and handed it to Zach. Zach shook their hands and left.

Zach's next stop was similar to his visit with the Benson brothers. Troy Hayes lived in a rural area not far from Dinkman. He was as suspicious of Zach's offer as Beau and Chandler had been at first. Troy had been removed from an abusive home, but his early years hadn't snuffed out his desire to better himself. Troy was eager to escape from his current aimless existence and try something new. Zach made the same promise he'd made to Beau and Chandler—he would let him know his final answer before the week was out. He was certain that Sophie would approve of hiring the young men he'd met so far, but he'd promised her that he wouldn't make any decisions without first talking it over with her.

Zach next drove west to the small town of Beaver Creek. From the looks of the town, even the beavers had pulled up stakes and left. Dilapidated shacks and a sleazy motel made up the town's center. Zach's stop here was not successful. Jake Newsome answered the door with glazed eyes and was unsteady on his feet. Jake's record indicated that he had left his last foster family early. Perhaps he had been asked to leave. Through the open door, Zach spotted two other boys lying on a ratty sofa, giggling uncontrollably. They were all high on something.

Zach excused himself, claiming he had knocked on the wrong door, and returned to his car. He couldn't even talk to them in their current condition. Zach hated turning away from someone in obvious need of help, but one bad apple could spoil all his efforts to help the others. Taking on someone with an apparent drug problem was not part of his plan or something he was qualified to handle. His best course of action would be to find a social services organization and alert them to Jake's obvious need for help.

No one answered the door at his next two stops in a rural area south of Kingsville. The places looked deserted, so he drove back to Kingsville for his last stop at 301 Kenny Avenue. Johnny Tackett had been born in Nashville, but his parents had brought him to rural Kentucky. Shortly after the move, they were arrested on drug charges and were currently serving time in prison. Johnny's neighborhood was located on the far eastern side of town and across the railroad tracks. The tiny ramshackle houses on the street looked much like the others he'd visited today. Zach knocked on the door, and a blond young man answered the door.

"Johnny Tackett?" Johnny had the same suspicious look Zach had seen on the faces of the other young men he had visited. He nodded but continued to stare at Zach.

"Who is it, Johnny?" a female voice asked, and an almost-identical face appeared behind Johnny's head. The face had more feminine features and long blond hair, but it was obvious that these two were twins.

"I don't know," Johnny replied to the girl behind him. He stuck out his chin and glared at Zach. "Who are you, mister? And what do you want?"

"Zach Whittaker. I'd like to talk to you."

Johnny opened the door further and invited Zach inside. He pointed to a worn, overstuffed chair where Zach could sit.

Zach looked around and took in the small room as he explained that he was there with an offer of employment as a stable hand on a horse farm.

"A job? Before you go on, this is my sister, June." Johnny introduced his twin sister. "If I go work for you, she goes, too. We've been separated for three years and just found each other. You hire me, you hire her." Johnny stood with his arms folded, his mouth in a straight line as he stared stubbornly at Zach.

"Johnny and June? Named after Johnny and June Cash?" Zach asked, pretty certain he had guessed right.

"Apparently. Our parents were originally from Tennessee. I guess they liked to listen to Johnny's music while they cooked their meth." Johnny didn't hide the disgust in his voice. "'Folsom Prison Blues' was one of their favorites, which is funny, because prison is where they ended up."

"Funny—or maybe karma," June commented with a shrug.

"As I said, June and I come as a pair," Johnny continued. "We won't be separated again."

"You were separated in foster care?" Zach asked.

"We were," June replied. "We couldn't stay together, but we were fostered by nice people. We were very lucky. Our foster families wanted to adopt us but couldn't afford to."

"Yes, you were lucky," Zach said, nodding.

Many foster parents were open to adoption, but their hearts

were often bigger than their bank accounts. They needed the money the state paid for fostering children. Most couldn't afford to adopt. Zach had found himself in a similar predicament, but he hadn't stuck around once he graduated from high school to find out for sure. He still didn't know if he was brave for having left or if he had taken the coward's way out.

"Can you hire June, too?" Johnny pressed.

Well, this complicates things, Zach thought. If he took a young girl into his home, he *would* be seen as a pervert. And there was no way he'd let her live in the bunkhouse with the boys, even though they'd all have individual rooms. He had been eighteen once and knew that if he added a female into the mix, it would only cause trouble among the young men. Before he could commit, he'd have to first consult Sophie and see if she had a solution. Foster girls had not been in his plans.

"Let me talk to my partner and see what we can work out. I see you have a phone." Zach nodded to a phone lying on the table.

"My foster parents gave it to me," Johnny replied. "The service is paid up through the end of the month. They gave me some money for rent until I find a job."

"Your rent is paid for the month?" Zach asked.

"No, I'm paying weekly," Johnny said. "The owner wanted me to prepay the whole month, but I refused. I don't trust him. I didn't want to give him all our money, then have him lock us out and cheat us. I'm not about to be conned."

This boy has a head on his shoulders, thought Zach. He was right to be distrustful, and he was either street-smart or on his way to becoming a future business mogul.

"Smart move," Zach acknowledged. "Let me have your phone number, and I'll call you with details when we decide."

"How do we know you'll do that? You could be lying." Johnny was naturally suspicious. Opportunity probably had never knocked on his door before.

"Why would I lie to you? What's in it for me? You'll hear from me by Friday," Zach promised them. "Here's my business card. Call me anytime or turn me into the authorities if you think I'm a conman." Zach understood how Johnny felt. It would take him a while to fully trust anyone again.

Zach left the neighborhood and drove out of the city and back toward Thornton Farms. He had potentially five people to hire, including June. Ms. Williamson had sent him two more names, but he'd try to locate them later. Or maybe, if the current group worked out, he'd ask if they knew someone they could recommend.

Zach expelled a sigh as he took the two-lane road leading to Thornton Farms. He was exhausted by the day's experience, although not at all surprised by what he found. The cynicism in the young peoples' eyes as they bravely tried to hide their fears and insecurities reminded him of his own days in foster care. The families he lived with were kind and caring people. They had given him a place to live, but he always felt like an outsider, a visitor who was just passing through. No one paid special attention to his needs or problems until he met George Cameron. George listened—really listened—and quickly cut through Zach's swagger and BS to lay things out plain and simple. And he did it frequently. George was blunt, and he didn't bury Zach in the vague platitudes he'd heard so often from social workers.

As Zach drove by the turnoff leading to Cameron Stables, he recalled his last day at the Cameron place so many years ago. A torrential rainstorm had rolled in as he and George were moving a new delivery of hay into the barn. They had to stop and cover the remaining bales of hay in the barnyard with a tarp to keep them dry. With their clothes soaking wet, they ran into the barn to escape the rain and waited for the storm to pass. They stood just inside the barn and watched the rain stream down in sheets over the door.

The rain must have made George philosophical because his tone was frank and even more blunt than usual. He began talking and giving Zach advice—something he was very good at. Zach could still hear George's firm voice: "You don't belong here, Zach. You have great potential. You're eighteen now. You should leave, join the Army, learn a trade, and go to college. You need to make something of yourself. Be more than what you are right now—a farm hand."

Zach had missed the message and only heard rejection—a repeat of the same old story he'd heard—or thought he'd heard in foster care. He didn't belong with the families—or anywhere. He was an outsider. They wouldn't miss him if he left. None of his foster parents had ever actually uttered such words, and he now realized that the rejection he heard was mostly his inter-pretation. But that day, standing in the barn with George, he let his hurt and anger motivate his actions. Late that night, after his work was done, he packed his belongings and left Cameron Stables.

Zach had walked to Kingsville and purchased a bus ticket to Lexington. As fate would have it, the bus dropped him off right next to an Army recruiting office. Tired from his trip and with his anger spent, he saw this as a sign. He curled up on a bench nearby and waited for the recruiting office to open the next morning. As soon as the door opened, he walked in and began the induction process to join the US Army.

That whole period now seemed like a lifetime ago. Actually, it *was* a lifetime ago. He'd changed in many ways. He had turned his anger into goals and purpose, and that had led him to be-come a success in business.

George had been right, as usual. The structured life of the Army was exactly what Zach needed at the time. It gave him a surrogate family and taught him teamwork. During deployments, depending on each other was a matter of life and death. He learned to trust people again.

Zach parked his car, and as he walked toward the house, he thought about his meetings with the young men today—and June. They seemed to be a solid group on the surface. It wouldn't take him long to determine whether they were living up to their potential in whatever job they were assigned. He had been there and could quickly recognize slackers and anyone who was just going through the motions or looking for a free ride. That didn't mean they had to be perfect and not make mistakes. He certainly wasn't perfect when he came to work for George. But Zach needed to see that they were curious and motivated to find a better life than what they currently had. If they worked hard to overcome the bad hand given them and used this job opportunity as a springboard to whatever their talents allowed them to achieve, he would help them go as far as they wanted to go.

That was the objective of his plan and the one lesson Zach was qualified to teach them.

CHAPTER ELEVEN

S ophie's hand hovered over the keyboard on her computer. She pulled back, hesitating to hit the key that would send the website live and announce to the world that Cameron Stables was open for business. The website's design was exactly what she wanted, but would it be enough to persuade visitors to come and relax in a pleasant and friendly atmosphere in central Kentucky?

It was now the beginning of June and less than four weeks until the date Sophie had targeted for the business's grand opening. Four weeks wasn't a lot of time to build a list of reservations, but that was alright in the beginning. A less-than-capacity crowd would make it easier to smooth out any hiccups in the operation. Sophie didn't expect a stampede at first under any circumstances. Advertising could sometime be slow in reaching the masses.

This morning, she had added photos to the website showing the cabins, the rolling pastures with the horses grazing peacefully, and the tree-shaded nooks tucked into the shadows of Mystic Hills. The tents on the high meadow near the tree line looked comfortable and inviting. Two diverse groups with entirely different tastes in camping could choose the experience they preferred. On top of all that, the refurbished and comfortable cabins, the elegant catered menu, and the entertainment venue reflected Sophie's vision of a new definition of the rustic experience normally found at a horse farm.

Sophie had also added a review section to the website so guests could leave comments—good or bad.

As Sophie added the finishing touches to the website, her mother and Aunt Rachel made final changes to the rose and flower garden. Jean had called Sophie out earlier that morning to the site with several suggestions for improvements.

"I think we should add some blue delphiniums in the back row there. They're taller and will add the perfect contrast to the mass of yellow daises in front," Jean suggested. "The roses, peonies, azaleas, dahlias, and other plants all look perfect, but I want to add a trellis for a climbing red rose at the entrance nearest the entertainment pavilion. And what do you think about six large planters placed throughout the garden? We could switch out plants according to the seasons—warm-weather flowers during spring and summer, but something like pansies for color in the winter."

Sophie laughed when Jean paused to take a quick breath. "I love it all. It sounds beautiful, and you two are the experts in this area." Sophie was pleased by her mother's enthusiasm and glad to see a spark of interest in something that might replace the deep sadness in her eyes lately. "We'll do whatever you think is best. You're the design expert."

"Glad you agree," Jean said. "We also need to run bubblers to the planters so they won't need hand-watering. Drip irrigation for the rest of the beds is adequate. The path lighting is perfect, too. But we should trim back that maple tree over

there." Jean pointed to a large tree that shaded one of the benches. "It spreads out too far. We need the shade for the bench, but
it's blocking the sun from reaching the flowerbeds on the other
side of the path."

"You know what would also look beautiful?" Aunt Rachel
said, catching Jean's excitement. "If we wrapped the tree trunks
in some white lights. Just think how magical and romantic that
would look at night."

"This all sounds wonderful," Sophie agreed. "Call Ian at the
landscape company and tell him what you want. You two are in
charge. Go for it! Make it romantic and make me proud."

Sophie, Jean, and Aunt Rachel met later in the kitchen for
lunch. As they ate the sandwiches Aunt Rachel had prepared,
Jean commented, "You're planning to serve an evening meal for
guests, right? Darlene will be providing the food and serving
staff?"

At Sophie's nod, Aunt Rachel spoke up. "I want to volunteer
to supervise and coordinate the dinners unless you have someone else for the job. You know, make sure things run on time
and handle any problems that might arise."

"Wonderful! Glad you thought of that. I had forgotten that
detail," Sophie replied. Aunt Rachel was the amateur chef in the
family and the perfect coordinator for anything food-related.
"Of course, Aunt Rachel, that means you need to extend your
visit indefinitely."

"Maybe I will. As a book editor, I can work remotely. Once
I get released to go back to work, I can drive back to Paducah if
the publisher wants to meet in person," Aunt Rachel said.

"But don't feel like you're just one of the staff," Sophie assured her. "This job is temporary until I get all the kinks worked
out and hire a permanent coordinator."

"I want to help and to stay busy." Aunt Rachel smiled. "This
shouldn't be that hard. And you know how I like to organize

and order people around."

"With you both assisting me, I'm starting to think we can make this work."

Sophie returned to her office after lunch. She heard Ian and his landscape crew arrive in the midafternoon. Her mother and Aunt Rachel went out to meet them and direct the crew on changes to the rose and flower garden. Sophie soon heard the sound of chainsaws as they trimmed the large maple tree in the garden.

The flower garden was in good hands. Ian might even learn a few things about landscape design and plant selection from Jean and Rachel. As far as what was needed to create a romantic atmosphere, they definitely knew more than Sophie.

Patsy had been a valuable resource for Sophie in filling some important staff positions. She knew most of the area's residents and had recommended several people she knew who were looking for employment. Maggie Garrett was Sophie's first hire after Ben. Maggie had worked the ticket window at the racetrack until she was laid off, so she had experience in customer service. She would start on Monday to take reservations by phone—if there were any—and check guests in at the gate.

A married couple had been hired to work security. Sam and Rita Hudson were both former security guards for the racetrack before it closed. They happily accepted the offer to live in the apartment over the garage and be readily available for any security problems, day or night.

Mark Hughes, a former racetrack handyman, along with his son, Tommy, had accepted the job of handling maintenance and repairs and keeping the facilities in good working order.

Patsy had also assigned three ladies from her staff to clean the cabins after guests checked out and do on-demand cleaning while the cabins were occupied.

Sophie's most important position left to fill was an operations manager. She had his or her office ready—a small room in the barn her father had once used as an onsite office. Zach had texted yesterday that he had visited the young men on the list Ms. Williamson had given them. He promised to come by sometime soon to go over those he thought she should hire for stable hand positions. Ben had been assigned to be their immediate supervisor once they were onboard.

Zach was probably still entertaining his visitor, the woman he had mentioned when they returned from their trip to Frankfort. Sophie knew that the visitor was a young woman because she'd passed Zach's truck on Tuesday as she drove into Kingsville to visit the wine distributor. As his truck turned off the highway in front of her to take the road leading to the interstate, she clearly saw a blonde woman sitting in the truck's passenger seat.

Sophie had felt a quick stab of jealousy at the sight of Zach with another woman. Was this his lost love? She'd spent the rest of the drive into town admonishing herself over her reaction. Finally, she convinced herself that she was only curious as to the visitor's identity and how long her stay would be.

But having the flower garden and almost all of her staff positions filled didn't quell Sophie's sudden hesitation about taking the final plunge and launching the website. Going all-in on a risky business venture was a scary step. What if it was a total flop? She would lose much of her life's savings in the process. She had already tied up a big portion of her savings in the bank loan, so that horse had already fled the barn.

So, why was she still stalling and dawdling? It was getting to be late in the afternoon, the website was done, and still, she hesitated. She reviewed the website and its embedded links again. Everything was working properly. Nothing had changed since she last checked it earlier. There was nothing left to be done, and she was out of excuses. The time had come to launch.

But what if she had missed an important detail?

"Argh," Sophie groaned as she put her head down on her arms on her desk. She sighed again, disgusted by her cowardliness. What was she afraid of? She'd do it eventually, but maybe if she closed her eyes for a moment and did some deep breathing exercises—perhaps even take a short nap—her courage would return.

Sophie wasn't serious about taking a nap, but she did take several deep breaths. She relaxed and closed her eyes. She quickly drifted into a state somewhere between awake and a light sleep. Sophie heard her mother talking somewhere in the house. She was probably calling Ian with another new idea for the flower garden. Ian didn't know what he was in for in dealing with her mother. Jean's boundless ideas matched her energy. The hum of voices further relaxed Sophie, and she sank deeper into sleep.

"Hey," a male voice said as a hand touched her head. "Sophie? Sophie? Sweetheart, are you okay?" The hand moved to her shoulder and gently shook her.

Sophie opened her eyes, blinked, and looked up. Zach was looking down at her with a look of concern. His hand rested on her shoulder.

"Oh my goodness!" Sophie's eyes widened as she raised her head from the desk. She wiped her mouth, relieved that she didn't find drool on her chin. "I was… uh… just resting my eyes."

"Yeah, I always snore when I rest my eyes, too."

"I don't snore," Sophie objected heatedly before noticing that Zach's eyes twinkled in mischief. She rolled her eyes. "Not funny. But what are you doing here?"

"Didn't you get my text that I was on my way over?" Zach gave her shoulder a squeeze, then moved to the other side of the desk.

"No. I wasn't expecting you to come by today." Sophie looked around for her phone. "I must have left my phone in the kitchen. I thought you'd still be busy with your *visitor.*" Her comment sounded petulant. She got up, stretched, then walked around the desk and stalked to the window. "I was trying to get up the courage to push out my website. Not that this event is of interest to anyone but me." She rolled her shoulders to relieve the tension and pressed her mouth firmly together, suppressing the pout that her lips wanted to form. She was behaving like a toddler, awakened before she had finished her nap. But at the moment, she couldn't seem to stop herself.

"Did I do something to make you mad?" Zach asked as he crossed the room to stand next her at the window.

"No," Sophie replied grumpily. "I'm just… I don't know, scared to jump off the cliff. And I'm disgusted with myself for stalling and afraid to dive headfirst into the unknown world of running a resort."

"You're ready. You've done a great job of setting everything up. Have faith that you've considered everything possible at this point. Just go for it." Zach reached out and pulled her into his arms. He massaged her tense shoulders. Sophie wanted to sag against him, forget everything, and lose herself in the comfort of his soothing hands and encouraging words—maybe even fall asleep on his shoulder.

"Has your girlfriend left town?" Sophie pulled back abruptly and looked up into Zach's face. At his confused look, she added pointedly, "I saw her with you in your truck the other day." She was behaving more childishly by the minute! She bit down on her lip to keep further comments from escaping her mouth.

"Oh! You mean Eli's sister, Lisa? Is that why you're mad at me? Are you jealous? She's a friend, but not a 'girlfriend,' if that's what you're implying. That was Eli driving the truck. They were on their way to the livestock auction in Louisville. And yes, to answer your question, my *friend* flew home the next day."

"Oh! Why would I be jealous? Of course I'm not!" Sophie backtracked. "And it's your business, either way." Sophie felt the heat rise in her face, and she added lamely, "I'm sorry. I know I'm making a fool of myself, but I can't seem to stop. And I don't even know why."

"Hmmm… If your eyes weren't naturally green, I'd think the green-eyed monster, Jealousy, was lurking in there somewhere."

"I… no." Sophie shook her head and looked away, embarrassed. "No further comment." She'd said enough. If the floor opened up right now and swallowed her, she would consider it a good thing. And on the plus side, she wouldn't have to launch the website.

From the corner of her eye, Sophie saw her mother start to enter the room, notice Sophie and Zach together at the window, then retreat back into the hallway. "Mom, you can come in. Nothing to see here. Zach's just trying to keep me from jumping out the window."

"Doesn't he know we're on the first floor?" Jean asked with a chuckle as she entered the room with Jamie on her hip. She averted her eyes from the window, where Zach was still holding Sophie in his arms. "Jenny came to pick up Pete, and I thought Zach might like to see Jamie."

"Cowboy Zach," Jamie said as she reached out to Zach. He removed his arms from around Sophie, gave her shoulder one last squeeze, and crossed the room to take Jamie out of Jean's arms.

"Hi, Jamie. I do want to see you," Zach said as he sat down and bounced Jamie on his knees. She giggled, then reached for his phone in his shirt pocket. Zach pulled his phone out and gave it to her.

"She might make some international calls," Sophie cautioned as Jamie began pushing buttons on the phone.

"No problem, but let's find you something better to do. Like a cartoon." Zach searched for a kid's cartoon video, turned down the volume, then handed the phone back to Jamie. She settled back against Zach's chest, her attention on the phone's screen. Zach turned to Jean. "Mrs. C, while you're here, I need to run something by you and Sophie." Zach went on to describe the results of his visits with the foster kids on Tuesday.

"Do you think they're all suitable for this work?" Sophie asked.

"All those I talked with appeared to be nice young men and willing to accept the job. And all seem well-adjusted, despite all they've been through," Zach replied. "But as your friend Darlene put it, it's like hiring 'a pig in a poke.' I think they're good kids, but we won't know for sure until we hire them and see how they work out. But…"

"But there's a problem," Sophie finished his sentence.

"Yes, a slight one," Zach replied. "Johnny and his sister June come as a pair, just like Beau and Chandler. Johnny won't hire on without June. Undoubtedly, there would be gossip if we were to hire June and I let her live in my house. More than once, the young men accused me of being a pervert. They're naturally cynical and don't believe a good opportunity would just drop out of the sky unless it's somehow unethical." Zach laughed at the memory, then continued, "And I was once a young man myself, so I know I can't let her stay in the bunkhouse with the boys, even though there are separate rooms."

"That is a problem," Sophie agreed. "Boys being boys."

"A pretty girl put into a group of young men—it'd be like lighting the fuse to a bomb. It would cause all kinds of trouble. Jealousy makes people react in crazy ways." Zach looked at Sophie. "Isn't that right, Sophie?"

"I wouldn't know. What do you think, Mom?" Sophie

didn't look at Zach but turned to address her mother. She didn't miss the smile Zach didn't try to hide.

"We should be able to work something out," Jean said. "We have two extra bedrooms upstairs. She could stay with us. And I'm sure we could find lots of things for her to help us with. We can work out her job description after we see what our needs are and we judge her capabilities." Jean came across the room and took Jamie off of Zach's lap. She handed the phone back to Zach. "Stay for dinner, Zach, and we'll discuss it more. Rachel is making her delicious pot roast tonight."

Jean settled Jamie on her hip, then looked from Zach to Sophie and back again at Zach. She paused for a moment, as if hesitant to say what she was thinking, then spoke. "I don't know the meaning of the undercurrents I feel in this room right now or of the cryptic comments. I won't ask for an explanation. Just know that I notice them. So, I'm going to leave you to it and take Jamie back to her mother. Jenny and Pete are probably ready to go home."

"I'm just teasing Sophie," Zach assured Jean.

"His favorite pastime," Sophie interjected.

"And," Zach continued, "she's wound pretty tight right now about launching her website. She's afraid to take the final leap. And dinner sounds great. I'd love to join you."

"Mom, before you go, watch this," Sophie said, shooting a challenging look at Zach. She had regained her confidence. Nothing ventured, nothing gained. She had prepared for most contingencies, and if there was anything to be added or changed, she would adjust them on the fly. Fear of sending her fledgling business out into the world had been replaced by the desire to wipe the amused look off Zach's face.

Sophie walked behind her desk and touched the computer keyboard. The screen lit up. "Ta dah! Done!" she said as she hit the 'Publish' button and the Cameron Stables' website went live. "We are open for business."

"Congratulations! Well done! Come to the kitchen," Jean said. "We'll have a glass of wine before dinner to celebrate."

Sophie and Zach joined Jean and Rachel in the kitchen. Zach opened the bottle of wine and poured a glass for each of them.

"To a successful launch of the new and improved Cameron Stables," Sophie said as she raised her glass in a toast. "Rustic redefined."

They all touched their glasses, took a drink, then sat down together at the table to enjoy Rachel's pot roast. As they filled their plates, the conversation turned to Zach's short tenure at Cameron Stables. Zach recounted how he had tried to brazen it out when George found him asleep in his barn.

"He should have kicked my backside when I said, 'Yeah, I spent the night here. What're you going to do about it?'" Zach shook his head, amazed by his rudeness. "I started to add 'old man,' but thought better of it. That *would* have earned me a butt-kicking, for sure."

"George admired your grit and your efforts to bluster your way out of it," Jean said. "But he saw through your act and recognized that you were just a scared kid. Though calling him 'old man' might have taken things a little too far."

"I'm glad he didn't have me arrested for trespassing. He put me to work cleaning stalls, saddling horses, and rubbing them down when they came back to the barn. What was that girl's name?" Zach asked as he turned to Sophie. "The one with the huge, bedazzled glasses who rode with you sometimes?"

"That was Darlene."

"*That* was Darlene? She certainly looks different now, but I couldn't actually see her face through her glasses back then."

"You remember her, but not me?" Sophie asked.

"I think it's the other way around. I remember you, but

you don't remember me," Zach asserted. "I remember Darlene mainly because of her fear of horses and those crazy glasses. She was the talk of all the guys that day when she sat down in the middle of the paddock and refused to get up. Mr. C eventually coaxed her to sit on the horse while he led it around the paddock. She got over her fear and learned to ride thanks to George."

"Ooh! Here's Wild Bill criticizing someone else's riding ability!" Sophie teased.

"Good point. But I was never afraid. I just didn't know that bouncing a foot off the saddle wasn't the proper way to ride," Zach said with a smile. Then, he grew serious. "Mrs. C, I want you to know how much I appreciate you and George for giving me a job and a place to stay, even if it was just for one summer. I learned more about life that summer from George than I have since."

"Call me Jean. George wanted you to make a good life for yourself, and it looks like you have."

"I've done alright. I'd like to give the foster kids I met a similar boost. Pay it forward, so to speak. But I doubt I can ever advise them as well as George did."

"George did talk a lot and was never short on advice." Jean laughed fondly. She wiped moisture from her eyes. "He was really pleased when you listened to him."

"I wasn't very good at listening, but George's words stuck with me, even when I pretended not to hear them." Zach turned to Sophie. "What else do you need to do before opening?"

"Some reservations would be nice," Sophie said with a laugh. "Mostly, I need an experienced manager, someone who can multitask, is organized, and can help me keep the operation running. I can keep an eye on most everything for now as we get up and running, but I'd like to turn over the scheduling of staff, personnel issues, and maintenance problems to a manager. My concentration needs to be more on the marketing and business side."

"Do you have a mobile site or application?" Zach asked.

"Not yet," Sophie replied, "but those are on my 'to do' list."

"I can do those for you," Zach offered. "You've already designed the landing page—your website—so designing the mobile site should be relatively easy. I can do both quickly, but the mobile site can go up first. An app will need to be listed on a platform so users can download it."

Sophie nodded. "Both sound great. I hadn't thought about much beyond the website."

"Your data would all be in one place, but you'd be able to download it in multiple forms—by reservation, work schedules by employee names, by date, or by individual activity. This gives you the ability to assign personnel wherever they're needed on a specific date. I can build a link to all your ad campaigns so you can track the metrics on individual platforms. See the ads that are working and those that aren't."

"Sounds easy. No problem for a techie like you, but I don't want to impose," Sophie said. "I hate to admit it, but I could use your help. My hands are full right now. I could probably design it, but who knows how long it might take for me to get to it. I had staff at my agency that did all the web design work, so my trial and error method might take a while."

"My methods are a bit different from yours and much less frustrating," Zach said with a laugh. "But what are neighbors for? I'd be happy to do it. I'll get started on it right away."

"I don't know what to say. There must be something I can do to repay you," Sophie replied. Her cheeks warmed when she saw the mischievous glint back in Zach's eyes. Sophie narrowed her eyes at him—a cautionary warning not to say what he apparently was thinking.

"Hmmm… I'd say this dinner is payment enough. And

you're taking in June, which saves me from being labeled a pervert. That's a big deal, according to our perspective new hires." Zach smiled, then looked at Aunt Rachel. "Aunt Rachel, you do know how to make pot roast. It was delicious."

After they finished eating, Zach stayed to help Sophie clean up the kitchen while Jean and Rachel cleared the table.

With the cleanup finished, Sophie walked Zach to the door. He touched her arm briefly, then opened the door and, with a slight wave, left her standing in the doorway. What? No teasing or flirtatious remarks?

Zach Whittaker, you flirt bravely when we're in a crowd but lose your nerve and run when we're alone, Sophie thought as she returned his wave. Did she want a more passionate goodbye from him? Maybe. But she was also being hypocritical, since she hadn't given him any indication that she wanted more. *She* was the coward.

CHAPTER TWELVE

W ill do. Friends discount will apply," was the message Robert texted back the next morning after Sophie had finished editing advertising copy and emailed it to Robert. She had asked for his assistance in adapting the written copy into sixty-second ads that would run on some of the TV stations they had working relationships with when she was with the company. She had already posted ads on all the social media sites.

"Thanks, but no funny stuff," Sophie replied.

Robert's reply came back quickly. "What funny stuff? Will let you know the costs."

Advertising was expensive, so she could use any discounts Robert offered. Sophie foresaw another large payment coming out of her account soon. But pushing out the website yesterday was of little use without simultaneously launching an advertising campaign. Next, Sophie finished up Cameron Stables' initial advertising buys by placing a print ad in the *Equestrian Gazette* in Lexington for inclusion in two of their forthcoming issues.

This morning, as she'd showered and dressed, a new idea had come to her—a trial run of the grand opening by inviting people from around the Kingsville area, similar to what Zach had done for Thornton Farms. A trial run wouldn't be the same as when the cabins and tents were filled with paying guests, but it would be an operational test to see how smoothly the dinner and entertainment went. Feedback from her neighbors about what the property now offered would be very useful in refining her plans for opening day.

She had decided to add a dance floor to the pavilion and hire a band for weekends, holidays, and special occasions, such as weddings and anniversary and company parties. The deck and dance floor would be installed tomorrow, just in time for the trial run.

Sophie's phone pinged with a notification of a text. It was from Zach.

"My manager Jack recommends a buddy of his for the job as your manager. A recently retired Marine, master sergeant. Grew up on a horse farm. Name is Hal Sherman."

"Great!" Sophie texted back. "Have Jack send him over around 9:30, if possible."

Only a few seconds passed before a new text arrived from Zach. "That time works. He'll be there. Leaving now to pick up your new hires. Will bring them by around 3ish."

Sophie started putting together the guest list for the trial run party, since the advertising was now taken care of. A week from tomorrow, Saturday night, would be the perfect time to invite the locals to a party. She couldn't invite the whole town, even though she'd like to, but she could invite a cross section of the people of Kingsville, including her neighbors, her staff, and city officials. It always helped to have local government on your side. Darlene could do the taste test on the food that night since

Sophie and Zach hadn't had time to go into town and do it at the Cherry Blossom.

The doorbell rang, and Sophie looked at the clock. It was nine-thirty. Mr. Sherman was right on time. Sophie answered the door. A man whom Sophie judged to be around fifty years old stood on the porch. "Grizzled" would not describe her visitor exactly, but his hair was cut in a short flat top and was heavily streaked with gray. "Unflappable no-nonsense leader" would more accurately sum up her first impression of him. Even if Zach hadn't given her a heads-up as to Hal Sherman's background, she would have recognized by his bearing that he was military and experienced in leadership.

"Mr. Sherman?" Sophie asked.

"Sergeant Hal Sherman, US Marines, retired, ma'am, but most people call me 'Tank.'" He extended his hand to Sophie.

"Tank?" Sophie asked, wondering how he got that nickname. Suddenly, she got the connection. "Oh! Tank! I see! As in Sherman tank?"

"That's right, ma'am," he said with a chuckle. "The nickname seems to stick wherever I go, whether I want it to or not. I just gave in and started using it."

"We'll do the same then, Sergeant Tank," Sophie said as she invited him inside. She led him to the office. "But we need to dispense with the 'ma'am.'"

"I'll drop the 'ma'am' if you drop the 'sergeant.' Just Tank will do."

"Okay, Tank. Have a seat." Sophie indicated a chair in front of the desk. Tank sat down facing her. "My dad served in the Air Force near the end of the Vietnam War. We have a lot of respect for veterans in our family. Thank you for your service."

"Thank you, and thanks for your dad's service, too. I served in Iraq, but I spent much of my twenty-five years as a boot camp training instructor at Paris Island."

"You're a retired Marine, and you grew up with horses, but that's about all I know about you other than that your friend Jack highly recommended you for the job. If you were a training instructor, I guess I don't need to ask if you have experience with organizing and keeping things running on time." Sophie smiled.

"I do believe I'm experienced at that. I grew up just north of here. My parents bred and trained racehorses—thoroughbreds. I know the workings of a horse farm, but I've never been involved in running a resort or anything like that."

"Well, Tank, neither have I." Sophie laughed. "How hard can it be, right? We can learn together. But tell me about you personally."

"I have three grown kids and three grandkids. They're scattered about. Two of my kids live in South Carolina, and one lives in Florida." Tank added quickly, "I lost my wife about three years ago—auto accident."

"I'm so sorry." Sophie nodded. Tank's face closed at the mention of his wife's death. Clearly it was a painful topic, and he offered no further explanation. Sophie moved on. "Let's take a walk out to the barn and stables, and I'll show you the layout of the property."

Sophie and Tank left the office and walked through the kitchen toward the side door leading to the stable area. Aunt Rachel was busy in the kitchen, prepping something for dinner that night. Sophie introduced her to Tank.

"I have a pot of coffee made," Aunt Rachel said. "Would you both like a cup to take with you?" She looked from Sophie to Tank.

"That sounds great. A soldier's fuel is coffee. Even a retired soldier," Tank replied with a smile.

Rachel took paper cups from a cupboard, filled them with coffee, and placed cream, sugar, and lids on the counter beside the cups. Tank and Sophie added cream to their coffees, left the kitchen, and walked to the barn.

Sophie introduced Ben and Pete as the stable managers and experts on horses, then showed Tank where his workspace would be. A desk and chair, a small bookcase, and two straight-backed chairs facing the desk filled the room. The internet provider had run cables to the office, and a laptop now sat on top of the desk. A small refrigerator stood in the corner.

"This looks very comfortable. Air conditioned, even. Very different from the swamps of Paris Island." Tank smiled and pointed to the window unit. "I'll become soft working in here."

"Soft is okay. My biggest fear is that you'll be pulling your hair out the first week," Sophie replied. "We want our employees to be comfortable. You may have to occasionally share the space with Ben and Pete."

"Not a problem," Tank replied.

Sophie then led him outside and across to the pasture. They stood by the fence and watched the boarded horses and Rose as they grazed.

"These are the boarders, except for the sorrel there. She's mine." Sophie then explained that three more horses that belonged to Cameron Stables were just over the ridge in an adjoining pasture. "We keep our boarders in the closest pasture just in case the owners come out to ride them."

Tank nodded, then followed Sophie farther away from the barn. She stopped and pointed out the other amenities offered, in addition to riding lessons, trail rides, and guided hikes. She explained her vision of offering a rustic stay, but with touches of refinement that would make the property appeal to more people than just horse lovers.

"Oh, I see," Tank said. "It's a combination of the horse farm experience with resort amenities."

"Exactly," Sophie replied, pleased that Tank got the concept she imagined. "I want to give guests an experience that fits our bluegrass and thoroughbred history—include horses, but not make it totally about farm life. My goal is to eventually expand even more, always with the goal of mixing stylish and classy with rustic."

Sophie and Tank returned to the main house and sat down in the office again.

"Your duties would include being the problem-solver before the problems get to me. You'd mostly be in charge of scheduling staff and generally keeping things moving along each day." Sophie described the manager's duties as she envisioned them. In addition to scheduling staff, he would sometimes need to move personnel around to make sure the events the guests requested were covered and ran on time. "You'd also be a clearinghouse to coordinate things like calls for maintenance or any security problems. I can pitch in if you become overloaded or during your time off. We'll work the kinks out of the operation together."

"If you need someone who can adjust at a minute's notice and keep to a schedule, I'm your man. That's what Marine boot camp is all about," Tank assured her.

They discussed salary and the work schedule, and then, Sophie offered him the job. Tank seemed perfect for what she needed in a manager. She held her breath as she waited for his answer.

"I'd be happy to become part of your operation. The job sounds like it was made for me—hard work but also fun. When do you want me to start?"

"Monday morning would be perfect, but if you can, I'd also like you to be here this afternoon. Mr. Whittaker is bringing by four young men for stable hand positions. They're very green and without experience, especially at the jobs we're offering them. It's another experiment of mine. I'd like you to meet them."

Tank returned at three. He had just joined Sophie in the office when Zach arrived with the new stable hands, plus June. Chairs were lined up in the center of the room for the five of them, while Jean, Rachel, Ben, and Pete sat in chairs near the back wall. Zach introduced everyone, then took a position against the wall behind Jean.

Sophie leaned back against the front of the desk and addressed the group. "I'd like to welcome you to Cameron Stables. We are starting a new venture together."

She went on to describe what the property was about, plus their duties, scheduled hours, and how they would be paid.

"Your hours may need to be flexible at times, but you'll be paid overtime for any hours worked over the standard forty-hour work week. If for any reason you can't work a scheduled shift, please let Pete, Ben, or Tank know. Does anyone have questions?"

Troy Hayes leaned over and whispered something to Chandler. *Ah,* thought Sophie, *Chandler has already been designated the spokesman for the group. He's the eldest, so that makes sense.*

"What do we do about lunch?" Chandler asked. Sophie had expected a question about wages, work hours, or job duties. Lunch was Troy's biggest concern? She understood, though. This was probably their first real job without a foster family to fall back on. She started to answer, but Zach spoke first.

"You have a kitchen where you're staying. You can pack your lunch there each morning or order delivery if you want." Zach glanced at Sophie and tried not to smile. "You'll be given a lunchbreak, but if your job requires it, lunchtime will have to be flexible, too."

Sophie introduced Tank, gave a short description of his work history, then asked him to address the group. He rose from his chair and stood in front of them. He rested his hands on his hips, and in a calm but firm voice, he spoke, his eyes moving from one to another. "As I always told my Marine recruits, a mile traveled begins with the first step. That's a worn-out expression, I know, but it's still as true today as the first time it was said. Your buddies will help you get back up and back on track if you stumble or fall. That's what teamwork is about. And that's what I expect." Tank's motivational speech was obviously the same one he had made many times to young Marine recruits. "Mr. Whittaker is giving you a place to live, and Miss Cameron is giving you a job. What you make of it is up to you."

Tank finished his speech, then returned to his seat. The voice was different, but the words could have come from Sophie's father. Tank's pep talk had gotten the young men's attention. They straightened in their seats. They were part of a team. Most likely, no one had ever encouraged them to work toward a unified goal.

"If no one has any questions," Sophie said. "I have a packet of information for you to fill out, sign, and bring back to me on Monday. You will also get your work assignments on Monday." She turned and picked up a stack of envelops from the desk.

"We're not signing any contracts." Beau's voice was filled with distrust. "We can quit and leave anytime we decide to."

"Of course, Beau," Sophie replied. "No contact. These papers are payroll forms. I have to report your wages to the IRS. That's all. You are not bound here in any way, but I hope all of you will stay and help us get Cameron Stables off to a good start. But yes, you can quit at any time. I just ask that you let me, Ben, Pete, or Tank know so they can assign someone else to cover your duties. And please don't leave in the middle of the night without saying goodbye." She looked pointedly across the room at Zach, a reminder that he had once done just that.

He shrugged his shoulders and mouthed, "Sorry."

Zach left soon after with the young men to take them to

their quarters at Thornton Farms. Aunt Rachel offered to take June and her bags upstairs, show her to her room, and help her get settled.

As they all left her office, Sophie checked her website again. Hallelujah! Someone had found her website. Maggie had recorded a phone reservation for a couple for the opening weekend, and a family of four had booked a visit for the Fourth of July weekend.

"A mile begins with the first step" Tank had told the new hires. The two reservations, though a very small start, was still a first step.

CHAPTER THIRTEEN

S ophie turned away from her computer and spun her desk
chair around to look out the office window. The sun was
beginning to rise over the tree line along the back of the
property. Its rays, not yet as strong as they would be later, left
light and dark patches across the high meadow and pasture. The
view, though pretty, didn't take her mind off the low number of
reservations that taunted her from her computer screen.

The total bookings this morning had not increased from the
two families that had booked at the end of last week. Not exactly a stampede. Of course, some people might rather stay home
on Father's Day than visit a property that was still unproven.
The ten percent opening weekend discount hadn't yet increased
numbers in the way she thought it would—or hoped it would.

It took time for a new business to get noticed—she knew
that—so she needed to stifle her impatience. Slow had its ad-
vantages since she had no idea what to expect or how to anticipate the many things that could go wrong.

Tank's pickup truck passed by on the service road that led to the barn. He was on his way to meet Ben and Pete at the stables. Sophie looked at the time. It was not yet six-thirty a.m. Tank was early, but Sophie expected no less from him.

A short time later, the van from Thornton Farms passed Sophie's window. She couldn't see if Zach was driving, but she expected he would follow Tank's example. Sophie was certain Zach had heard her father's oft-repeated refrain: "If you're not fifteen minutes early, you're late." Sophie's observations of Zach and his success in business indicated that he would instill good work habits in the young men he'd taken under his wing.

Sophie swung her chair back to her desk and turned her attention to the trial run party on Saturday. Providing an evening of free food and entertainment would be expensive, but there were benefits a new struggling business would gain from word spreading through the community that Cameron Stables lived up to its advertising.

Time was short to get the invitations sent out. Calling it a trial run party didn't set the right tone and had all sorts of bad connotations. "Preview Party" was more accurate and would certainly look better on the invitations.

She had just finished the list of invitees and had drafted what she wanted the invitation to say when June walked into the office.

"Aunt Rachel sent you a cup of coffee and a blueberry muffin," June said as she set the coffee and the plate holding the muffin on the desk.

"Bless Aunt Rachel and you." Sophie picked up the cup of coffee and took a drink. "Ah. Just what I needed. How are you doing? Is Aunt Rachel keeping you busy?"

"She's super nice," June replied. She turned and looked around the room. Her eyes fell on the bookcase piled high with papers. "What's that?"

"*That* is my sweet dad's filing system." Sophie smiled fondly at the mention of her dad. "Thirty years of papers and who knows what else. Hopefully, rats haven't built nests in there. I'm kidding," she added quickly when June took a step away from the bookcase.

"Wow! That's a lot of paper." June turned back toward Sophie. "Aunt Rachel sent me to ask if you need help. She's done in the kitchen and doesn't have anything else I can help her with right now."

"Yes, I could actually use some help," Sophie replied. "I need to go to the barn and see Tank, so if you could put this list of names and emails into a group email for me, that would help me a bunch. I should have thought of the preview party earlier but didn't, so now, I'm running out of time. There's not enough time to get invitations printed and mailed since the party is this Saturday night. An email is the best I can do. I'd like to get it sent out today. I can show you how to copy the written invitation into the email once you've set up the list. But don't send anything out until I look over it."

"Sure, I can do that," June replied. She came around the desk to see what Sophie was asking her to finish. "Oh! You have a design software program. I've used that program before. I can design an invitation for you that can be attached to the email. That is, if you want me to. That might be better than just a written message."

"You can do that?" At June's nod, Sophie said, "That would be perfect!" She showed June the information that she wanted on the invitation. "Get creative if you feel like it. I'll look it over when I get back." She couldn't believe her luck. Young people were almost all computer savvy, since computer skills were a common part of their education, but having someone with design skills just fall into her lap? That was a break Sophie hadn't expected.

Sophie left June sitting at the computer, engrossed in designing the invitation. She walked through the kitchen toward the side door to take the shortcut to the barn and stables. The kitchen was empty, but the delicious aromas that hung in the air indicated that Aunt Rachel had been there just a short time ago.

Aunt Rachel loved to cook. Jean was a good cook but not as passionate about it as Aunt Rachel. Aunt Rachel coming to live with them, even if it turned out to only be for a short while, was another piece of good luck. And not just for the delicious meals she cooked. She was company for Jean. Actually, they were company for each other. Both were widows now and knew what the other was going through. And Aunt Rachel's cooking expertise was another boon, since she was coordinating the dinners at the pavilion with Darlene.

Sophie met Aunt Rachel returning to the house as she neared the barn.

"I took the guys some blueberry muffins for their morning break," Rachel explained as they paused on the path.

"Thank you! That's very nice of you," Sophie replied. "My food coordinator is already on the job!"

"Just a little welcoming treat. No big deal." Rachel shrugged. "I thought it might make them feel more at home."

"That's a sweet thought! Where are you off to next?"

"Jean asked me to come to the flower garden. She has a new idea to run by me." Rachel turned and began walking along the path.

"Of course she does!" Sophie laughed as she waved goodbye to Aunt Rachel, then continued walking toward the barn.

She entered the cool interior and walked to Tank's office just inside the door. She knocked on the doorframe. Tank looked up from the paper he was writing on. He put down a half-eaten muffin on a napkin on the desk, then beckoned her to come in.

"I've brought company mobile phones for the new guys so you can keep in touch with each other," Sophie said as she lay the phones on the desk. Then, she sat down in a chair next to the desk. "Here's the list of numbers. They're all activated. All employees now have a phone. What are you working on?"

"I was drawing up a list of chores that need to be taken care of around the stables on a daily basis. Pete also gave me the scheduled delivery of supplies. I've included those, along with daily feeding, watering, cleaning stalls, currying the horses, etc.," Tank said, tapping his pen on the paper on his desk. He put down the pen, then leaned back in his chair. "I'll adjust the duties once we have guests that need to be taken care of and after I assess the guys' individual skills. Things work better when everyone is on the same page and knows what's expected of them."

"I agree." Sophie nodded. "How are things going with Zach's squad so far?"

"They've only been here a short while, but when I talked with them this morning, two of them seemed more aware of what needs to be done than the other two. But they all seem eager to learn."

"We can't ask any more of them than that. We knew they were inexperienced," Sophie replied.

"No problems otherwise. I sent Mark over to look at the air conditioner in the office at the front gate. Maggie says it's not cooling properly."

"I have an account at the local hardware store if Mark needs to buy parts. Did Zach bring the boys over personally this morning?"

"He did," Tank replied. "He said Jack would do it from now on, but he wanted to drop them off on their first day. I reminded him that this wasn't kindergarten." Tank laughed at his joke.

"I guess it's important to him that this experiment works out well. Has he left?" Sophie had looked around the area on her approach to the barn but hadn't seen the van.

"Yes. He said that he and Miss Thornton had a plane to catch. Is there something I can help you with?"

"No," Sophie replied, disappointed that Zach had left already. She didn't have anything pressing to discuss. She just wanted to ask if the young men had everything they needed at the bunkhouse. And maybe she just enjoyed seeing him.

Zach hadn't mentioned an upcoming business trip to her last Friday, but she hadn't had a private conversation with him, either. He left right after the meeting to get the new hires settled into the bunkhouse.

And now, he was on a trip with Lynn? Was it business or pleasure? With Lynn, most likely a pleasure trip. Ugh, Sophie was sounding more and more like Patsy. *Petty thoughts regarding Lynn are becoming a habit of late*, Sophie scolded herself.

Zach's travel schedule and personal life were his business, not hers. And she needed to stop letting it bother her. "I just wanted to invite Zach and others from Thornton Farms to our preview party on Saturday. I'm sending out invitations but wanted to invite him in person, since he was here. You're invited, too, as are all the staff. And bring a plus-one, if you like. The party will include food and drinks with a band and dancing at the pavilion."

"That's a nice gesture. I'm sure everyone will have a great time. My plus-ones are scarce these days, so it'll just be me," Tank replied.

"Well, the party is not without motive. I'm hoping to spread the word of what we offer. I'm inviting the editor of the town paper in hopes of some free press. The mayor, city council, and other business leaders in town are also invited, because their support is always helpful. Darlene and I also plan to ask everyone to vote for their favorite dishes, which will give us an idea of which foods are best received. That will be useful information when we officially open."

"Sounds like fun and a smart strategy. I'll be there," Tank replied. "Let me know how I can help."

Sophie said goodbye to Tank, left the barn, and walked back to the house. June was taking something out of the printer when Sophie walked into the office.

"What do you think?" June asked nervously as she handed Sophie the invitation she had designed. The party details were artistically displayed on the page. A portrait of Sophie's horse, Irish Rose, encircled by a horse shoe, was placed below the caption, "Cameron Stables." The tag line, "Rustic Redefined," was centered on the page beneath the picture. It matched the logo on the website. June had found the picture of Rose in a file on Sophie's computer—proof that she was resourceful as well as creative.

"I love it. This is perfect." Sophie nodded. "You did a super job."

"Thanks," June replied, pleased by the compliment. "I have the email blast ready to send."

After a cursory look, Sophie gave June the okay to send the invitation out to the list of invitees.

"How would you like to become my office assistant?" Sophie asked June. "I definitely could use someone with your skills. But if you'd rather work with Aunt Rachel, that's alright, too."

"Really? I'd like that." June grinned happily. "I love this kind of work, but I can still help Aunt Rachel when you don't have anything for me to do."

"Great! You're hired," Sophie replied. June grinned, pleased by the offer. If all the people involved with Sophie's resort experiment were like her new office assistant—and if enthusiasm was an indication of success—this business was going to work out. "And when there's time, maybe you could go through my dad's filing system." Sophie pointed to the paper-laden bookshelves. "I know it looks overwhelming, but if you could just sort the papers into different categories, I'll look through the different piles and decide what to keep and what to shred."

"I'll do that." June nodded in reply. "By the way, you got a text while you were out. You left your phone next to the keyboard. I saw from the notification on the screen that it was from Mr. Whittaker. But I didn't read it."

"Thanks," Sophie said as she picked up her phone and opened the text message from Zach.

It read: "Finished your mobile website. The mobile app will be available for download soon. Check out site. If a keeper, download the link. Send changes or questions. Gone to CA. Can still make changes. Be back soon."

Sophie was pleased that Zach had not forgotten his promise to design a mobile site after deciding to go to California with Lynn. She took a seat facing the desk while June finished up sending out the invitations for the preview party. Sophie followed Zach's suggestion and linked the mobile site to the company website. She then scrolled through its features, selecting a cabin, a morning trail hike, and an afternoon trail ride, and then added payment information. She submitted the test reservation.

"Two more notifications for reservations just came in," June said in response to the notification on the computer screen.

"One of those is probably me testing the mobile site," Sophie replied. She came around the desk and looked at the screen. "That one under SC is me. See if you can pull a report for Saturday of the opening weekend and print it. I want to review the data. It should show a breakdown of guests and activities for that day."

Sophie walked to the printer and waited for the report to print. She picked up the paper from the printer tray. There were six reservations, including hers and the other new one that had just come through. The report showed the reservation data, events each guest had signed up for, and confirmation numbers. Payment data was displayed at the bottom of the page.

"This is exactly what we need," Sophie said to June. "Delete my test reservation, and we're good to go."

Sophie returned to her seat and replied to Zach's text: "Tested mobile site. Linked to website correctly. Works as if designed by a pro."

Zach's reply came back quickly. "Who knew? Just cowboy savvy, ma'am."

"Enjoy your time in CA, Cowboy," Sophie replied.

"Yup! See you in a few, Miss Sophie," Zach replied.

CHAPTER FOURTEEN

Sophie and Robert spent the next few days coordinating and fine-tuning the TV ads. Using videos and photographs Sophie had taken of the property, they created ads that would fit audiences in different locales, both urban and rural. Once Sophie gave her approval, Robert purchased spots in broadcast markets in the Mid-Atlantic and Midwestern states. Robert's "friends discount" meant he didn't charge her for the time spent putting the ads together, just for the airtime. It was a break Sophie's bank account appreciated.

The preview party invitations were well received, with RSVPs coming in quickly and almost at a one hundred percent participation rate from all who were invited. The response was as Sophie expected, since it was a night of free food and entertainment, as well as a chance for invitees to catch up and visit with their neighbors.

Tank, Ben, and Pete quickly became a smooth, well-coordinated management team. Sophie met with them a few times to iron out minor kinks in the operation. Her involvement was rarely needed, though, because Tank expertly handled most operational problems on his own.

"Zach's Squad," as Sophie had come to think of them, were under Ben's tutelage and were all working out well and quickly becoming friends. Sophie frequently heard shouts of laughter coming from the stables and barn when she walked the property. And most importantly, according to Tank, there were no slackers in Zach's group. They had fun together, but they always completed their assignments well and on time.

At Ben's suggestion, Sophie had hired his friend, Kenny, an experienced hiker and rider who knew how to manage a hiking or riding group. With Kenny onboard, the current staff seemed adequate to handle all aspects of the business at this time.

With her employees taking care of the stables, Sophie devoted her time to finalizing the arrangements for the preview party. She and Darlene had consulted and agreed on a menu. An order and delivery time were set up with the wine and beer distributor in Kingsville. Sophie hired a local band for the party and promised that if they were well-received, she would offer them a contract for a steady gig when Cameron Stables opened permanently.

By Saturday morning, Sophie was confident that she had done all she could to make the party a pleasant experience for all the invited guests. Even the weather was cooperating. The forecast was for a clear, starry night, which meant a bright Kentucky moon would rise and add even more ambiance to the evening.

Sophie added the finishing touches to her hair and make-up, then made her way toward the party's entertainment area. She should be nervous, but she wasn't. She had attended clients' launch parties throughout her career in marketing, so she was ready for this. It would be nothing like the large corporate launches she had previously hosted, but experience had taught her that if you offer a pleasant atmosphere with good food and entertainment, most people will overlook any small glitches that might pop up during large gatherings. Sophie had tried to anticipate and hopefully avoid even small glitches, but there was often a surprise or two with such events.

Darlene's catering vans had arrived, and the catering staff, with Aunt Rachel's help, were putting the finishing touches on the meal in the prep kitchen. They would soon transfer the dishes to a long buffet table located on one side of the pavilion.

Sophie paused at the entrance and looked over the room with satisfaction. Tables, decorated with vases of roses from the flower garden and lighted candles, were set up around the space. A few tables were placed outside on the dance floor, and a small number were stationed on the grassy lawn that surrounded the pavilion—different choices for different tastes. The food service area and the inside dining tables were surrounded by magnetic net curtains to keep away mosquitos, moths, and other insects. Since it was a warm night, the heavy canvas curtains had all been raised, giving the diners a view of the dance floor, the landscape, and the beautiful night.

Sophie wasn't offering a sit-down dinner, but rather self-serve dishes that could pass as a full meal and be easily eaten whether the guests sat at a table or milled around the room visiting with other guests. Darlene had supplied strips of paper with the names of the main dishes and stacked them in front of labeled glass jars so guests could vote for their favorite dishes.

Tonight's menu would be pared down and adapted when they fed paying guests. Tonight's party was a dress rehearsal to help Darlene fine-tune the logistics of preparing a catered meal, determine which dishes were favored, and figure out how to pull it off as smoothly as possible.

Some of the food choices were dishes offered at Churchill

Downs on Derby Day, in keeping with the regional cuisine. Burgoo, a meaty stew; hot brown, a kind of turkey bacon slider; and beer cheese soup were all on the menu. Darlene also added dishes from her personal recipe collection, as well as an array of desserts that she offered at the Cherry Blossom.

The guests began arriving around six-thirty p.m. Sophie stood at the entrance of the pavilion to welcome each one. The local city government leaders arrived, followed by a steady stream of other invitees, along with the Cameron Stables' staff. Stephen brought a date and was accompanied by his father and mother. Mrs. Hampton seemed impressed by the set up as she stopped in front of Sophie and looked over the room. Her nose didn't turn up even a little bit, and to Sophie, that was a major coup. Mrs. Hampton had a reputation for not approving of any events outside her own parties.

Jack, the manager of Thornton Farms, and his wife brought Zach's Squad. Zach arrived with Lynn, Cal, and Eli.

"It all looks fantastic." Zach greeted Sophie at the pavilion's entrance. A soft breeze blew through the net surrounding the pavilion, flickering the candlelight on the ceiling. Music from the band played softly in the background. "Very nice, indeed. Save me a dance later?" At Sophie's nod, he moved along in the receiving line.

Some of the guests sat at tables while others milled around the room visiting with people they knew. Sophie moved from group to group, chatting with each of them. She listened to them describe what was happening in their lives or tell stories about their children or grandchildren. A few reminisced about her father. Everyone was very complimentary about the wonderful evening they were having.

When the dishes were cleared away and couples started filling the dance floor, all heads turned toward the band. But Sophie had only one thought, and it wasn't joining in the dancing.

Since everything was going smoothly, all she wanted was to find a quiet place where she could relax for a few minutes. Actually, her biggest need was to find a quiet spot where she could take her shoes off and rest her feet. Her sandals had felt comfortable four hours ago, but now, the little toe on her right foot was screaming for relief.

Sophie quickly looked around the room and dance floor. Her mother was engaged in a conversation with Jack and his wife on the other side of the room. Zach was standing by the mayor's table, laughing at something the mayor had said. And was that Aunt Rachel and Tank on the dance floor together? Everyone was occupied at the moment, so no one would miss her if she snuck away for a few minutes.

Sophie slipped out the back side of the pavilion and walked toward the flower garden. The smell of roses perfumed the air even before she entered the rose-covered trellised gateway. She followed a winding lighted path to a bench in the middle of the garden. Sophie sat down, leaned her head back against the bench, kicked off her shoes, and gazed upward. The night sky was filled with stars, and a bright moon peaked through the leaves of the tree that shaded the bench.

Sophie closed her eyes and slumped against the bench as the sound of music from the band floated through the garden. She completely relaxed and took a deep breath for the first time in what felt like hours. She raised both feet off the ground, moved her ankles in circles, and flexed her toes. Oh, relief! Even her right little toe was happy.

Warm hands closed over her toes and began to rub her feet. Sophie's gasp at the sudden contact quickly faded into a drawn out "ahh" as the gentle pressure soothed her burning feet.

Sophie knew who it was even before she opened one eye in a small slit. Zach was standing on the path, holding both her feet while gently massaging them.

"You can stop now," Sophie said as she reluctantly pulled her feet from his grasp and sat up. She moved over, giving him space on the bench.

"You don't like your feet rubbed?" Zach asked as he sat down beside her.

"Crazy question," Sophie replied. "Who doesn't? But I probably should get back to the party soon. The hostess falling asleep on a bench in the garden during a foot rub probably wouldn't be good advertisement for my business. But how are you? I guess you and Lynn had a good trip to California?"

"More assumptions, Miss Sophie?" Zach asked. He added with a smile, "As I've said before, you need to lose that habit."

"Not an assumption. Tank told me," Sophie replied.

"Did Tank also tell you that my plane is parked at the Lexington airport? And that I took the helicopter there and dropped Lynn off for a visit with her mother? I went to California alone—for business."

"No, he didn't explain that part," Sophie admitted slowly, feeling foolish. But she wasn't done with being snarky, so she repeated something Zach had previously said: "I guess the boss can't work from just anywhere after all."

"Not when you have to fire someone for selling proprietary information to a competitor. I prefer to do that in person." Zach looked over at her and added, "Hmmm? Is it the admission that her assumption was wrong that has the lady in a snit, or is it jealousy again? This isn't the first time we've discussed both conditions, is it?"

"Assumptions. I'm sorry. I was wrong. There, I said it," Sophie replied, happy that the darkness hid her embarrassment. "I sometimes wander into territory I know nothing about."

"That you do. But you promised me a dance. I'll take the dance as your apology." Zach stood up, took her hands, and pulled her up from the bench. His arms closed around her, and he pulled her close as the band started to play a slow dance tune.

Sophie hadn't realized how physically tired she was until she rested her head on Zach's shoulder, let go, and allowed him to guide her through the dance. She barely noticed the tiny pebbles on the pathway beneath her bare feet as they moved in unison to the music.

The last few months had been very busy and more stressful than any other time in her life. She often felt as if the weight of the world rested on her shoulders. One wrong decision, and she would lose her mother's and her family home. What would it be like if she had someone like Zach to share her burdens and worries with all the time?

When the music ended, Zach didn't turn her loose. Instead, he raised her chin and kissed her softly. He pulled back with a question in his eyes, seemingly hesitant to continue.

Sophie's head cautioned her to go slow, to not let a bright Kentucky moon and the feel of Zach's arms holding her tempt her, to not get sidetracked from her mission. The job of rescuing her father's business was not yet finished, and it still demanded all her attention. But her heart's longing pushed her toward forgetting duty and to just enjoying a brief moment with a handsome man in a magical moonlit garden.

Zach still hesitated, waiting for Sophie's answer. Overwhelmed with longing, Sophie ignored her head's warning—an impulsive and unusual move, since she was usually a coward in such situations. Sophie rose up on her toes and locked her arms around Zach's neck. She pulled his head down and kissed him, surprising herself with the passion she poured into the kiss.

"I'm sorry. That just happened," Sophie whispered in a breathless voice as the kiss ended. She blinked and drew back slowly. She tried to pull away, but Zach held her firmly against his chest. "I should get back. My guests."

"Sophie," Zach said in a soft voice as he lowered his head and kissed her again. When the kiss ended, he said, "Never apologize for a rash decision when it turns out to be the right one. This is right." He raised one hand and cupped her cheek. Pushing back her hair, he bent and nuzzled her neck just below the jawline. He sighed. "Mmm, you smell so good."

"That's not me. It's the roses." Sophie laughed, using humor to get control of the fire she had started. While she longed to further explore this new side of her relationship with Zach, duty to her guests cooled any additional romantic thoughts. "I... I just got caught up in the moonlight, the dancing, and the party. It meant nothing."

"Nothing, huh? Are you lying to this cowboy or to yourself, Miss Sophie?" Zach looked skeptical.

"We had better go. My guests will be leaving soon." Sophie ignored his question.

"I know, but the excuse that 'the moonlight made me do it' isn't good enough. Whatever it was, it's not over. And next time, there'll be no kissing, then running," Zach promised. He released her but took her hand to steady her as she slipped back into her shoes. He continued to hold her hand as they walked along the path leading back to the entertainment pavilion together.

"On a different topic, I bought two thoroughbred horses while in California that I'd like to have Pete train, if he has time. At prevailing rates, of course. They'll arrive in the next few days."

"He can do that, but at no charge. You've done so much already."

"What have I done? Found four green farm hands for you to hire, train, and pay?"

"There's Tank and June. They're all working out great. And the apps. They're extremely helpful."

"Yes, there is Tank and the apps, but there's also your bottom line." Zach stopped and took both her hands in his. He turned her to face him. "Don't let your soft heart override your business head like your father did."

"You're right," Sophie agreed, acknowledging the truth in what Zach said. While her father was loved by everyone he came in contact with, his generosity was one of the reasons she was having to rebuild his business now. "But I can't be dishonest and greedy, even if it means the business will fail. Or take charity."

"You couldn't be dishonest if you tried. And accepting payment for a service you offer isn't charity. It's income that will help you pay your staff," Zach replied.

"Okay, we'll charge you double." Sophie laughed, happy that they were both ignoring what had just happened and were back on a safer topic.

"I'm serious. As the former owner of a firm, you know that starting a business is hard. Sometimes, it requires decisions you don't want to make. It was hard for me to fire my employee last week. He was someone I liked and trusted. I contemplated giving him a second chance—but only for a second. It wouldn't be fair to the other team members because he was trying to personally profit from their hard work. You owe it to the people who depend on you to make the business as profitable and financially secure as possible."

"Ahem!" A voice interrupted them. Eli stood at the edge of the garden. "Is Professor Whittaker wasting this beautiful setting on a business lecture? We need some remedial training on pickup lines, I see."

"What do you want, Eli?" Zach showed an unusual irritation with his partner.

"Your mother is looking for you, Sophie. Some of your guests are leaving. I told her I'd find you. I figured if I found you, I'd also find my partner and my ride home. You ready to leave, partner?"

"Yes," Zach replied, his tone more even this time. He looked at Sophie and nodded toward Eli. "It's his bedtime. He gets cranky when he misses it. Thanks for the dance and for the…" he paused, then added, "and for an enjoyable evening. I'd call it a success, wouldn't you?"

"I would. And thank you for the foot rub and… the dance," Sophie had almost blurted out "the kiss." She suspected that was what Zach had almost said, too, but for once, he didn't say what he was thinking. He bypassed the chance to tease her over what just happened between them.

"Foot rub? Dance?" Eli ribbed Zach as Sophie and Zach walked past him. "Now, *that's* what I call a pickup move—a definite improvement. Good job! My here work is done."

◆

Sophie was alone in her office on Monday morning. Just as she opened her computer to check the reservation page, the doorbell rang. June had gone to the barn to visit with Johnny before she tackled the job of sorting the papers in the bookshelf. Jean and Aunt Rachel had gone into town on a shopping trip. Sophie rose from her desk and went to answer the front door. Lynn Thornton was standing on the porch.

"Lynn! Good morning," Sophie said in surprise. "Please come in."

"I want to talk with you. I tried to catch you Saturday night, but you were always busy. But it's easier to talk here, so this is actually better," Lynn said as she stepped into the entryway.

"Sure," Sophie replied. What was this about? "How about a glass of iced tea in the kitchen? We can talk there."

Sophie led Lynn into the kitchen and poured each of them a glass of iced tea. They sat down at the table. "What can I do for you?"

"Congratulations on the party Saturday night. It was very nice and obviously a huge success. And thanks for inviting me. You've done a wonderful job with this property."

"Thank you, Sophie replied. "I appreciate you coming by to give me your feedback."

"That's not really why I'm here." Lynn's face took on a serious look as she pulled her chair closer to the table. She took a drink from her glass of tea, swallowed, then looked directly at Sophie.

Sophie felt a tightening in her stomach. As small children and neighbors, they had been friends, but as teenagers, the friendship had died. Lynn and the crowd she ran with could, at best, be called obnoxious and rude to anyone not in their clique. As adults, she and Lynn had nothing in common.

"I want to apologize for the way I treated you in high school. I was an awful person. And I'm sorry."

Sophie was caught off guard, but she waved away Lynn's apology. "You don't have to apologize."

"Yes, I do, if for no other reason than to selfishly make myself feel better." Lynn smiled.

Even Lynn's apology was all about Lynn, Sophie thought. But even that was more than she had ever expected.

"I need to clear the air," Lynn continued. "In high school, I thought I was mistress of the universe and only those who had an ego as big as mine were allowed to be my friend." Lynn leaned back in her chair and took a deep breath. She was sincere. Selfish or not, this was important to her, and she was barreling through with an apology whether Sophie wanted to hear it or not. "When I lost my father, I learned a cruel lesson: I was not immune to the bad things I thought only happened to other people. I was knocked off my pedestal. A pedestal I had put myself on. And my parents had never told me any different, especially my doting father."

"I... don't know what to say." Lynn was baring her soul with an honesty Sophie had never heard from her before. Sophie didn't have a response to her confession, but Lynn didn't seem to expect one. And she wasn't through yet.

"When my mother moved me to Lexington and I entered a new school, I was a stranger—a vulnerable, fatherless child who was alone and without her supporting crowd. It was a real eye-opener for me. I no longer had the power to decide who was popular and who wasn't. Now, looking back, it seems ridiculous and unbelievable that I was as conceited and misguided as I was when I lived here. I want to apologize if my actions ever hurt you."

Sophie was taken aback. Lynn had been what Sophie and her high school friends called a "snot" behind her back. Lynn was probably unaware then—and maybe even now—that there were classmates who were not enamored with her or her status. Sophie's reaction to Lynn at the time had been more confusion than hurt. She couldn't understand why someone would be that dispassionate and hurtful to others. But Sophie never seriously aspired to be part of Lynn's pack.

As a teenager, Sophie was a skinny girl in glasses, more interested in horses and getting good grades than competing with Lynn, a self-anointed goddess in the latest designer clothes. Lynn apparently thought she had made more of an impact on Sophie than she actually had. She may have had that effect on some classmates, but Sophie wasn't one of them. Sophie was a realist and knew she couldn't compete with Lynn, so why try?

"You don't need to apologize. We were just kids. But... apology accepted," Sophie replied slowly. She didn't want to sound ungracious, since Lynn was making an effort. "Truthfully, I haven't thought about the high school hierarchy since… well, actually never. Definitely not since I graduated. That was a lifetime ago, and hopefully, we've all matured by now."

"I just wanted you to know that I'm aware of what a pain I must have been back then. I've changed and am not that person anymore," Lynn said. "And there's something else I want to share. I'm getting married!"

"You're getting married?" Sophie felt a stab to the heart and almost choked on her drink. She hadn't expected an apology and certainly not an engagement announcement. She slowly set her glass down on the table. Was this the real purpose for Lynn's visit? To gloat? Maybe Lynn did have designs on being "mistress of the manor," as Patsy had said.

Zach had kissed Sophie in the garden Saturday night. Had he kissed her while engaged to Lynn or was planning to ask her to marry him? She didn't want to believe Zach would do something like that, but she had a long track record of only seeing what she wanted to see where men were concerned.

"Yes, I am. Cal asked me to marry him this past weekend. We haven't decided on a date yet, but as one of my oldest friends, I wanted to tell you personally and invite you to the wedding whenever we do set a date."

"Cal? Oh!" Sophie felt ashamed for instantly thinking the worst of Zach. But mostly, what she felt was relief that once again, her *assumptions* had been wrong. "Congratulations! That's wonderful! Have you known Cal long?"

"We've known each other for several years but never spent much time together. When Zach bought our property and needed a decorator, Cal suggested me for the job. We fell in love, and now, we're getting married." Lynn glowed with happiness.

"I'm very happy for you. I really am. Thanks for inviting me. But you don't need to apologize for the past. We were just kids."

"I do, and I feel better now that I have." Lynn soon stood up to leave, and Sophie walked her to the door.

"Thanks for listening to my *mea culpa*. You'll get an official invitation to the wedding as soon as we settle on a date," Lynn said as she hugged Sophie goodbye. "There are others I need to visit now on my 'apology tour.' Some I dread more than others, but I feel I have to do this."

"I'm sure that once they know you're sincere, they'll all accept your apology," Sophie assured Lynn. But would that be true of Patsy or her brother?

"Before I go…" Lynn smiled as she paused at the door. "Sometimes, it's more than moonlight magic on my momma's terrace that brings two people together—two incredible people. Maybe you can't see it, but anyone else can see the attraction between you and Zach. Wake up! Go for it, Sophie. Don't let a great guy get away. Just friendly advice from a friend." Lynn pointedly looked at Sophie, then left through the door and walked to her car.

Lynn's apology for her behavior years ago was admirable, but she wasn't above inserting herself into other peoples' business. For her to conclude that she knew more about Sophie's feelings toward Zach than Sophie did showed that she was still opinionated and felt her opinions mattered. Like the old Lynn, the new version had nerve and wasn't shy about bossing people around.

Lynn opinionated? Yes, she was, but was she wrong about Sophie's feelings toward Zach?

CHAPTER FIFTEEN

S ophie dropped a flashlight into her backpack, then checked the contents one last time to make sure she hadn't left anything out that she might need if an emergency arose. She had her phone, a couple of protein bars, two bottles of water, and a rope, just in case they needed to remove any large objects that blocked the trail. She added a fixed-blade knife, more for cutting back vegetation than anything. Snakes were frequently sighted in the woods, but they were usually more afraid of humans than the other way around. "Live and let live" was her motto, but she also believed in preparedness, so she added a first aid kit to the backpack.

Finding everything in the backpack she thought she'd need, Sophie zipped it up and swung it over her shoulder. She left the house through the kitchen side door and took the path toward the stable yard where Pete, Chandler, and Kenny were waiting astride their horses. Rose, also saddled, blew and pawed the ground impatiently waiting for Sophie to mount and begin their night ride toward Mystic Hills and Fairy Woods. She had thought at one time that Zach might join them, but Chandler had driven alone from Thornton Farms.

Fairy Woods, dark and foreboding during the day, saved its spectacular show for the darkness of night, when even the brightest moon didn't penetrate the thick stand of trees.

According to family stories passed down through the generations, Sophie's ancestors had believed that fairies lived in the dark woods. As evidence, they pointed to the mysterious blue-green glowing patches that moved around and kept spreading in an ever-widening swath. The glowing patches were only vivid at night—further proof to them that the fairies came out to dance, though only in the darkness. The Cameron settlers dubbed the mysterious glow "fairy fire."

Scientific evidence later indicated that the glow was not mysterious at all. Commonly called "fox fire," it is due to the oxidation of fungi that live on rotted stumps and fallen trees in cool, damp, dark places like Fairy Woods. Still, having a scientific explanation didn't alter the Camerons' stories about a large group of fairies that were supposedly encamped on a section of the woods they owned.

The Camerons had a reputation as fun-loving pranksters and great storytellers. They could spin a yarn that could turn the most skeptical person into a believer. Those who gathered to have a pint were entertained by stories of fairies that magically appeared at night and danced by the light of fireflies, which were also drawn to the spot by the fairies' magic. The Camerons loved to entertain, even if it meant exaggerating and embellishing the truth to hold an audience's attention.

But Fairy Woods *was* a magical place, and Sophie planned to take advantage of that by including it in the trail hikes offered by Cameron Stables. No other property she knew of had anything that could compare with Fairy Woods. She would use the mystery and magic of Fairy Woods to attract visitors to the property to witness the spectacle of dancing fairies.

Sophie and the other riders were making a preliminary ride to Fairy Woods tonight. They would inspect the trail to ensure its safety and judge if the area still qualified as a worthy attraction. Sophie had only been there at night once before, and that was a long time ago. Tonight would be her last chance to make the trip before opening day.

Kenny—or maybe even Chandler, whose riding ability improved daily—would lead the ride with the couples who won the lottery drawing for the exclusive trip to Fairy Woods. Sophie planned to keep the number in the party limited to four guests and a guide. A small group was needed for the safety of the guests on the trail as well as for the protection of Fairy Woods. A larger group would be harder to manage and keep from trampling all over the site and ruining the area's fragile nature.

Pete was leading the group this evening, with Sophie bringing up the rear. It would be part trail ride and part hike. They would ride to within half a mile of the darkest section of the woods, dismount, and go the rest of the way on foot. Horses would cause even more damage than humans if brought into the area of fairy fire.

Twilight was just beginning to settle over the land as Sophie mounted Rose and they started riding toward the mountains. The sun had dropped behind the tree line, creating an orange glowing ball that resembled a forest fire along the ridge. It was the perfect weather for an evening ride, pleasantly cool with only a slight breeze.

Pete led the riders toward an established trail just west of the tents in the high meadow. The trail inclined slowly and was easier on horses and riders than the rougher trail that branched off toward Mystic Peak. This particular trail would also be easier and safer should novice riders win the Fairy Woods lottery.

They rode across the meadow in silence until Pete started singing a medley of songs from once-popular Western movies. Kenny and Chandler joined in. They knew at least some of the words to the old movie tunes.

The lyrics about riding the range and the lonely life of a cowboy reminded Sophie of Zach and the letters he had written to her father about his plans to move to Texas with Eli. What a culture shock that must have been! But if anyone could adjust to a change in culture with aplomb, it would be Zach. Wild Bill would "fake it until he made it" and do it with humor and a self-deprecating style.

Before long, the small procession had crossed the meadow and entered the woods. The blossoms on the redbud and dog-wood trees were mostly gone now, replaced by thick, green, leafy foliage. Scrub pine and small cedar bushes lined the trail. Their scrawny branches struggled to survive in the scant light that managed to penetrate the taller trees that were wrapped in a thick mass of vines.

Pete and Kenny took the position of lead riders, and Sophie and Chandler fell in behind them. As they rode, Sophie made note of any areas on the trail that needed to be reworked or altered for the safety of horses and riders. In most places, the trail was wide enough for two riders to ride side by side, but they had to stop a few times to cut back thick vines and vegetation that had crept out onto the trail. In another area, a large boulder had become dislodged and rolled onto the trail. The men quickly pushed it back, clearing the way.

As the group rode deeper into the forest, the light disappeared, and the trail was visible only a few feet in front of them. The sun's glow had completely disappeared, and the faint light of the rising moon rarely pierced the blackness of the woods. Pete fastened a light to his saddle and lit the path for the riders.

Soon, they reached the clearing where the horses would be left. The rest of the way would be on foot.

As Sophie slid from the saddle and started to tether Rose to a nearby sapling, a loud crashing sound came from the woods on her right. A wild animal? A robber? Sophie grabbed at her backpack as she tried to formulate a response. Whatever was plowing through the trees was coming straight toward them. She fumbled nervously with the zipper on her backpack to retrieve her only weapon, the knife, but the backpack slipped from her hands and landed with a thud on the ground.

A large bay gelding appeared from under a poplar tree and walked into the clearing. Pete, Kenny, Chandler, and Sophie all stood gaping as Zach pulled Big Boy to a halt.

"What are you doing here? Other than scaring us to death?" Sophie asked heatedly as Zach dismounted and attached the gelding's bridle to a nearby tree. There was a large scratch on his cheek, a sign of an altercation with a tree limb.

"Sorry. I didn't mean to scare you. I wanted to join the ride but got delayed by a business call," Zach replied. "I cut through the woods from the other side of the hill on Thornton Farms." He looked around, pleased with himself. "I'm actually surprised I came out at the right spot."

"That was a reckless thing to do," Sophie said angrily, still shaking from fright. She was frustrated, too, that her reaction to possible danger had been a fumbling attempt to retrieve the knife in her backpack. As a defensive plan, it wasn't much to begin with, and it would have been an utter failure if the danger had been a wild animal. But she was most angry at Zach's nonchalance over what he had done. She added loudly, "You could have been shot!"

"Do you have a gun?" Zach asked, smiling at her bluster.

"No, but..." Sophie replied weakly. She recharged her outrage and shouted, "You could have been hurt. Taking an unbroken trail is dangerous for horse and rider even in daylight." An experienced rider like Zach was capable of avoiding dangers on the trail, but at night, getting hurt was a real possibility for anyone on an unbroken trail.

Sophie's pulse was still pounding, so she lashed out at the person responsible. "And you're hurt. Sit down and let me attend to that gash on your cheek." She unzipped the backpack and removed the first aid kit and a flashlight. She turned it on and handed it to Pete. "Hold the light so I can see the cut."

"It's nothing more than a scratch," Zach objected as Sophie stalked toward him with the kit in hand.

"Sit." Sophie pointed to a boulder beside the trail.

"You're overreacting!" Zach threw up his hands in surrender and sat down on the boulder. "Are you worried my handsome face will be scarred?"

"Hush, Mr. Tough Guy. I've seen scratches like this turn into infections. This is going to sting—I hope." Sophie dipped the swab in antiseptic and dabbed at his cheek. She not-so-gently placed an antibacterial adhesive strip over the cut.

"You didn't take the Hippocratic Oath, did you? 'First, do no harm,' you know? The oath where you swear not to kill your patient?" Zach grabbed Sophie's hand and held it in his. "It's nice to see you're concerned for my safety. I knew you cared, but not this much," Zach added softly, though loud enough for the other riders to hear. The mischievous sparkle in his eyes broadcasted his intent: putting her on the spot in front of her employees as payback for insisting on treating the scratch. Plus, he just enjoyed teasing her. From the corner of her eye, Sophie saw Pete, Kenny, and Chandler staring at them.

"I'm concerned for your sanity," Sophie shot back as she pulled her hand free and returned the first aid kit to her backpack. "But since you are here, we're finishing the rest of the trip on foot. Do you think you can keep up, Cowboy?"

"Yes'm, Miss Sophie," Zach replied, smiling. "Lead the way, Little Lady."

Sophie turned and stalked toward the trail leading through the woods. She almost tripped over a boulder as she pushed past the others to get to the head of the group. She quickly found her footing and lifted her chin—a message that dared any of them to laugh.

Sophie continued stalking ahead, but soon, Zach fell into step beside her.

"Hey, I'm sorry I didn't let you know I might come by way of a shortcut," Zach said. "I didn't know exactly when my call was going to happen or how long it would last. You know how Californians are on their own time and expect everyone else to adjust."

"Maybe I did overreact… about you scaring us to death. Not about treating the cut. These damp woods are petri dishes for bacteria," Sophie said by way of apology. "But I'm not sure what I would've done if it had been a bear or a mountain lion charging through the brush."

"You have three strong, healthy males with you, so you aren't alone," Zach pointed out. "It wouldn't surprise me if Pete is armed."

"Oh! Maybe, but I feel responsible for them, too. I'm just stressed about everything. The opening is soon, so it doesn't take much to send me over the edge."

"You don't have to shoulder all this alone." Zach reached out and took her hand in his. "If you want to bounce ideas about the opening off of me, feel free to do so."

"Frighten me like that again, and it won't be ideas I bounce off you," Sophie returned. Despite her words, she didn't pull her hand from his. The warmth of his hand wrapped around her fingers was comforting, and his offer of help was reassuring. She hadn't seen him since the night of the preview party. He'd probably bring up the scene in the garden before the night was over.

"You have my permission." Zach squeezed her hand, then brought it to his mouth and kissed it. "Are we good?"

Sophie nodded, then looked ahead, checking their location. She spied a large boulder beside the trail just ahead. It marked the edge of the largest tract of "fairy fire" in the woods. As they neared the site, she stopped walking and removed her hand from Zach's. She turned off her flashlight and turned to the three men behind her. "We're here. Fairy Woods." She pointed to the area in front of them.

Kenny and Chandler stared at the large area of eerie blueish-green light that glowed from years of fallen tree limbs and rotted stumps. It spread across the dark tree-sheltered ground like a blob from a science fiction movie. A jumble of blue-green crisscrossing paths spiraled off through the darkness and swirled up tree stumps. If one believed in the mystical, it would be easy to interpret the scene as one inhabited by fairies.

"Amazing!" Zach whispered beside Sophie.

"Shush. It's best enjoyed quietly," Sophie whispered as she placed her finger across her lips and looked around. "There's more. Watch!"

Sophie picked up a stick from the side of the trail and tossed it into the trees further into the tract, hitting the branches. It was a trick her father had showed her when he brought her here years ago. As the stick bounced off the trees, an explosion of what looked like a million fireflies burst from the leaves. They gathered in a huge blinking cloud that hovered above the glowing patch of fairy fire.

Sophie looked around at the group. They stood transfixed by nature's spectacle. Even Zach seemed lost for words.

"It's like a firework display," Kenny whispered in awe. "'Bombs bursting in air.'"

"Or a huge bonfire sending out sparks," Chandler added.

"Or a swarm of tiny drones. Or aircraft on a dark night."

"It's awesome. I've hiked here in daylight but had no idea it was like this at night," Pete said.

The group stood silently and watched the display until the fireflies stopped their blinking and returned to their roosting places in the trees. Without the fireflies, the fairy fire, while still interesting, had lost much of its drama.

"The light show's over. But pretty special, don't you think?" Sophie turned and motioned for them to begin the journey back to where the horses were waiting.

"I've never seen so many fireflies in one place," Zach commented as he walked alongside Sophie. "What draws so many to this spot?"

"I'm not sure. Maybe they're also fairies at heart and think they've found some long-lost relatives," Sophie replied with a smile. "According to scientists, it's because of them and other insects that the fungi spores are carried around the tract. That's what spreads and sustains the fairy fire—keeps this sight alive and growing."

When they reached the clearing and had saddled up, Zach urged his horse toward the opening in the underbrush he had broken through.

"You're not planning to go back that way, are you?" Sophie asked in alarm.

"Sure, but don't worry! Big Boy and I broke the trail on the way here—as evidenced by my face." Zach laughed as he rubbed the gelding's neck. He sobered when he saw that Sophie's concern was real.

"You can leave your horse in our pasture and come back for him tomorrow. Catch a ride home with Chandler."

"Sophie," Zach said as he guided his gelding closer to her. He lowered his voice to a soft whisper. "The trail isn't that bad. It was already broken up to about a quarter mile from here. And don't worry. I'll let you know as soon as I get home."

Sophie's outburst had drawn the interest of Pete, Kenny, and Chandler again. They waited for her signal to begin the ride down the trail. She realized suddenly that she was treating Zach as she might treat Jamie. She was embarrassing herself, as well as Zach. But it *was* dangerous to ride an unbroken and unfamiliar trail at night.

"I won't fall off any cliffs or into any ravines. I promise," Zach assured her. "I like that you're worried about me, though." He reached out and pushed a tendril of hair behind her ears, letting his fingers linger on her cheek before pulling his hand away.

"I was worried for your horse," Sophie replied louder, hoping to divert attention from her whispered conversation with Zach and her worry about him and Big Boy on the ride home. Her trail mates were probably wondering what was going on—and drawing the wrong conclusion.

"Funny! But trust me," Zach replied.

"I'll do that," Sophie replied shortly. "We'll be off, then. See you later." Zach's mind was made up, so Sophie gave up trying to change it. She quickly turned and guided Rose toward the trail that led back down to the meadow. At the bend in the trail, she looked back, but Zach and the gelding had already disappeared into the trees.

The group arrived back at the stables still talking about the sight they had witnessed in the Fairy Woods. Pete, Kenny, and Chandler's awe over the spectacle indicated that the twilight trail ride to the attraction would be a hit with anyone who witnessed it.

She turned Rose over to Chandler's care, bid them goodnight, and walked toward the house.

She had just entered the kitchen when her phone pinged with a message from Zach. "Home safely. Thanks for caring," it read.

"Glad Big Boy is safe," Sophie typed in response.

"He is, and so is his horse," Zach answered.

Sophie smiled and responded with a smiley face. She added, "Goodnight," and ended the thread. Zack could play text-volleyball all night long. Before long, he'd no doubt reach into his trove of Western idioms and use them to tease her. While jousting with Zach was entertaining, she had more boring things to do.

Opening day was a week away, and another review of the schedules and personnel assignments might ease the apprehension she was feeling. Plus, she wanted to check the performance stats of the digital ads and the website before going to bed.

CHAPTER SIXTEEN

When the opening weekend arrived, Sophie felt confident in her preparations. The preview party had demonstrated that operationally, she had adequately considered almost everything. But when dealing with the public, there were always small hiccups here and there.

Opening day began with one of those hiccups. One family brought an extra person—a friend of their daughter's. The girls bunked together, though, so it wasn't necessary to move the group to a larger cabin. Then, opening day closed out with a child getting sick from eating too much ice cream after dinner at the pavilion. Jean's nursing skills took care of the child's overindulgence, but the incident reminded Sophie that she needed to have an emergency plan in case a more serious illness or injury occurred.

The band and dancing at the pavilion on Saturday night were well-received, and the dinner Darlene and her catering staff provided received wide praise and compliments. Darlene gave out coupons for a free meal at the Cherry Blossom before the guests left town as an inducement to leave a review on Cameron Stables' website.

The luxuriousness of the safari tent was even more than the young couple from Philadelphia had expected. They came for an outdoor experience but wanted more pampering than a camping trip. The guests who reserved the regular tent enjoyed their more rustic stay in the high meadow. Making s'mores outdoors under the stars as moonlight poured over Mystic Hills was a much-needed change from the New Jersey apartment they called home.

Sophie let one of the children pull the winning lottery names for two couples to take the twilight ride to Fairy Woods. They had never heard of fairy fire, much less seen it. The spectacle turned out to be the highlight of the winning couples' weekend stay. Kenny led the ride, and staying true to the tradition of the original Cameron storytellers, he kept the couples entertained by embellishing the folktale and mystery of the fairy fire.

Kenny later shared with Sophie that when the trip was over and they returned to the stables, he confessed to the couples that there was an alternate and more scientific version of the story about fairy fire. According to Kenny, the guests preferred the original version, even though they knew it was a made-up folktale.

Cameron Stables had been at just over forty percent capacity for the opening weekend. And since that first day of operations, the property had settled into a consistent pattern. Reservations had steadily increased for Fridays through Mondays but were still low for the rest of the week. As word spread and vacationers began looking for summer getaways, Sophie expected—or hoped—that more people would book longer stays. But an encouraging sign was that reservations for the upcoming Fourth of July holiday were already at sixty percent capacity, and there were still several days left before the holiday.

Traffic on the website was also increasing—another positive sign. The new and improved Cameron Stables hadn't been a total flop, as Sophie had feared. Even with her continued worries over finances, Sophie felt good about the direction the business was headed. Current trends indicated that they were moving ever so gradually toward profitability.

And Sophie still thought about expansion. The spa and tennis court were still in her future plans once the profit margin became more dependable and consistent. In the more immediate future, some people had shown interest in scheduled day trips to visit famous tourist sites in the area. Those would cost very little to arrange and would add another revenue stream. Mammoth Cave National Park and Cumberland Falls State Park were within driving distance and would make nice excursions for those who wanted to spend a day visiting other parts of the region. Several breweries offered guided tours, which might interest other groups. Some guests would probably enjoy dipping into the Scots-Irish culture and attend the Celtic Festival east of Kingsville that was open during the summer months.

June continued to make herself invaluable to Sophie and Rachel. When she wasn't helping Rachel in the kitchen or Sophie in the office, she voluntarily entertained the children of the guests. She babysat the children for the couples who made the twilight trip to the Fairy Woods. At other times, she would wander into the game area and join in volleyball, horseshoes, or other games with the younger visitors.

One day shortly after opening day, Jean and Sophie were having a cup of coffee in the kitchen when Jean remarked, "June is such a wonderful addition to our staff. She's indispensable to Rachel and to you in the office. That girl is going places… if Chandler doesn't distract her."

"She's wonderful. I couldn't get along without her," Sophie agreed. "But what does Chandler have to do with June's future?"

"You haven't noticed? June goes to visit Johnny when he's here, but Chandler miraculously appears, and she spends more time with him than with Johnny. They seem to enjoy each other's company, too. She has a very bright future, so I'd like to see her pursue an education before getting sidetracked by romance. Reminds me of you and Zach when he worked here."

"What do you mean? Me and Zach? I don't even remember Zach."

"Exactly! Your father made sure you didn't get to know Zach." Jean smiled and added, "But I suspect it wasn't because Zach didn't try."

"Dad didn't approve of him?"

"Quite the contrary. He saw in Zach what I see in June. Despite the setbacks Zach had faced, George saw great potential in him. He didn't want you or Zach to get distracted by a teenage romance before both of you figured out what you wanted in life. If you appeared in the barn, George would send Zach on an errand someplace else. He kept all the young men away from you, but especially Zach. He thought he was doing the right thing."

"Huh! I never knew that. Where was Dad when I met and married Robert? I could have used some interfering then."

"By then, he thought you were old enough to know what you wanted. And by that time, you were established in your career."

"Did he take our divorce hard?"

"No, I don't think he did. You both handled it like adults without much drama. You and Robert made the decision together and had an amicable break. You went on with your lives. We didn't see a lot of emotion from either one of you. If your heart had been broken, your father might have reacted differently."

"Dad could be very practical at times," Sophie said. "A practical Irishman. A novelty for sure."

"Yes, that was your father," Jean replied with a faraway look in her eyes. "What is that saying? 'A conundrum wrapped in an enigma'? He could be extremely stubborn about some things and a softie where other things were concerned. At times, he let his heart overrule his head, but other times, his head was what got him in trouble."

♦

Sophie grabbed a pair of garden shears from a basket on the back porch and headed to the rose garden behind the house. The roses of the early-blooming varieties were starting to drop petals, a sign that the blooming season was almost over for them. Sophie intended to cut some for the house before that happened. She left June in the office sorting through George's papers in the bookcase. June had already partially filled three plastic tubs labeled "Junk," "Business," and "Don't Know." Two other empty tubs sat nearby, ready to hold other classifications as June thought necessary.

Sophie walked past the rose garden, deciding to first visit the training area and see what was happening around the stables. As she passed the hay barn, she stopped briefly to say hello to Tank and three of Zach's Squad as they unloaded a delivery of supplies.

She walked to the training ring and found Ben showing Danny Sampson how to place a saddle on the back of a golden palomino mare, tighten the cinches, and properly mount the horse. The horse belonged to Dr. Sampson, a new resident of Kingsville who wanted his twelve-year-old son, Danny, to learn how to ride. It was his first riding lesson. Chandler was observing Ben in hopes of learning how to teach a novice horseman how to properly ride.

Sophie left the training ring and walked to an adjoining fenced-in paddock. She waved to a couple of guests who leaned on the fence, engrossed in the activity in the paddock. Pete was in the ring, slowly walking in half-circles around one of the horses Zach had purchased and transported from California—a black chestnut quarter horse. His racing bloodlines were evident in the shape of his head, lean body, and long legs. Zach had said he didn't plan to race him but preferred to have him trained as a riding horse. The horse had been broken, but was still skittish, not used to Pete or his new surroundings, and hesitant to accept the bridle and saddle.

Training a horse was an arduous chore, but Pete had the patience needed to get the horse settled and at ease before attempting to put on the bridle and saddle. With each circle, Pete got closer and closer to the horse. He moved to within inches of the horse's head, reached out, and rubbed the white blaze on his forehead. Speaking softly, Pete soon slipped the bridle slowly and carefully over the horse's head and began to lead the chestnut around the paddock. Pete would first get the horse used to the bridle before attempting to put on the saddle.

Sophie gave Pete a thumbs-up, then left the training area. Concerns about how her staff was working out was one thing she didn't have. She had Zach to thank for much of that, since he had done an excellent job of finding and vetting the four young men and had sent Tank her way.

Sophie walked back toward the rose garden behind the main house and finished cutting the roses. A hot day was in store for central Kentucky. Her cotton shirt was already stuck to her back. The mist had completely burned off along the tree line on Mystic Hills, and not a cloud marred the clear blue sky. The humidity was high, even in the shade. In a hurry to return to the air-conditioned house, Sophie quickly filled her basket with the cut roses.

The noise of an approaching vehicle and the subsequent slamming of the door at the front of the house caught Sophie's attention. She walked toward the front of the house. A courier service's truck was sitting in the driveway. She called out to the driver as he approached the front door.

"I have a certified letter for George Cameron," the driver said as he turned and walked back toward her.

"My father passed away a few months ago. I'm his daughter." Sophie met the driver on the sidewalk.

"Sorry to hear that, Miss Cameron. I just need an adult to sign for it." The driver handed her a mobile device, and Sophie signed for the letter. *What's this about?* she wondered as she retraced her steps to the back of the house, picked up the cut roses, and entered the house. She laid the roses on the kitchen counter, found a vase, added water, then placed the roses in the vase. She'd rearrange them later after she checked out the contents of the letter.

Sophie leaned against the counter and looked closely at the return address on the letter. She blinked when she saw the California address: Whittaker & Co. What could Zach's company be contacting her father about?

Sophie opened the envelope and spread out the letter. It was clearly official company correspondence because the company logo was centered at the top of the page. As she read, her heart stopped. The words swam before her eyes. No! This couldn't be! Sophie sagged into a chair at the table. She reread the letter.

Dear Mr. Cameron,

With your failure to respond to our earlier notifications about the interest-only balloon mortgage payment, this is your final notice. Although this is not a normal business line of Whittaker & Co., you are contractually obligated to repay the loan by a fixed date, as shown on the copy of the contract enclosed. A lien has been placed against your property, Cameron Stables, located in

Kingsville, Kentucky.

The rest of the letter jumbled together and swam before Sophie's eyes. She made out a few more words: *...satisfy the debt...$250,000...July 31ˢᵗ...foreclosure...Sincerely, William Jenkins, Chief Financial Officer, Whittaker & Co.*

Sophie unfolded the enclosed contract and inwardly groaned. Oh God! Yes, that was indeed her father's signature. The meaning of the signed contract, and the notice of the lien against the property hit Sophie like a punch in the stomach. Her breath came out in short gasps as the reality settled in. Her father had mortgaged the property. It was in foreclosure! Impossible! This couldn't be happening!

Sophie tried to swallow the bile that clogged her throat. In a trance, she vaguely heard her mother and Aunt Rachel come into the kitchen. Their hollow laughter seemed to come from far away. Sophie's head spun, and for a moment she feared she was going to pass out. She bent over, holding her stomach, hoping the dizziness would pass.

"Sophie? What's wrong?" Jean grasped her by the shoulder and tried to raise her into a sitting position.

Sophie gulped in deep breaths as her body began to shake. Aunt Rachel took the letter from Sophie's trembling hands and began reading it.

"I… the letter…" Sophie stammered. "Oh God! Mom, I don't know… what to do. I think I'm going to be sick."

Aunt Rachel handed the letter to Jean. As Jean began to read, Aunt Rachel went to the refrigerator and filled a glass with water. She held it to Sophie's lips while rubbing her shoulders with her free hand.

"There must be some mistake," Jean said, her face blanched white. "We don't have a mortgage. Have you talked to Zach? This is… this can't be true."

"It is true," Sophie replied between gulps of air. "Mom, the contract has Dad's signature. It's true. Zach did this behind my back. He didn't even have the courtesy to let me know this was coming." Sophie swiped tears from her cheeks, then took a drink of water from the glass Aunt Rachel handed her. "Did you know about this?"

"No." Jean's voice was barely above a whisper. She shook her head. "This contract was signed almost two years ago. I knew we were in financial trouble, but George never told me about this. We weren't making much money, but I thought we were at least breaking even." She sat down at the table across from Sophie. "I can't believe Zach would do this."

Anger over her naïveté for believing Zach actually cared about what happened to their property replaced Sophie's initial shock. She lashed out, "We've been duped! His pretense that he cared was a ruse. All this time, he knew this was coming. He offered to help save our business because he knew it would soon be his."

"I still can't believe that, Sophie." Jean shook her head sadly. "What are we going to do?"

"I'm not sure, but I've got to do something. Otherwise, in less than thirty days, we'll lose our home as well as our business. I'm calling Stephen!"

Sophie stalked to her office, sent June off for a break, and dialed Stephen's number. Stephen listened to her story, but he didn't offer any advice to avoid foreclosure, as she had hoped.

"Sophie," Stephen said, "I'm afraid that based on what you're telling me, the contract is airtight. With you and your mother as owners of the property with your father, you own this debt, too. Have you talked to Whittaker? Maybe you can get an extension on the foreclosure date. At least find out what happened."

"No. I'm done with Whittaker. I want this resolved now."

"Okay. Since you or your mother didn't sign the loan contract, do you want me to try to nullify it?"

"No. My father took out the loan. It's his signature, so I want it paid. I'm not letting this hang over my head. I need to think." Sophie hung up the call, cutting Stephen off as he tried to argue with her. Her mind was already busy reviewing Cameron Stables' assets and debts and what, if any, options were available to her. She was right back where she had been just over three months ago—in debt up to her eyeballs and now with a foreclosure notice to boot.

"Oh Dad," Sophie groaned. She put her head down on the desk and asked the same question she'd asked many times over the last few months. "Why didn't you come to me?"

Her slow-burning anger at Zach burst into a raging fire. So, this was how Zach had built his empire. Not through hard work, as he had boasted, but by swindling people out of their property. Somehow, she had to stop this. She was determined that Whittaker & Co. would not get their property. A merger of Thornton Farms and Cameron Stables, which included all of Mystic Hills, would be a big deal—a masterful maneuver for diversifying his business. Something else was clear now, too—the *real* reason he had purchased Thornton Farms.

She would not help him expand his empire. Not this time. Zach Whittaker had met his match. If she went down, she would go down fighting to the bitter end.

Sophie couldn't use any of the money in her business account because that was already dedicated to expenses that soon needed to be paid. That left her with one remaining option. Sophie logged into her investment and brokerage accounts. This was supposed to be for her future and her retirement years, but if she lost her home, her future would be ruined and there wouldn't be any retirement. She had to do everything she could to save Cameron Stables.

Sophie went through her investment accounts and wrote down the current balances. She had more than enough without dipping into her retirement accounts. There would be a large tax implication on this solution, but she'd worry about that at tax time.

She called her brokerage account manager, and after refusing to be talked out of her request, he reluctantly agreed to process the transaction. The money would be in her bank account by the day after tomorrow.

Two days? She couldn't wait that long. The debt and foreclosure notice had set off an anger that surged through her whole body and consumed her thoughts. She couldn't let it go. She would draw on her business funds tomorrow, then transfer the amount back once the money from the brokerage account cleared the bank.

There was stunned silence around the dinner table that evening as Sophie told her mother and Aunt Rachel what she had done—selling her investments to pay off the loan.

"Have you talked to Zach?" Jean asked.

"No, I'm done with trusting Zach or anyone else. His company's bottom line is all he cares about." Sophie stubbornly crossed her arms over her chest.

"Honey, you know that's not true," Jean said. "He may have an explanation."

"I'll handle this tomorrow and be done with it," Sophie promised. "I have to do this. For Dad and for you. I will not be the Cameron that loses our property. No one is taking our home. If I start listening to Zach and let him sweet-talk me into another *deal*, I know I'll regret it. Listening to Zach is probably how Dad got into this mess in the first place."

◆

After a restless night, Sophie was at the bank the next

morning when it opened for business. She purchased a cashier's check for the amount specified in William Jenkins's letter. Still seething with anger, she drove straight to Thornton Farms. Mattie opened the door at her knock.

"Is Mr. Whittaker in?" Sophie asked, bypassing any pleasantries.

"He and Mr. Reardon are in the main office. Is he expecting you?" Mattie asked.

"No," Sophie replied shortly as she pushed past Mattie and stalked toward the office. She knew the location from the tour Zach had given her during his open house. That night now seemed like a hundred years ago.

Zach and Eli were involved in a discussion when Sophie neared the open office door. Zach looked up as Sophie walked in.

"Hey there. Come in. I didn't know you were coming over today. It's good…" Zach stood up. He stopped talking when he saw Sophie's face. "What's wrong?"

Sophie walked to his desk and threw down the check and the foreclosure letter from the CFO of Zach's company. "You can call off your collector. This check should take care of my father's debt." Sophie tore the copy of the contract into several pieces and dropped them on top of the check. "Don't ever darken my door again." She turned on her heel and strode back toward the office door.

Zach caught her just before she stepped into the hall. "What's wrong? I don't understand," Zach said as his hand closed over her shoulder.

"Take your thieving hands off me," Sophie said through gritted teeth. "You've got your money. Now leave me alone."

"Sophie. Wait," Zach said.

Sophie ran through the hall, out the front door, and to her car with Zach right behind her. She locked the door as soon as she sat down in the driver's seat. Zach pulled on the door handle and attempted to open it, but he was blocked. He quickly stepped away from the car as Sophie backed up, put the car in drive, and sped down the driveway.

Tears blurred her eyes as she glanced in the rearview mirror. Zach was standing with his hands on his hips, staring after her. By the time she had reached the end of the driveway and pulled out onto the gravel road, he was walking back toward the house.

"Fool! Fool! Fool!" Sophie slapped the steering wheel. "I'm such a fool!" When she divorced Robert, she had promised herself that she'd never let her life be controlled by another relationship again. She had generally stuck to that promise. Yet lately, ever since that night in the garden, her thoughts frequently centered around Zach. She had to keep reminding herself that attraction was not the same as commitment and that he could leave for California at any time.

If she was being truthful, she'd admit that she had let herself briefly contemplate what it would be like to have him permanently in her life—that she had toyed with the idea that there was something stronger than just attraction. But each time, she squelched that thought. It was easier to avoid involvement than risk getting hurt. Zach's actions had now confirmed that her decision was the right one. But he'd managed to inflict hurt anyway.

Sophie swiped her fingers across her cheeks, removing the tears. Taking a deep breath, she straightened in her seat and stiffened her spine. She was over this latest hurdle, unexpected as it was. Her heart was no longer involved in her decision-making. Her head was back in charge.

The check she had just given Zach would settle the foreclosure debt. Cameron Stables was safe. She was through with Zach Whittaker, and if she never saw him again, that would be ideal.

CHAPTER SEVENTEEN

S he wouldn't even talk to me," Zach said to Eli as he returned to the office. He ran his hands through his hair,
standing it on end. "I don't know what I've done."

"Read this letter," Eli replied as he held out the letter Sophie
had thrown on the desk. "You'll understand what she's mad
about."

Zach sat down behind the desk, picked up the letter, and
began to read. "Oh my God!" He groaned as the words sank
in. Sophie had good reason for being angry with him. "Damn!
I forgot all about this." Zach brought his fist down hard on the
desk, scattering a folder of papers. "I told Grayson to cancel this
contract. Apparently, he was too busy selling company secrets
to do his job. Jenkins wouldn't have known I wasn't going
through with the foreclosure. God, what a mess!"

"Your new CFO stays on top of things. He doesn't seem to
miss much," Eli replied.

"I didn't want to do this contract in the first place, but

George insisted. And I let him talk me into his crazy scheme. I'm at fault too because I forgot it even existed."

"Do you want me to call Jenkins? I assume you want this killed?"

Zach stood and picked up the cashier's check. "I'm so angry right now, I might fire Jenkins, too. So, yes, you'd better call. Tell him to take care of it immediately. I'm going to the bank to return this check. I can do that much."

Zach drove to the bank, his mind in turmoil. What must Sophie and Jean think of him? That he was such a lowlife he would take away their home? Something like that would never enter his mind in a million years. But he, Zach Whittaker, was entirely at fault for the current mess he found himself in. He had listened to George Cameron when he knew he shouldn't. But he thought he could control the situation. That's what he got for depending on the company CFO to handle a personal matter. Bad idea. Bad results.

Zach entered the bank and walked to Mr. Taylor's office. He didn't have an appointment, but that wasn't going to stop him from seeing Mr. Taylor if he was in. Mr. Taylor looked up as Zach opened his door.

"Zach! Come in. Welcome. What can I do for you?" Mr. Taylor stood and greeted Zach effusively. He pointed to a chair, inviting him to sit down.

Zach was still slightly uncomfortable with the amount of deference he received now that he was a wealthy, accomplished businessman, as compared to the way he was treated when he was a homeless orphaned teen. But he had realized early on in his business that this was the way the world worked. He often used that deference to his advantage. Today was one of those days.

"I need to get this cashier's check canceled and the funds put back into Miss Cameron's account." He handed the check to

Mr. Taylor.

"That's highly unusual," Mr. Taylor said as he looked over the check in his hand.

"Can you do it? If not, I'll write a check to cover the amount," Zach said brusquely. He was angry that the situation had gotten this far, and his mood hadn't improved on the drive into town. He was impatient to get the funds back into Sophie's account. Small talk only increased his impatience.

"Yes, I can do that. But it's very unusual," Mr. Taylor reiterated. "Can you share the reason why?"

"No," Zach replied shortly. "It's personal."

"Alrighty then. No problem. Fill out this form, and I will personally take care of it for you."

Once Zach had completed the form, he stood, impatient to be on his way.

Mr. Taylor walked him to the front door. "I'll notify you when it's done."

Zach nodded, left the bank, and drove back toward Thornton Farms. When he came to the turnoff leading to Cameron Stables, he swerved onto the road that led to the Cameron property.

Jean answered the front door when he knocked.

"I need to see Sophie," Zach said without greeting Jean.

"I don't think that's a good idea," Jean replied. "Not right now."

"This is all a mistake. I have to tell her that," Zach insisted. "You need to believe me. Jean, I would never take your home."

"I don't know, Zach. George signed a contract, and we always pay our debts, which he obviously didn't do this time," Jean replied. "I don't think Sophie is in the mood to listen, but you can try. She's out on the back porch." She held open the door for him to enter.

Zach walked through the house to the back porch and

opened the door.

"I don't want to talk, Mom," Sophie said without turning around. Her back was ramrod straight and her shoulders stiff—not a good sign.

"Sophie, I need to talk to you. Please!" Zach stepped out onto the porch.

Sophie's head whipped around at the sound of his voice. She sprang out of her chair, ducked his outstretched hand, and quickly entered the house. She slammed the door, and a click followed as she turned the lock. A very bad sign. "Go away! I'm not interested in listening to your lies," Sophie yelled from behind the locked door. "You got your money. We're done."

"This was all a mistake. You have to believe me."

"Here's the thing, Zach. I don't have to believe anything you say." Sophie's laugh lacked humor as it came muffled from behind the door. "This tactic may be the way you built your business, but I don't plan to help you expand it further."

"Hear me out," Zach pleaded. "I can explain all of this."

No other sounds came from behind the door. Sophie was not budging and not open to hearing his explanation—or opening the door. After a few minutes, Zach gave up, left the back porch, and walked around to the front of the house where he had parked. He was *persona non grata* in the Cameron household, especially with Sophie. He couldn't blame her for feeling that way, but her comment about his tactics in building his business had cut deep. His business had been built on integrity and the highest ethical standards.

"Jenkins has removed the loan from the books and canceled the lien," Eli said as he met Zach in the foyer when Zach returned home. "But from the look on your face, I'm guessing that doesn't help with Sophie."

"I don't know how to fix this," Zach said as he threw his hat toward the coat and hat tree in the coat room next to the foyer.

It missed the tree in the corner by several feet, but Zach didn't notice. His mind was on Sophie and their friendship that had crashed suddenly with a resounding thud.

"By the way," Eli continued. "Ed Lindsay called while you were out. VironTech Solutions' Chicago site is having problems with the software for their navigation system. The connectivity link to the smartphone keeps dropping. Do you want me to send one of the engineers up there to see what the problem is?"

"I guess," Zach said distractedly. "No, wait! I'll go. I could use something to focus on right now. Distance might give me some insight into my problem with Sophie. I have to find a way to make things right with her, if that's possible. What the hell's happened with VironTech?"

"I don't know. They're building their navigation system from the ground up. It might be in their design, not the software. You sure you want to go?"

"I'm sure. I'll call Patrick and see how soon he can have the plane ready to go. Can you call VironTech and let them know I'm on my way? I need to pack."

"Of course," Eli replied.

♦

Zach landed in Chicago around five that afternoon. A rental car was waiting for him. He drove straight to VironTech, located in Elgin, about thirty miles west of the airport. He met with company executives, and together, they reviewed the data from the test runs. Zach quickly recognized the source of the problem: the smartphone link for voice control and the screen display for text messaging were not connecting with Bluetooth. But he couldn't tell if it was a problem with his company's software or a problem with VironTech's system's design. He called the home office in California and arranged for two software engineers to come to VironTech immediately and remain until the problems were fixed.

It didn't matter who caused the problem. He took ownership when things didn't work as designed. *That* was how he built his business—with integrity and standing behind the promises made to his clients. He didn't steal property from anyone, especially two defenseless women. He smiled sardonically at the thought. Neither Jean nor Sophie could be called defenseless, especially Sophie. She'd rip his eyes out if she knew that description had even crossed his mind.

Zach spent the night in a nearby hotel. The next morning, after he grabbed a quick breakfast, he spoke with the software engineers who had arrived late last night. They were already at VironTech and just beginning to analyze the navigation system. No update yet.

Zach next called his personal assistant and informed her that he would be off-grid for a good portion of the day. He had some personal business to take care of.

Zach drove north to the city of Barrington. It had been almost twenty years since he was last here. Lately, he had begun to think it was time to put old nagging memories and nightmares behind him. Since he was in the area, this seemed as good a time as any.

Zach drove to an older section of the city. Less affluent than some newer areas, it was still an upper-middle-class neighborhood. He drove around looking at familiar landmarks until he came to Rose Hill Drive and found house number 2601. He parked across the street from the house and gazed at the property—his boyhood home.

The house seemed smaller now than it did the last time he saw it when he was thirteen years old. He hadn't been back to the house since his life had crashed along with the plane that had taken his parents. It still looked much the same, though, except the shrubs across the front were bigger and a subsequent owner had added a sunroom to the back of the house. The sunroom took up part of the lawn, but the large oak tree in the backyard was still visible from where Zach was parked. It reminded him of his dad's constant nagging for him to clean the oak leaves out of the pool. He could still hear his dad's voice today: "You've got one job, Zach. Just one job." Zach now smiled over his logic for stalling. "More leaves will fall, Dad. Why clean them up now?" he'd whine. It drove his dad crazy. As an adult, he now understood his dad's reaction, but as a kid more interested in playing sports or video games, his logic seemed reasonable to him.

The shade tree was the bane of his teen years—and his father's—but his mother would've been disappointed if a new owner had cut it down. In the shade of the tree was her favorite place to sit and read medical journals and research papers. He could still picture her sitting there with her reading glasses propped low on her nose and a glass of iced tea in one hand as she reviewed the latest techniques in children's orthopedic surgery. God, he still missed them both.

With a sigh, Zach said a silent goodbye to his boyhood home and drove out of the city and south to Rolling Meadows. He entered a neighborhood of modest homes and drove around until he found the place he was looking for—the Webb home. The Webbs were the foster family he had lived with for almost two years before he aged out of foster care. Two years with the same family had been a record for him.

He was moved to the Webb home after a year with the Allen family. They had decided that with three biological children, they couldn't support a foster child any longer. Before that, it had been a year with the Carson family. He couldn't remember why they had let him go. Apparently, back then, his expiration date was about one year after he arrived in a home. It might have been his sullen attitude and disinterest in everything that caused them to decide they no longer wanted him around.

The Allens and the Carsons weren't his parents, so nothing they did could fill the hole in his heart or lessen his silent anger at the world over how his life had fallen apart. He wasn't a troublemaker. He just didn't open up or try to blend with the families he lived with. Even knowing that his life could be even worse than it was didn't ease any of the hurt and anger he carried over what had happened to him.

The Webbs were good people and treated him fairly, but he started life with them as he had with all the others. But the Webbs had a teenage son about his age, and that was what helped him adjust and finally come out of his shell. Richard was a nonstop talker, and he talked whether he got a response from Zach or not. Eventually, Zach began to join Richard's running dialogue, if for no other reason than to get a break from his constant chatter.

Zach parked on the street in front of the Webb home and exited the car. He walked to the door and rang the doorbell. He figured the Webb family had probably moved in the ensuring years. He would be disappointed not to see them, but he wanted to at least make an effort while he was in the area.

A man about Zach's age answered the door. Zach stared at the familiar-looking face. He looked older now, but the face belonged to none other than his foster brother, Richard. "Richard Webb?" Zach asked in surprise.

The man nodded and recognized Zach in the same moment. "Zach?" He held the door wide. "My God! Come in, man. You've changed a lot, but I'd know you anywhere. How long has it been?"

"Around seventeen years," Zach replied as he stepped into the house and looked around. "I was hoping to see your mom and dad."

"We lost Dad two years ago, and Mom lives in an assisted living home. It's just me here now," Richard replied. "But how are you?"

"I'm sorry to hear that. Your dad was a good man. I'm doing well. How about you?"

Richard motioned for Zach to take a seat in the living room. "I'm doing alright. I opened my restaurant three years ago. You know, the one I talked about nonstop when you lived here?"

"I remember. I also remember the mess you frequently made in the kitchen concocting new dishes. Sometimes, you even tried to blame the mess on me, but your mom was too smart for that." Zach laughed at the memory.

"You can't blame a guy for trying," Richard replied, smiling. "I was better at making a mess than cleaning it up. I have people who do that for me now. But has life been good to you, Zach? Do you have a good job? You left so quickly—just disappeared—that we always wondered what happened to you."

"I was good at disappearing back then," Zach said. "I'm doing fine. I was in the area and wanted to stop by and thank you and your family for taking me in after my parents died. I bought a place in Kentucky, so if you ever get down that way, come to Thornton Farms and look me up."

"You're a farmer? I didn't see that coming. You were a techie extraordinaire when you lived here."

"No, not a farmer, but some of the land is leased to farmers. I still dabble in the tech world a bit."

"Have you had lunch?"

"No." Zach shook his head.

"Let me take you to my restaurant. We can visit more over lunch."

Richard drove to the outskirts of Rolling Meadows and parked in the lot next to his restaurant—Rich's Bar-B-Que. The place was evidently popular because it was packed with the lunch crowd. At Richard's suggestion, they ordered barbecue sandwiches and fries, then spent the next couple of hours sharing stories and reliving the two years they had lived as brothers.

"So, what have you been doing?" Richard asked. "You haven't said what business you're in now."

Zach briefly described his time in the army and how he ended up in California, where he became involved with a technology firm and later started his own company.

"And is there a Mrs. Whittaker in your life?" Richard asked.

"No," Zach said, "I'm not married. Maybe I'm not the marrying kind. A rolling stone can't be tied down."

"I'd hate to think that's true. It's sad, really," Richard said. "'A rolling stone gathers no moss,' is the accurate saying. I don't see any moss on you, and you're not exactly an old man. You lost your family, so now, it's up to you to make one."

"Maybe, but I've spent most of my time since college getting my business started. What about you?"

"I'm engaged. Marjorie and I have been together two years. She's a veterinarian, so she keeps very busy, and I've been tied up with starting my business, too. But it's time we made it official. We're planning a fall wedding but haven't set an exact date."

"You should come down to my neck of the woods for a destination wedding. There's a resort and horse farm next to Thornton Farms. Marjorie would probably love being around animals that aren't patients. There are cabins—enough for a large group—and food and entertainment. Of course, you could also stay with me. I have lots of room."

"That a great idea," Richard replied. "It sounds like a place we'd enjoy."

"Here are the details." Zach wrote the information for Cameron Stables on a napkin and handed it to Richard. He didn't have any of Sophie's business cards, and he'd probably receive a broken leg if he asked for some now. What he wanted more than anything was for her to talk to him. Getting business cards would probably be the easier job.

Zach and Richard finished their lunch, then drove back to Richard's home. They shared a brotherly hug as they parted in the driveway.

"It's been good visiting with you, and be sure to tell your mom I stopped by. Make sure you call and reserve Cameron Stables and bring your mom to the wedding," Zach said in parting. With Richard's assurance that he would let his mother know about Zach's visit as well as discuss the wedding plans with Marjorie, Zach climbed into his car and drove back to his hotel near Elgin. He reported in to his personal assistant that he was available once again.

After a final meeting with his software engineers the next morning and getting an update on the fix for VironTech's navigation system, Zach boarded the plane for his trip back to Kentucky. As he settled into his seat and readied for takeoff, he opened his briefcase and pulled out a new contract proposal Cal had given him to review during the flight. He soon set it aside, though, unable to concentrate on the dry legal language in the documents. His thoughts kept wandering back to his visit with Richard and the trip to his boyhood home.

The plane soon left the runway and quickly climbed to cruising altitude above the clouds. Zach relaxed in his seat, stretched out his legs, and let his mind objectively analyze the devastating loss of his parents. There was something about hurtling through the air at forty thousand feet that gave a person a clearer picture of their past.

He had not been singled out, as his thirteen-year-old self had angrily thought. He had been randomly selected by fate and dealt a tough blow. He subconsciously knew this even at the time, but reasoning was not something he was good at back then. He let built-up resentment at "something" consume him.

Zach had another epiphany as he leaned his head back against the headrest and closed his eyes. After the death of his parents, that tragedy had ruled his life. He had bottled up his grief, unwilling to share it with anyone. While scars of self-isolation didn't show on his person, he'd carried deep scars within for many years. He should have handled things differently. The one thing he'd had control over, he hadn't done. He could have stopped disappearing and hurting the few people who were trying to help him. But wrapped in self-pity, he had locked himself into sullen bitterness. He had punished himself for what happened.

He spent years blaming unseen forces for devastating his life, but now, in hindsight, he had to give those same forces credit for randomly leading him to Kentucky. Fate had chosen the road that dark night that took him to Cameron Stables instead of into Kingsville, where he meant go. Taking the wrong road led him to a chance meeting with George Cameron. George became a surrogate father to him, but Zach had disappeared again and almost destroyed that relationship, too.

George never gave up on him, though. He prodded and nagged the homeless kid he found asleep in his barn until he turned himself around and started using his skills and intelligence—along with some hard work—to build a life for himself. Zach wasn't ultrawealthy by any means, but he was comfortable and, more importantly, satisfied that he had managed to overcome the tragedy and not let it destroy him.

As the pilot neared the landing field in Lexington, Zach sighed contentedly. A burden had been lifted by his visit to his past. The sharp edges of his memories had softened, giving him closure and a new perspective on that part of his life. Old ghosts had finally been laid to rest. Why he had waited so long to go back to Chicago was a question he couldn't answer.

Now, if he could convince Sophie that he wasn't a low-class thief, his personal life might look as promising as the other aspects of his life.

CHAPTER EIGHTEEN

S ophie was out early on Friday morning making a last-minute check on the property. They were just short of full capacity for Saturday, which was the Fourth of July holiday. Some guests had included Friday in their stays, while others would stay through the holiday until Monday. Four of the cabins were occupied already this morning, and other guests would check in throughout today and tomorrow.

Sophie arrived at Tank's office to go over the scheduled events and the staff work assignments. This would be their busiest weekend yet, and it was important that all details—even minor ones—had been considered.

After going over the schedules with Tank and finding that, as she expected, he had things under control, Sophie left the barn. She was nearing the main house when she heard the throb of a helicopter coming over Mystic Peak. She stopped and looked up at the noise. There was no mistaking who the 'copter belonged to, even if the blue-and-white lettering on the sides wasn't visible. Was Zach coming back from a trip, or was he leaving on one? Or was he out surveying the new addition to his empire?

Zach had canceled the cashier's check, and the funds had been returned to her bank account. She had also received an email notice that the lien against the property had been removed. So, he wasn't surveying his property—yet.

Refusing to accept the payment only complicated her problem. Zach had boxed her in. He was calling the shots by eliminating her best method of settling the debt. In Sophie's view, the debt of over two hundred thousand dollars still hung over her head, and nothing Zach had done had changed that.

Sophie was still at a boil over the foreclosure letter. It was a slap in her face that still stung. A lien placed against her property for defaulting on a debt was both humiliating and a blow to her pride as a businesswoman. It was another black mark on Cameron Stables' credit record, which she had worked so hard to clean up. Currently, her bottom line was not just red, but blazing fire-engine red after the addition of Zach to her list of creditors.

Camerons did not accept charity, as implied by his refusal to accept the cashier's check. Sophie had many reasons to be angry, but she was angriest at Zach for negotiating an interest-only note with her father in the first place. Zach was an experienced businessman and should have known better than to engage in a risky financial deal like that.

Sophie had looked through the bank statements from her father's papers that June had unearthed and placed in the tub marked "Financial." She'd found a deposit in Cameron Stables' operating account of one hundred seventy-five thousand dollars made almost two years ago. Another twenty-five thousand had been deposited in the household account at the same time.

Over the last two years, Sophie's father had used the mortgage money from Zach as a reserve fund to fall back on when his income did not cover expenses. Purchases of hay and feed during last summer's drought and then a recession that caused reservations to drop had stressed the business's finances to the breaking point. There was no way her father could have made the large final payment when it was due.

Her father's habit of "winging it," as he put it, and not writing information down until he assembled it at tax time made this all speculative on Sophie's part. She had yet to come across any comprehensive accounting records that detailed how he had used the money, and she hadn't found his tax filings, either.

When Sophie returned to her office following her inspection of the property, she decided to call Stephen to schedule a meeting with him. Maybe he had come up with an idea by now on how she might extricate herself from the debt owed to Zach. She was fresh out of ideas herself.

"I'm tied up this afternoon and tomorrow, but why don't you meet me tomorrow night at The Golden Palomino Bar and Grill. You need to take some time off. Clear your head," Stephen suggested. "We could relax over a drink and see what we can come up with together."

"That's the Fourth of July holiday. I have guests to take care of," Sophie said. "I'm needed here."

"You've got staff to take care of all that. Paid staff! That's mostly why you need money to operate, remember?" Stephen countered.

"You're right," Sophie conceded. She could use a short break, and the debt wasn't going anywhere, whether she went out or stayed home. "What time?"

They agreed to meet at seven p.m. Sophie then went to find her mother and ask if she could be on-call while Sophie was out should anything major come up.

"Of course," Jean replied. "And don't worry. You need to get out for a change and forget about business."

Sophie was nervous about taking a night off as she drove to The Golden Palomino the next night. Which was crazy, she told herself. It wasn't as though she was leaving her child in a stranger's hands. Her mother had been involved with Cameron Stables longer than she had. Jean had assured her that she would call if anything came up that needed Sophie's attention.

The Golden Palomino, a country-and-Western club and restaurant, was decorated in festive red, white, and blue in honor of the nation's birthday. And it was packed to capacity.

Stephen stood up from a table located not far from the dance floor and waved to her when she walked in the door. Shortly after Sophie sat down, they ordered drinks and placed their food orders.

"So, did you come up with a solution for my financial predicament?" Sophie didn't wait to bring up the reason she had agreed to meet him. The problem constantly tumbled around inside her head and nagged her even in her sleep. She was ready to move on from it.

"I've thought about it—a lot—but I'm at a loss as to what you can do other than what you tried to do with the cashier's check. The lien is now canceled and so is the loan. You don't technically have a debt to pay off, since Whittaker refuses to accept payment."

"I don't understand."

"You have to admit this is an unusual situation. It doesn't fall into any legal situations I've ever been involved in. You're trying to pay off a debt you don't legally owe," Stephen said. "Have you talked to Whittaker?"

"No. I don't even want to see him, much less talk with him," Sophie replied.

"Well, that might be difficult. He's sitting three tables over—that way." Stephen nodded in the direction behind her. "I expect you to dance with me, and we'll go right by his table to get to the dance floor. He'll be hard to miss."

"Is he alone?" Sophie resisted the urge to turn around and see for herself.

"Is that relevant?" Stephen asked. "I could get my feelings hurt over my date wondering if another man is cheating on her. You want me to kiss your hand—make him jealous?" He picked up her hand and started lifting it toward his lips.

"Do you want your face clawed?" Sophie countered as she pulled her hand out of his grasp. "I'm not worried about him being with someone else. Just curious, that's all. And this isn't a date," Sophie insisted.

"I know," Stephen replied, smiling. He reached across the table again and took her hand in his. "We've been buddies since tenth grade, but it never hurts to make someone you have the hots for think otherwise."

"You are misinterpreting my relationship with Zach. We were just friends until I discovered his plot to take our land."

"Uh-huh," Stephen replied, sounding unconvinced. "But to answer your question, he's with Lynn and Cal and another woman I don't know."

"Oh," Sophie said. Stephen smiled at her reaction. Sophie started to explain that she wasn't bothered that Zach was with another woman, but the waiter interrupted her as he brought their dinner.

Sophie and Stephen chatted as they ate their dinner. Sophie tried to ignore the feeling that eyes were boring into her back.

Stephen ordered another glass of wine for each of them, then held out his hand to Sophie. "The time of reckoning is here. Let's dance."

"He's still there?" Sophie asked.

"Yep," Stephen answered. "What? You're scared to go near him?" Stephen made a clucking sound like a chicken.

Sophie scowled at Stephen's challenge. She took his hand and let him lead her toward the dance floor. Her eyes met Zach's briefly before she looked away as she passed his table. She and Stephen began moving to the music in a slow dance. Only minutes passed before a hand tapped Stephen on the back.

"May I cut in?" Zach asked.

"You may," Stephen replied, quickly stepping away.

"Traitor," Sophie wanted to shout as she watched him walk to Zach's table and ask the unknown woman to dance.

Zach took Sophie's hand, then wound his arm around her waist. "Relax. I'm not going to wrestle with you here on the dance floor. Though that might be interesting."

"Very funny," Sophie replied without smiling or looking at him. She forced herself to relax. No use letting him see that her heart was thumping so hard in her chest that it rivaled the staccato rhythm of the band's drummer onstage.

"I'm sorry all this happened," Zach apologized as he pulled her closer.

"You should have thought about that when you tricked my father into a crooked deal," Sophie countered as she pulled back at arm's length. "I'm an idiot for thinking you had more class than that."

"Stop! I said I wasn't wrestling with you or chasing you across the dance floor." Zach pulled her back in, closer to his chest. "Your father wasn't tricked." Zach's mouth tightened to a thin line. "This situation is not what you evidently think it is. I can explain if you would only listen."

"I saw the legal documents you sent us. That's all the explanation I need. I have a plan. I'll pay you back." It was an empty promise, but she didn't care. Let him wonder what she meant. The music ended, and Sophie stepped away from him. "Goodnight, Mr. Whittaker."

"'Night, ma'am," Zach said with his fake accent. With a

mocking smile, he touched his hand to an imaginary hat in a salute. "You can't run forever. I'll be seeing you, Miss Sophie."

Sophie and Stephen reached their table at the same time.

"I'm going home," Sophie said as she picked up her purse. "Thanks for dinner. If you come up with anything regarding the debt, let me know, will you?"

"I will," Stephen replied. "I'm ready to go, too. I'll walk you out."

When they reached Sophie's car in the parking lot, he said, "I know you aren't interested in this little tidbit of news, but the unknown woman at Zach's table is Lynn's wedding planner. Married with two kids." He grinned, then added, "But you probably don't care. Am I right?"

"Hmmm, so Romeo struck out again," Sophie countered, attempting to wipe the smug grin off his face. "Maybe you should try one of those dating sites." She hugged him, then climbed into her car. "Call me if you come up with something." She started the motor, then drove out of the parking lot.

Sophie had just left the city limits of Kingsville when lightning lit up the sky in the distance in the direction of Cameron Stables. She had checked the weather forecast that morning, and there hadn't been any mention of rain, but storms could build quickly during the heat of the summer. Hopefully, the guests were inside and out of the storm. It was after ten p.m., and all organized outside activities at Cameron Stables would be over by now.

Sophie was about a mile away from the turnoff to Cameron Stables when a flash of lightning lit the sky directly in front of her. It was followed by a loud, rolling rumble of thunder. Suddenly, the air around her changed, and another bolt of lightning crackled just outside her car.

With a roar, strong winds moved in, rocking the front of her car as rain began to splatter the windshield. Sophie started the wipers, hoping to remove the debris the wind had plastered against her windshield, blocking her view. It was only a matter of minutes before she met the deluge head-on. Long shafts of lightning and ear-splitting thunder rolled around her as the rain came down in sheets. Blinded by the rain, Sophie slowed the car to a crawl.

An eye-scorching brilliance suddenly streaked across the sky directly in front of her car, followed by a deafening crash of thunder. Sophie's car hit a water-filled pothole and bounced toward the side of the road. She fought against the wet, slippery pavement and tried to steer the car back toward the middle of the road. The car lost traction and skidded further off the shoulder of the road.

Softened by the rain, the embankment immediately crumbled under the weight of the car. Another flash of lightning illuminated a ditch of roiling muddy water. Her car careened down the embankment rushing straight toward it. On the opposite side of the ditch, a large tree stood surrounded by swirling water—directly in the path of her vehicle.

Sophie screamed and pressed her brakes as hard as she could—a natural reflex and the only thing she could think to do as the car slid down the embankment and plunged into the water. The car barreled toward the tree. Sophie closed her eyes and waited for impact.

Suddenly, the car's front bumper hooked on something beneath the water. Miraculously, it lurched to a stop only inches from the trunk of the tree. The seatbelt tightened across Sophie's chest, but the car's airbags failed to deploy. Sophie was tossed forward like a rag doll, and her head slammed hard against the steering wheel.

Stunned by the blow from the steering wheel, Sophie sat for a moment, unable to move. She gulped in breaths of air, sucking it deep into her lungs. Finally, she was able to raise her head from the steering wheel. Shaking it from side to side, she tried to clear the fog left by the blow. She gingerly touched her forehead. A large egg-sized lump was already rising in the middle of her forehead just above her eyes, but miraculously, only a smudge of blood stained her fingers. She slowly moved her arms, legs, and torso, checking for injuries. Other than the large lump on her head, no other injuries were apparent.

She had little time to think about how fortunate she was to sustain what seemed like only a lump on her head. A sudden gush of water flowed over her feet as the water broke through the door seal. Terror-stricken, she looked down at the trickle of muddy water that was quickly covering the floor mats. At the rate the water was flowing in, it wouldn't take long for the car to fill with water.

Despite the raging storm outside, Sophie's instincts told her to move and get out of the car before it was engulfed by the rising water. The water was already lapping the top of her front tires. The "turn around, don't drown" slogan had been drummed into her head ever since she learned to drive. It was too late to turn around, but she was determined not to drown in a muddy ditch while trapped in her car.

Sophie unfastened her seat belt, grabbed her purse, and shoved hard against the door as she pulled the handle. The door wouldn't budge. From somewhere in her past, another safety precaution came to her—don't open the car's door because that would cause the water to fill the vehicle faster and sink it even more rapidly. She had no idea how much deeper the water in the ditch would eventually become, but she didn't intend to stay in the car and find out. She had seen this ditch full and over-flowing during heavy rains in the past.

Go out the window! her mind screamed at her. In a panic, she pressed the button for the power windows, but the electrical system was apparently damaged and didn't respond. She'd have

to break the glass. Using what? Sophie searched the floor behind the front seat until her hand closed over a large plumber's
wrench Mark had asked her to pick up while in town. With so
much going on recently, she had forgotten to give it to him.

Using all her strength, she struck the corner of the window
with the sharp edge of the wrench. It bounced off the window
and back at her. Using the light from her phone, she inspected
the window. A small chip and a crack had appeared in the glass.
She kept pounding that spot with the wrench, making the crack
expand as sections of glass fell out. Each strike took out bigger
and bigger pieces of glass until only a few shards remained.
Most of the window was now clear, leaving a hole large enough
for her to wiggle through and hopefully avoid getting snagged
by any remaining shards.

Sophie dropped her phone back into her purse and wrapped
the purse around her shoulders crossbody-style. Rising up on
her knees on the seat, she twisted around and began to slowly
work her upper body out through the window. She grabbed
onto the car's doorframe and driver's side mirror to keep herself
upright as she slowly wiggled her body through the window.

Once Sophie had pulled her legs free and while still holding onto the doorframe and the side mirror, she lowered her
feet and legs into the muddy water. It swirled around her body,
lifting her into a floating position in the water. Another flash of
lightning showed her the way to the embankment and the path
leading up to the roadway.

A large bush grew on the side of the embankment, with a
branch extending over the water's edge close to where Sophie
floated. Half-swimming and half-walking, Sophie lunged for the
branch. She grabbed hold of it and, using it like a rope, pulled
herself toward the side of the ditch. When she reached the
embankment, she paused to rest for a moment before beginning
the slippery ascent up to the roadway.

Using clumps of grass and weeds as leverage, Sophie dragged herself hand-over-hand up the embankment until she reached the shoulder of the roadway. She lay panting for a few minutes, waiting for her strength to return. As the cold rain pelted down on her, Sophie struggled to her feet and pushed wet strands of hair from her eyes. She was shaking, unsure of whether it was from the cold rain, the exertion of her escape, or the relief that she was out of the muddy water.

Sophie turned and looked down into the ditch at her car. Rushing water was now over the hood, and the rear end bobbed up and down. The front end was still hooked on whatever had stopped it earlier, preventing it from washing away as the rushing water filled the ditch. Who knows where it would have ended up without that piece of luck? Another flash of lightning showed that water had filled the inside as it flowed through the broken window. Relief that she had freed herself from a watery death made her knees weak.

Now what? There was only one thing she *could* do. Sophie started walking along the edge of the road toward home. She silently prayed that the lightning and rain would soon move past her. After escaping the water-filled ditch, it would be ironic if she was killed by a lightning strike.

There was no way she would call her mother and have her come rescue her as long as the storm raged as it was now. There was a farmhouse near the turnoff to her house, so if she could make it that far, maybe they would give her shelter until the storm passed and she could call her mother to come get her.

Sophie had taken only a few steps when headlights lit the road behind her as a vehicle came around a curve, driving in her direction. A pickup truck came to an abrupt halt beside her, splashing more water over her feet and legs. Her first thought was, *How rude!* If she wasn't so cold, she'd have laughed at her reaction. A little more water certainly wouldn't hurt her waterlogged body and was also acceptable if the driver—whether friend or stranger—would give a ride. She looked over as the driver exited the truck. The driver was neither friend nor stranger.

Zach raced around the front of the pickup toward her. Now was no time to be choosy about her rescuer. Relief that someone would help her surged through Sophie.

The rain had picked up in intensity again and streamed off of Zach's hat brim. He carried a yellow raincoat over his arm. When he reached Sophie's side, he placed the coat over her and put his arms around her, sheltering her with his body. She was shaking with cold and pressed close to him, thankful for the shelter of his body.

Sophie actually did giggle as Zach straightened the raincoat around her shoulders. She was soaked to the bone, had waded through chest-high water to get to safety, and had more water splashed on her thanks to him, so a raincoat was like putting a Band-Aid on a gushing wound. It would do little to keep her dry.

"My God, Sophie! Are you okay?" Zach had to yell to be heard above the crackle of lightning and thunder. He hugged her tightly and looked down into her face with concern.

Sophie nodded, still shaking from the cold. Relief that she had been rescued was suddenly replaced with the memory of what he had done and why she was angry with him. She hadn't forgotten. She didn't want his help. She pulled away from his arms. "I'm fine. I don't need help. I'm going to call a wrecker."

Zach didn't answer. With a noncommittal grunt, he bent over, picked her up, opened the passenger side of the pickup, and deposited her in the seat. Sophie was too tired to argue with him or try to get out of the truck. She didn't have any other place to go, anyway. Zach hurried around the front of the truck, climbed in behind the wheel, and slammed the door. The storm still roared, but the sound was muted somewhat inside the cab of the truck.

"Stop being ridiculous. A wrecker won't come out in this," Zach commented as he reached toward the truck's dashboard, turned on the heat, and directed the vents toward her. He removed the wet raincoat from Sophie's shoulders, then pulled a blanket and a towel from the back seat. He handed her the towel, raised the middle console out of the way, and straightened the blanket over her. "Do you hate me so much that you'd risk your life to avoid my help?" Zach asked sadly as he tucked the blanket around her. "Never mind. Don't answer that."

Sophie didn't reply. She suddenly felt foolish for her comment about waiting for a wrecker. Zach was right. A wrecker wouldn't venture out in a storm that still raged with little evidence of letting up soon.

"You scared me out of my wits," Zach said. He hunched over the steering wheel, then straightened and gripped it hard with both hands. "I saw your car in the ditch before I saw you on the road. You shouldn't have tried to drive in this storm. Why didn't your *date* drive you home?"

"Are you jealous?" When Zach just looked at her without answering, she added, "It wasn't storming when I left the restaurant. It came out of nowhere. And I'm a big girl. I can get myself home." Sophie began to rub her wet hair with the towel.

"Yes, I can see what a great job you're doing. How did you end up in the ditch?"

"It just jumped out in front of me." *A dumb question deserves a dumb answer*, Sophie thought.

"Hmph. That lump on your head didn't turn you into a comic, I see." Zach looked at her briefly, shook his head, then reached over to further turn up the blower on the heater. Without further comment, he put the truck in drive and began to ease along the roadway. The rain was so heavy, the headlights lit the road for only a short distance.

Now that she had dried some of the water from her hair and it no longer dripped down her face, she felt a little better. But her clothes were still wet, and she was cold. She pulled her feet from her wet sandals and placed them on the seat directly in front of the warm air from the heater vent.

Without taking his eyes off the road, Zach reached over and tucked the blanket closely around her legs. His warm hand remained on her feet. Sophie was reminded of his tenderness with Jamie when he fed her breakfast that morning when Jamie spent the weekend with her. Lulled by the warmth of his hand and the air from the heater, Sophie leaned her head back against the seat and closed her eyes.

"You have a foot fetish," Sophie remarked without opening her eyes. She was also remembering the night in the garden when Zach had rubbed her tired, burning feet.

"Ha! I have a fetish says the woman whose stubbornness can be classified as a compulsive disorder." Zach didn't elaborate further. He removed his hand from her feet so he could make the turn onto the wet road that led to Cameron Stables.

Sophie opened her eyes to narrow slits just as Zach finished a text message on his cell phone, then laid it down on the seat beside him. A late-night date that he needed to inform that he'd be even later, perhaps?

The warmth of the truck's interior had removed some of the icy cold from her body, making her feel relaxed and languid—and more forgiving. She was sympathetic to his situation. She was sorry for disrupting his evening. Despite her anger toward him, she would always be grateful for his help. Her desperation to get out of her car and her struggle up the embankment to safety were still fresh in her mind. The fight had temporarily gone out of her. But she didn't voice any of her thoughts. He had broken her trust, and that was something she was not prepared to forgive anytime soon.

Zach was quiet as he focused on guiding the truck through the downpour. The only sound was the wipers moving back and forth across the windshield. Sophie wasn't in the mood for conversation with him, anyway, since recent history had shown it would probably end in an argument. Her sympathy toward him was short-lived. Yes, she was grateful for his help, but she hadn't forgotten the debt she still owed him.

The rain had slowed to a heavy drizzle by the time they reached the driveway leading up to Sophie's house. Zach maneuvered the truck up the driveway and stopped as close to the front porch as the driveway would allow. He got out and walked around to open the passenger door.

Sophie was searching through her purse. "My keys. They're in here somewhere." She dug into another pocket.

"You don't need your keys," Zach said as he reached out. Before she could object, he plucked her from the seat and pulled her into his arms. He then turned and carried her toward the front porch.

"Put me down," Sophie insisted. "I'm not helpless." She slapped at his shoulders.

"Stop! Or I'll put you down in one of those mud puddles over there." Zach veered off the sidewalk and headed toward a large mud puddle in the middle of the yard. He added, "And leave you!"

"Alright! I'll stop." Sophie didn't have any doubt that he would follow through on his threat to drop her in the muddy water. Plus, she was too exhausted to physically fight him.

"You're not helpless, but you're stubborn to the point of recklessness," Zach said as he changed directions again, turning away from the mud puddle and stepping back onto the sidewalk.

"You'll scare my mother if she sees you carrying me in as if

I'm injured." Sophie gave Zach one last weak resistant slap on the shoulder.

"She's okay, Jean," Zach called out.

Sophie looked toward the front door. Her mother and Aunt Rachel stood on the porch. "How did they know... about my accident?"

"I let them know while you were napping. I didn't want to frighten them when they saw us looking like two sewer rats."

"Thank goodness you're both alright," Jean exclaimed as she held the door open for them. "I was so worried, Sophie! The storm spun up so quickly, and I knew you were probably on your way home by then."

"I'm okay, Mom," Sophie assured her mother. "Just water-logged."

"You're home, as promised." Zach bypassed Jean and Rachel on the porch, entered the house, and sat Sophie down in the entryway. "You need to get into some dry clothes," Zach said, still holding onto her arms.

"Stop treating me like Jamie!" Sophie tried to pull away from Zach's hold.

"If you were Jamie, I'd kiss you on the forehead, turn you over to your mother, and let her deal with you." He lightly touched her forehead with his fingertips, then dropped his hands to his side. "You need to get that injury looked at." He turned to Jean. "She's all yours."

Sophie waited for him to add, "And good riddance," but he didn't.

Zach looked down at the floor where water dripped from his clothing and puddled on the tiles. "Sorry about the mess." He turned toward Jean. "Her car's badly damaged, but the lump on her head seems to be her only injury—except for a case of extreme bullheadedness, but that's natural, not from the accident."

"I called Dr. Sampson after your text. He said that if her head is the only injury and there isn't an open wound, let her sleep, but wake her every two hours," Jean said. "Rachel and I will take turns. We'll update Dr. Sampson tomorrow on how she feels and see what else he suggests."

"I'm right here, you know. You can talk to me directly," Sophie interjected. "But I don't think you and Aunt Rachel should spend the night checking on me. I feel okay."

"Listen to your mother—the nurse." Zach scowled at her. "Do you want me to stay with you? I will."

"No!" Sophie exclaimed, horrified by the threat. "Alright! I'll do what you say."

"I'll go, then. Jean, Rachel, goodnight. Call me if you need anything." With a nod, Zach left the house.

Once Sophie had convinced her mother and aunt that she didn't have any broken bones, she went up to her bedroom. It wasn't until she'd had a hot shower and dressed in soft flannel pajamas that she finally felt warmth seep back into the deepest parts of her body.

She shivered, though not from cold, as she acknowledged how fortunate she was that she hadn't been badly injured or even drowned—and how lucky she was that Zach had come along to give her a ride home. She wouldn't let herself contemplate what might have happened to her if he hadn't arrived when he did.

Sophie disagreed with Zach's accusation that she was stubborn. *Determined* was more accurate. It was determination that spurred her to get free of the car, climb out of the water-filled ditch, and make it to safety. After surviving tonight's life-threatening incident, she didn't feel that determination was a bad trait to have.

Sophie climbed into bed and sank deep into the softness of the mattress. Exhausted by her ordeal, she soon fell asleep. Her dreams were filled with nightmares in which something pulled her down into deep, dark water and thick brown mud filled her mouth, choking her. As she struggled against the strong current and tried to breathe, a large hand reached out, pulled her from the raging water, and embraced her. She was so cold. She moaned in her sleep and thrashed about as she tried to snuggle closer to the warm familiar body that held her. Interspersed in her dreams were her mother and Aunt Rachel in her bedroom every two hours, as promised, shaking her awake to assess her condition.

At some point, a noise abruptly awoke Sophie. She pushed the hair out of her eyes and opened one eye to familiar surroundings. Relief! She was at home, in her bed, and not trapped in her nightmare. She stretched, rolled to her side, and snuggled deeper into her pillow. Then, slowly, she came fully awake. What time was it?

The light was already bright outside her bedroom drapes. She rose up on her elbow and looked at the bedside clock. It was 8:45 a.m., over two hours past her normal wake-up time. *Oh my God*, she thought. *I have a business to run!*

The noise that had awakened her started again and finally penetrated her sleep-fogged brain. She groped for the ringing phone on her bedside table.

At first, she had trouble making sense of what the voice on the phone was saying. "What? You have my car?" It was Ernie's Wrecker Service and Repair Shop in Kingsville. "But... how?"

Sophie lay back in bed and groaned as the horrifying events of the preceding evening rushed back over her. It hadn't been a dream!

Ernie explained that Mr. Whittaker had called him very early this morning, asking him to retrieve her car from the ditch on the road leading out of Kingsville. "I towed it to my shop," Ernie said. "I've just finished looking it over. My opinion?

The car is a total wreck. There's nothing much left to repair. The front end is badly damaged. Looks like the boulder also struck the engine block. All the electrical and computer systems were knocked out by the impact. Water and mud ruined the interior. The inside of the car is a mess."

"Okay. Thanks, Ernie. I'll be there tomorrow, after I contact my insurance agent."

Sophie was not surprised by Ernie's damage assessment, considering the conditions the car was in the last time she saw it. The surprise was that Zach had gone back to the scene of the accident early this morning, waited for the wrecker, and had the car towed into town. Why? Had he appointed himself her protector?

"We'll see about that," Sophie mumbled as she threw back the covers. "Oh," she groaned as her body reacted to the movement. Pain and stiffness hit her. She gritted her teeth, gingerly climbed out of bed, and slowly walked to the bathroom.

She began to rethink the idea of needing a protector once she had showered, brushed her teeth, and pulled on jeans and a shirt. Every bone in her body ached, and she could barely comb her hair because of the large black-and-blue lump on her forehead. Adding to her misery, she had a slight headache.

Despite her initial intention of showing Zach that she could take care of her car on her own, she was now reconsidering that, too. The car had been towed and was one less problem for her this morning. She couldn't be upset over that, but she still had an unforgivable grievance against him. His assistance with her damaged car hadn't made her forget that.

CHAPTER NINETEEN

Jean was in the kitchen pulling a pan of muffins out of the oven when Sophie walked in.

"Yum," Sophie said. "Can I have one with my coffee?"

"Of course. They're banana oatmeal, one of your favorites." Jean took one from the muffin pan, put it on a plate, and handed it to Sophie. "How are you feeling?"

"Like a truck ran over me. Otherwise, I'm okay."

"It'll take a few days for the soreness to leave. I'm just thankful that soreness is all we have to worry about. I talked to Dr. Sampson, and he advised that you take it easy for a few days."

"I don't have that luxury. I have a business to run."

"Rachel and I can help. Please don't try to do it all by yourself and do more than you can handle."

"I won't." Sophie pointed to two other pans of muffins cooling on the counter. "But what's with all the muffins?"

"Rachel and I are having a contest to see who can make the best muffins. She's been taking them out to the stables for the guys to eat during their break. But I'm beginning to think that maybe my sister has a crush on Tank. She wants to do *all* the deliveries."

"Really?" Sophie asked as she poured herself a cup of coffee, then sat down at the kitchen table. "Come to think of it, I ran into her out there one day, and she had a bit of a glow. I think that's sweet. It's been a long time since she lost her husband. And Tank is a nice guy."

"Who's a nice guy?" Aunt Rachel asked as she came into the kitchen. "Zach? He certainly is. Definitely a keeper, as they say. Thank God he was driving behind you last night! Are the muffins ready for me to take to the barn?"

Sophie ignored the comment about Zach. She exchanged a smile with her mother.

"Yes, they're ready. I'm putting them in a box right now," Jean replied. She handed the box of muffins to Rachel. Rachel quickly left the kitchen by the side door on her way to the barn.

"I'm sorry I left everything to you last night. Things wouldn't be such a mess today if I had stayed at home. My car is totaled." Sophie saw the question in Jean's eyes. "Zach called a tow truck this morning. It's at Ernie's Repair Shop now. Ernie called a bit ago to tell me the car is totaled."

"Well, Zach is everywhere, isn't he? Rachel is right. Definitely a keeper!" Jean smiled as she fixed herself a cup of coffee and joined Sophie at the table.

"Everywhere—as well as in my business," Sophie grumbled, then realized she came off as uncharitable and irritable. She didn't want to ruin the few moments she had with her mother. They used to have mother-daughter conversations quite frequently, and Sophie had missed that when she lived in Tampa. Since she had moved home, though, she'd been too busy trying to get the business back on track to take time for a leisurely tête-à-tête with Jean.

"As for leaving everything with us last night, Rachel and I are capable of helping out. No problems came up that we couldn't handle. And there was no serious damage from the storm, either. Just a few broken tree limbs. I've already had Tank, Rita, and Sam look around the property."

"I overslept this morning, too," Sophie apologized. "Sorry about that."

"You were exhausted, especially with being awakened every two hours. You know, you don't have to shoulder the entire burden of this place," Jean said. "By the way, last night, I moved the Ryan and Morgan families from the tents to the empty duplex because of the lightning and strong winds. I told them that we'd discount their stay for the inconvenience. They didn't seem to mind moving. When they checked out this morning, they told Maggie that they had never seen a lightning show like the one they saw last night from the high meadow. They promised to visit again s soon as possible."

"I haven't seen lightning like that before, either—or as up close," Sophie agreed. "And I hope to never see it again." She shivered at the memory of the blinding lightning strikes and deafening thunder.

She had wondered how the tents would hold up during a storm, but last night, caught up in her own personal horror story, she had forgotten all about them. That slip could have led to a disaster. *Note to self*, she thought, *I need to coordinate more of the management decisions with Mom and Aunt Rachel. They are indeed capable. But they were capable last night even without any coordination or instructions from me.*

"So, the tents didn't blow over or come loose from their posts or anchors?" Sophie asked.

"The winds were strong up there, but the anchors didn't budge from the ground. I think the hills and tree line kept them from getting a direct hit. It was the lightning that was the most dangerous."

"If they could survive the storm last night, they can survive almost anything. If we face another emergency like last night and happen to be fully booked, we can also move the tent guests into the main house. I'll redecorate the empty bedrooms upstairs so we can use them in a pinch. Maybe later, when—or if—our cash flow improves, we can build another duplex and keep it open just for emergency use."

"Good idea. But what are you going to do about Zach?" Jean asked, redirecting the conversation.

"I'm going to pay him back. I just don't know how yet, since he wouldn't accept my check."

"I figured as much," Jean replied, rolling her eyes. "But I mean in a personal way—what are you going to do about the obvious attraction between you two? A blind person could see that spark."

"Nope! Nothing there! I'm divorced! Not trying again! Not interested in anyone, especially Zach!" Sophie's response came out in short staccato bursts.

"Hmph! Things often change. But I'll leave that up to you. What are your plans for today?"

"Nothing very exciting on the agenda today. Since it's Sunday, I'll have to wait to take care of my car tomorrow." Sophie stubbornly focused her thoughts back on the day ahead and away from Zach. The spark her mother spoke of was anger—at least, since she received the foreclosure notice. "I have a few invoices to go over and some tax forms to complete. I might review the ads posted on social media to see if any need tweaking. Maybe I'll research how to pay a debt when the creditor won't accept payment. Stephen wasn't any help."

"You should turn the bill paying over to June," Jean suggested. "She's a great addition to the staff, isn't she?"

"She's certainly a sharp one. She absorbs information like a sponge. I can show her something once, and she gets it. I plan to give her more duties as soon as she gets through sorting Dad's papers."

"Lord help her," Jean said with a laugh. "Your father would barely finish one thing before he was ready to move on to the next great idea. He knew where the papers were if he ever needed them. Filing seemed like a waste of time, especially if he felt he wouldn't need the documents anytime soon."

"All his quirks made him who he was." Sophie smiled fondly at the memory of her father's business philosophy: "Act confident, and no one will know you're winging it." But that didn't always work, as evidenced by his unpaid debt to Zach. "I really miss him, quirks and all."

"I know. Not a day goes by that I don't long to see him and talk to him," Jean said sadly. "Hard as it is, it's one of those situations you have to accept. Life goes on. It just goes on differently." She stood up, took her coffee cup to the sink, rinsed it, and placed it in the dishwasher. "I'm going to go putter in the flower garden. Start the dishwasher after you get done with breakfast, okay?"

"Of course." At Sophie's nod, Jean left the kitchen, heading to her personal garden to take care of her plants. Gardening had always been her mother's hobby, but since she wasn't volunteering at the hospital, she now had more time to take care of her horticultural patients.

Sophie finished her coffee, cleaned the crumbs off the table, and started the dishwasher. Then, she went to her office to take care of the paperwork that sat on her desk, awaiting her attention.

The question of how to repay Zach nagged at her as she worked. She couldn't let it go. Settling the debt now bordered on an obsession with her. Her father was always adamant about taking care of his obligations—financial or otherwise—and she felt the same way about his debt. But this situation turned out to be an obligation she didn't have a solution for.

Sophie soon wrapped up her office duties, but she still couldn't bat away the question of what to do about her father's loan. Zach wouldn't take her money. What did she have that he might want?

Sophie groaned out loud as the answer came to her. Land! She had lots of land—including land that bordered Zach's property on Mystic Hill. The thought made her sick, yet she mulled it over anyway. This was the only way to get out from under the debt. Land was the one thing she could offer Zach that he couldn't refund and that he might accept.

She searched the internet for local sales of land around Kingsville. Bluegrass country land sold at a premium. The prevailing price for acreage was a little over two thousand dollars per acre. Mystic Hills was unique, so twenty-five hundred an acre seemed fair. Others might not think the hilly terrain was worth that much, but *she* wouldn't list the acreage on the real estate market for less. Maybe she was using personal reasons and her attachment to the hills to support the price, but that was what it was worth to her.

One hundred acres at twenty-five hundred an acre would pay her father's debt in full—the loan, plus the interest he hadn't paid recently. The section would have to be pie-shaped because she wouldn't include Mystic Peak and the Fairy Woods. Under no circumstances could she let those sections go. Those areas were special to her, and she needed them for business reasons.

Sophie knew that Stephen wouldn't help her, so she turned to a website called LegalEase. She signed in and searched until she found a form for deeding property to someone. Sophie filled out the form, leaving the exact coordinates blank. She would fill those in later after she arranged for a survey.

Sophie printed the form, then went in search of her mother

to share her latest plan. Since they were joint owners, she would need her mother's signature and approval to make the transaction legal. She found Jean under the shade of an elm tree, repotting plants on a table near the greenhouse.

"Sophie!" Jean exclaimed when Sophie showed her the document and told her what she planned to do. "This is crazy. Are you sure you aren't suffering from a concussion after all?"

"I know what I'm doing." Sophie hadn't expected her mother to be one hundred percent onboard, but disapproval dripped from her voice, and it was much harsher than Sophie had expected. Jean rarely questioned Sophie's business decisions, let alone this much.

"I think you're misreading the situation and misreading it badly," Jean added. "I don't believe Zach would ever take our home away from us." Jean pounded a bag of potting soil long past the time needed to break up the clumps inside. "I don't know why you won't just talk to him."

"I don't need to talk," Sophie insisted. "Dad's signature is on the loan papers. It's notarized. He made a deal and spent the money. I want to settle his debt, so the Cameron property is free and clear."

"By breaking up the land and selling a piece of it?" Jean turned away and stared into the distance for a few minutes. Then, she turned back to Sophie. "Alright," Jean said, defeated. "If this is what you want to do, I'll concur, but I'm not happy about it. You're making a huge mistake."

"I can't think of any other way," Sophie protested. Her mother's disapproval cut deep. For a minute, Sophie wavered, unsure if she should take this drastic step. "Do you have a better idea? I'd like to hear it if you do."

"No, I don't," Jean replied shortly. "I'll sign the papers if that's what you want. It's only a piece of land—and a friendship. I'll say no more." She turned her back on Sophie and began adding soil to the flowerpot on the table. The set of her jaw spoke volumes. Jean disapproved but would not discuss the matter any further.

Sophie's shoulders slumped as she walked back into the house. She hadn't seen her mother this angry with her in a long time. She wished there was another way, but she had gone over every scenario in her mind, and this was the only viable solution she could come up with. She couldn't seem to let it go or move on until it was done.

◆

The next morning, Sophie left June sorting through "Paper Mountain"—the name they had given her father's bookcase filing system—and drove into town. She had an appointment with her insurance adjuster at Ernie's garage at ten a.m. Gabe Ferguson arrived soon after Sophie parked the company truck in front of the auto repair shop. After Gabe spoke with Ernie, he and Sophie inspected her car together.

"Wow! You did all this in a roadside ditch?" Gabe asked Sophie. He forced open the car door and shook his head at the mud-caked interior. It was still wet, and the humidity from the July heat hung thick on the inside. The interior reeked of an unpleasant odor that promised to soon turn into mold. "How did you end up in the ditch?"

"A flash of lightning blinded me just as I hit a pothole in the road. Before I knew it, I was sliding down the embankment and into muddy rushing water."

"With damage like this, you're very lucky you escaped with just bumps and bruises."

"Today, I realize I'm lucky, but Saturday night, you couldn't have convinced me of that. A black cloud of trouble seems to be following me around lately. And this cloud was filled with trouble and rain—lots of rain."

"We used to call these sudden storms 'cloudbursts' or 'gully washers,'" Gabe said. "Lots of rain in a very short period of time." He walked around to the front of the vehicle. "Ernie tells me that the front end caught on a rock and saved you from slamming headfirst into a tree."

"Something stopped everything—except my head, which hit the steering wheel."

"Ernie said he'll figure out why the airbag didn't deploy. The failure might need to be reported to the Feds. My guess is that the rock dismantled the system that deploys it. Looks like the boulder that saved you also did a number on the engine. Yep, this car is totaled. Black cloud or not, luck and that rock saved you from serious injury."

Sophie and Gabe finished inspecting the car, and Gabe filled out the paperwork that declared the car a total loss. Sophie left Ernie's and immediately drove to a dealership in town. She picked out a midsized SUV and made the financial arrangements for payment—another unexpected expense—until she received the insurance payment. Someone would deliver the car that afternoon after it was cleaned and detailed.

Sophie's next stop was the surveyor's office. Without letting herself second-guess what she was doing, she scheduled a survey of the land she wanted to deed to Zach. Single-mindedly, she was on a mission to clear her father's debt, along with his reputation. She had gone over the situation in her mind ad nauseam. She refused to dwell on the repercussions of her decision to deed away a section of Cameron land.

She was tired and annoyed that she couldn't seem to get one problem solved before another one popped up. Hopefully, once Zach took ownership of the land, she'd be free of the debt and could go back to concentrating only on the business.

As Sophie drove toward home and took the turn leading to Cameron Stables, she looked up at a cloudless blue sky. Not a single black cloud appeared on the horizon this morning. But that didn't mean one with her name on it wouldn't come out of nowhere suddenly and zap her again.

CHAPTER TWENTY

Z ach rode through the woods astride Big Boy. A morning ride might clear the confusion that had gripped him over the last few days. Confusion? No, there was no confusion. His thoughts all centered around one stubborn green-eyed, auburn-haired woman named Sophie.

Since she had received Jenkins's foreclosure letter, Sophie's anger was like an impenetrable shield between then—except for a brief moment Saturday night when he found her on the side of the road. The mini-thaw was probably due to sheer exhaustion, and it had frozen over again quickly. He couldn't really blame her. His agreement with George had turned into the bad idea he'd warned George it would be. He could kick himself for not remembering and taking care of the problem before it reached this point.

"Live and learn" may be an appropriate cliché to describe his failure to intercede and stop the foreclosure letter from being sent to Sophie, but if eyes could actually shoot life threatening daggers, his days among the living were numbered—if he ever saw her again. Or spoke to her. He had called her several times, and she refused to take his calls.

Zach let Big Boy set the pace along the winding trail. Early-morning dew sparkled in the shafts of light that penetrated the thick undergrowth under the trees. He came out of the woods and stopped near the top of the hill bordering the meadow and the property line between Thornton Farms and Cameron land. He started to dismount to let Big Boy graze for a while when a flash of color drew his eyes to the Cameron side of the property line.

"What the hell? What are they doing?" Zach spurred his horse down the hill and toward the two workmen in the meadow below. The rising sun glinted off what looked like a surveyor's transit sitting on its tripod. The two men were lining up sites and points as they marked off a tract of land on the other side of the fence line. Red ribbons tied to stakes waved in the breeze. The stakes started farther to the north and followed a path that angled down the hill past Mystic Peak. Zach reined in Big Boy, dismounted, and climbed over the fence. He stalked toward the surveyors.

"What are you doing here?" Zach asked angrily. "Why are you surveying this land?"

"We have a contract with Miss Cameron to survey," one of the men answered, obviously offended by Zach's tone. "Not that it's any of your business."

"We jointly own this fence," Zach said, equally offended by the man's answer. "So, it's jointly my business, too."

"We're not bothering the fence. Just doing what we're told," the man replied. He shrugged and turned the palms of his hands upward in a "not my problem" stance. "I suggest you take it up with Miss Cameron."

"You're right," Zach agreed. "Sorry for the attitude." He

pulled his phone from his shirt pocket and dialed Sophie's number. It went straight to voicemail. Again. "Damn!" he said as he disconnected the call and put his phone back in his pocket.

Without another word to the surveyors, Zach turned and walked back the way he had come. He didn't have time this morning to find out why surveyors were surveying the land. He had to get home, shower, and leave for an appointment.

Ms. Williamson had recommended three more foster kids that lived several miles outside of Kingsville. He had visited them and offered them all jobs at Thornton Farms. He had promised to pick them up this afternoon. He couldn't disappoint them by not showing up while he chased Sophie down to see why she had ordered a survey of her land.

That would have to wait—if she would even talk to him. What was she up to with a land survey of her property? A survey was needed when property was up for sale. Was she letting her anger make her do something she'd regret later, like break up her land—and all because of him? That idea left a sickening feeling churning in his stomach.

♦

Jean was in the kitchen having a glass of sweet tea when Sophie walked in.

"There was a problem in cabin three with the air conditioner," Jean said as she wiped her forehead and took a sip of tea. "I asked Tank to send Mark to check it out. It's too hot and humid to be without air conditioning even for a minute." Jean didn't look directly at Sophie.

"The survey is complete. The men finished it a short time ago and emailed the report. All that's left to finalize the deal is for you to sign the deed. Tank is a notary and can notarize your signature. He did mine a while ago," Sophie said. "The hundred acres are identified and marked in detail. I've attached the deed that I filled out, too. They're all in this envelope."

"You're still going through with this crazy plan?" Jean asked in disbelief. "This is a bad idea, Sophie." Her mouth tightened in displeasure as she looked Sophie squarely in the face. "Your father had one quality that I never got used to—stubbornness. It's a good quality to have at times when you need to keep pushing forward and not give up, but at other times, it just leads to more trouble. If an idea took root in his head, he wouldn't let it go, even if it was a bad idea. You're sometimes very much like him in that way."

"It's not stubbornness that makes me want to take care of our obligations," Sophie protested.

"I'll handle this situation the same way I used to handle my disagreements with George," Jean said, ignoring Sophie's remark. "You can't be told. Just like your father, you have to be shown. I'm not happy with your decision, but I'll sign the deed."

"I can't come up with any other way to pay off Dad's debt," Sophie replied sadly. "I don't want you to be mad at me. I wish there were another way."

"I know you're doing what you think is best, but I disagree with you. You could talk to Zach and work this out. But I've suggested that before, and you won't listen. Leave the papers on the table. I'll take care of them," Jean replied brusquely. "I have to take Rachel to Dr. Sampson's office for an injection in her shoulder. She irritated the joint somehow and needs me to drive her home after the procedure."

"Sure," Sophie replied. "I have another favor to ask, then. Could you sign them, get Tank to notarize them before you leave, and then deliver the papers to Zach on your way back?"

"You're stubborn, but you're not usually a coward," Jean remarked. "Can't do your own dirty work, huh?" Jean was unable to hide her unhappiness with Sophie at the moment. She understood Sophie's desire to pay her father's debts—she felt that way, too—but did Sophie have to turn the situation into a battle? She could sit down with Zach, talk this out like an adult, and maybe come up with a payment plan. She didn't understand why Sophie wanted to break up the land when it could be handled in another way.

"I… uh… if I go over there, he'll either badger me or try to cajole me with sweet talk into accepting only *his* solution. You know how he is. He'll mock me with that fake folksy accent or refuse to even listen to *my* plan, which will just make me angrier."

"A sweet-talkin' man makes you nervous, huh? Afraid you might let yourself go and fall for someone worthy of your love?" Jean tried to hold her tongue, but the words flowed out of her mouth against her will. She couldn't stop. She was voicing pent-up thoughts she'd had for a long time.

For some reason, Sophie had always dated men she could never love. Or at least that's how it looked to Jean. It had started in high school with that boy Travis, and it had ended with Robert. Robert was a nice man—for someone else—but Jean never saw the passion between him and Sophie that she wished for her daughter. Their marriage was more like a business arrangement, and their careers were about all Jean could see that they had in common. Misguided as she felt Sophie was for marrying Robert, Jean never interfered in their relationship. Sophie had to learn that lesson all on her own.

A sweet-talking man? Yes, Jean was familiar with such a man. But she also knew about a passionate one, too. George Cameron had been such a man. He could add an Irish lilt to a conversation that would make a wild horse beg for the saddle. Except for one horse. That was how she met George. She was twenty-three years old and just out of nursing school when

George appeared in her ER. A horse had objected to a saddle George was trying to put on its back, and it had slammed him into a wooden gate, breaking his forearm.

George kept appearing in the ER waiting room over the next couple of weeks, even after he was on the mend. One day, he called out to her when he saw her in the hallway behind the registration window. Dr. Benson, the physician on duty at the time, yelled, "Jean, give the young man your phone number so he'll stay out of my ER." Jean complied and fell head over heels for George. They were inseparable after their first date and had married one year later.

Maybe her belief that a romantic spark existed between Sophie and Zach was just nostalgia for the time when she and George were themselves young lovers. Over the years, they had settled into a comfortable companionship, but the initial spark between them never dulled or burned out. Jean missed everything about George. He drove her crazy with his stubbornness and his foolish ideas that frequently led to heated arguments. But the anger could always be wiped away simply by him slipping his arms around her and hugging her for no other reason than it had been a few hours since they had last seen each other.

If she were in charge of choosing a mate for Sophie, it would be someone like Zach. From the first time she met the skinny, sullen young man, she could tell he was special. When she finally coaxed a smile out of him and he began to talk to her and George, they both recognized that Zach had huge potential. He hadn't disappointed them as he grew into adulthood. Jean believed in her heart that Zach would love passionately, deeply, and unconditionally. Was a love like that too much for a mother to ask for her daughter?

Sophie was so wrapped up in trying to save Cameron Stables right now, she wouldn't recognize love if it bopped her on the head. And her latest plan might be the death of any chance for that love with Zach. That was too sad to contemplate, but it was another lesson Sophie would have to learn by herself.

Jean sighed, then walked over to Sophie and hugged her hard. "I apologize, sweetie, for being snippy. I'm just irritable that there's not another way to do this. I'll deliver the papers to Zach after I bring Rachel home from her procedure at Dr. Sampson's."

♦

Jean dropped Rachel off at Cameron Stables to rest after the steroid shot in her shoulder. She then retraced her route and took the main road to Thornton Farms. Mattie let her into the house, then showed her to the main office.

Jean knocked on the frame of the office door. Eli was sitting behind the desk. He stood and motioned for her to come in.

"Mrs. Cameron, come in. What can I do for you?" Eli asked.

"I was hoping to see Zach. Is he here?"

"He had some business to take care of, but he should be getting back anytime now." Eli pulled out a chair for Jean to sit down. "Is there something I can do for you?"

"No, I'll wait a while and see if Zach returns, if that's okay," Jean replied as she took the offered chair. "Why don't you come over some weekend for the festivities at our place? We're neighbors, and you don't need to be a paying guest to come for the music, dancing, and food. Bring someone."

"I just might do that. I'm getting bored with only Zach's company," Eli said with a laugh. "But I have a girlfriend in California, so there's no one here I could bring. I'll be heading back to California the first part of September after I visit my mamma in Texas."

"Your mamma will love that," Jean said. She looked around

the room. "Zach has done a very nice job renovating this place."

"Zach's a master at finding things to rehab or businesses to turn around, but once he's done, he turns them over to someone else in the company and moves on," Eli said. "He likes to say that he's a rolling stone, but I see him putting down roots here more than anyplace he's been."

"We can hope," Jean replied. She added meaningfully, "Having him as a permanent neighbor would make me very happy."

"I see you've got the story all figured out, Mrs. C. It's the two main characters in our play that are messing up the ending."

Jean and Eli chatted for a while longer, but Zach still had not returned.

"Maybe I could just leave a note for Zach with these papers," Jean said, holding up a manila envelope. "Do you have a pad of paper?"

"I do," Eli said as he pulled a pad from the drawer. "Come around here and sit. I'll leave, and you can write for as long as you need to."

Jean settled into the chair behind the desk and drew the pad of paper toward her.

"Let one of the staff know if you need me, and they'll come get me." At Jean's nod, Eli left the room.

Jean had just started writing when someone entered the room. She looked up as Zach walked through the door.

"Mattie told me you were in here. Do you need to see me?"

"Yes," Jean replied. "Here, I'll move." Jean stood and started to walk around the desk, but Zach motioned for her to remain sitting. She picked up the envelope on the corner of the desk, sighed heavily, and handed it to Zach.

"What's this?" Zach opened the envelope and pulled out the papers. "Damnit! Is she kidding? I can't believe she thinks I'll go along with this! I saw the surveyor crew finishing up this morning, but they wouldn't tell me why they were surveying."

He looked at Jean with a hard glint in his eyes and scowled. "She barely let the ink dry on their report. She really thinks I'll take your property?" Zach raised his voice. "She thinks I'm that low?"

"She's *not* thinking," Jean replied. "I tried to talk her out of this, but she's on a mission to, as she puts it, 'clear her father's name.' It was a shock to get the foreclosure notice. She took it as a personal afront, and I don't think she's recovered yet."

"It's a shock to me that she believes I'd be this heartless. My CFO got carried away doing his job, but I blame myself for letting George talk me into this mess. I forgot the damn mortgage was even on our books." Zach stood up and walked to the window. He paced back and forth, then came back to the chair and sat down facing Jean. "Do you remember or even know how this mess got started?"

"No," Jean replied. "I wasn't even aware we had a mortgage."

"Around two years ago, during a phone call, George let it slip that Cameron Stables was about to go bankrupt. I offered to give him two hundred thousand dollars, which was the sum he said he needed to stay afloat until things turned around. He refused my offer of a gift, then said he'd give me his coin collection in return for the money. I didn't want his coins, but he wouldn't let it go. To get him to accept the money, we made a verbal agreement. I told him to keep the coins, and I'd pick them up the next time I was in the region. I had no intention of taking his coins, but three days later, I received a box of coins with a precious metal appraisal signed by a Bill McClain that valued the coins at two hundred thousand dollars—the exact amount George needed. George had been hoodwinked by one of the biggest scams in the world—precious metals. His original investment was small, thankfully. He'd been smart to buy when he did, McClain told him, because now, they were worth a lot more—which was, of course, a lie."

"Bill McClain was George's barber," Jean said. "He meant well, but he didn't know any more about precious metals or investments than George. But he wanted to be a player. I had no idea that George had become that deeply involved with Bill's shenanigans."

"Ah, yes," Zach replied with a hollow laugh. "Bill, the barber and wannabe investment guru and tax advisor. There's more to this story, though." Zach went over to the coffee bar on the side of the room and took two bottles of water from the fridge. He passed one to Jean, opened the other, and took a drink.

"George was very loyal to people he thought were his friends. That's how Bill was able to convince him to go along with many of his ideas," Jean said.

"The dream of secretly discovering the 'big one' before it becomes public knowledge has fleeced more than a few. But Bill wasn't done *advising* yet. Shortly after the coins arrived, George called again. Bill had told George that if he entered into a privately sourced, interest-only loan with me, George would be able to deduct the interest from his taxes, thereby reducing his tax liability. A 'win-win,' in Bill's words." Zach shook his head. "Even as I retell it, I can't believe I gave in again and agreed to the balloon mortgage. Maybe I'm the one that got conned."

"You were just trying to help. Both Bill and George were gifted talkers, so it was hard to say no to either of them. I think Bill McClain was an 'Irish Traveler' in a former life."

"I sent George a letter about his proposal. I thought that if I laid it out on paper, he would see why the interest-only loan with a balloon payment at the end of the term was a bad idea. I told him that the interest would give him very little relief, if any, on his taxes. But Bill said it would, so what did I know?"

"Did he make the interest payments?" Jean asked.

"He did. Monthly and on-time, up until early this year. I assume the late interest payments is where Jenkins came up with the final total of more than the initial two hundred thousand dollars. I set up a holding account just for the interest and planned to give it back to you and George. And I planned to talk to George again and make it clear that the money was a gift, not a loan. It's my fault that this spiraled out of control. I got busy, then George passed away, and I forgot there was a balloon payment coming due this summer. I changed CFOs and didn't mean for the foreclosure letter to be sent."

"Are we in trouble with the IRS?" Jean asked.

"No, George paid the applicable rate for a loan at that time. George later *gave* me his worthless gold coin collection, too, because I 'helped him out when he needed it,' he said. But I brought them back when I moved here. I intended to give them back. They're actually in the bottom of the bookcase over there. That's the whole story." Zach picked up the documents, then looked at Jean. "I'm not accepting this, you know. George was the only father I knew as an adult. The money was a gift I would have given to my biological father if he were alive." Zach tossed the papers back onto the desk. "I wouldn't accept a dry creek bed if she offered it, but this… I know how much this land means to her."

"I know. Sophie thinks she's doing the right thing. She's under a lot of stress. While trying to process and accept the loss of her father, she discovered that the business was in terrible financial shape. Since coming home, she's worked tirelessly to expand, hire staff, and try to save it. She's used her personal funds that she got from the sale of the ad agency and also sold some of her investments to raise cash. Then, on top of all that, she gets a foreclosure notice—which shocked us both," Jean said, hoping to explain Sophie's actions. "I'm not excusing her behavior. I told her to just talk with you and work this out—that together, you could come up with a less drastic solution." Jean paused, then added, "Maybe she wants to prove to you that she can handle business decisions as well as you."

"Oh, I understand. You don't need to explain her motivations. But if I'm such a great businessman, I never would have let George talk me into this mess. Sophie's done an amazing job. And as I've said more than once, she's as stubborn as... as... her father—with me, anyway. Now, she thinks I can be bought with one hundred acres of land."

"I don't think she really believes that, but I agree that she's stubborn. I blame her father for that trait," Jean said with a smile. "But maybe you could talk to her and tell her what you just told me. She won't believe me if I tell her."

"And you think she'll believe me? I've tried to talk to her, but she won't even answer my calls," Zach replied. He ran his hand through his hair in frustration. "My solution is that there's no debt to be paid off. That's it. I'll accept no arguments. Do you think she'll accept that?"

"Sounds like someone else might be pigheaded, too." Jean smiled as she leaned back in her chair with a thoughtful expression on her face. "I can't say this with absolute certainty, but Sophie mentioned that she's been neglecting Rose's exercise lately and that she needs to take her up the trails to Mystic Peak soon. We aren't that booked for this Sunday. So, if someone were to ride up there on Sunday morning, say around seven a.m., who knows? They might find her up there. Her mother might even encourage her to take a ride up there—at that exact time."

"Hmmm," Zach replied, then smiled ruefully. "And those green-eyed daggers might knock someone right off the edge of that cliff. Just saying!"

"No pain, no gain," Jean countered. "Just saying."

Jean was on her way home and almost back to Cameron Stables when she remembered that she hadn't signed or had Tank notarize the deed transfer. Because of the argument with Sophie and the trip with Rachel to the doctor's office, signing the deed had completely slipped her mind.

"Shoot," Jean said to the empty car. Sophie's effort to pay George's debt by deeding the land was going nowhere anyway, but she'd at least let Zach know about the missing signature.

Well, well, Jean thought as she drove through the gate at Cameron Stables. *Luck is a funny thing. Sometimes, it's as simple as forgetting to do something. This might work out in the end.*

Sophie was waiting for Jean on the back porch when she parked her car in the garage under the carriage house. She joined Sophie on the porch.

"Was Zach at home?" Sophie asked. "Did you give him the deed?"

"No," Jean replied slowly. "When I arrived, Eli said that Zach had gone someplace on business. I left the papers on his desk." The statement was not a lie... exactly.

"You were gone a long time," Sophie pointed out. "I wonder what he'll think when he opens the envelope."

"I visited with Eli while I waited," Jean explained. Also true. "It's not hard to imagine what he'll think. He'll be angry that you went to such lengths to pay off a loan he insists you don't owe." Another true statement. Jean had seen that in real time. "Are you going to talk to him? He'll probably call, you know."

"No, I think I'll let him stew for a few days," Sophie replied, shaking her head. "He needs to learn that not everyone jumps when he says jump."

"Putting things off is always a good plan," Jean replied sarcastically. "But since he has the deed, isn't the only thing left for him to do is file it at the courthouse?"

"Yes," Sophie agreed. "But I'd think he'd call me before he did that."

"Why? You're not taking his calls," Jean pressed. "So, why bother calling?"

"It's the polite thing to do," Sophie insisted. "We're neighbors, and we need to peacefully coexist. Get this episode behind us."

"Hmpf! Your logic escapes me." Jean shook her head at Sophie's reasoning. "Neighbors or not, you won't even have to see him when he goes back to California. Eli said he was going back at the end of the summer, so Zach might go back then, too." Also, not a lie.

"Oh," Sophie replied. "I guess that's true. Regardless, we're free of the debt now."

"Why all the questions?" Jean asked. "Are you having second thoughts about deeding away the land?"

"I…uh…" Sophie stammered. Much of her confidence that she was doing the right thing appeared to have evaporated. She sagged into a porch rocker. "No. It's the only way I know to resolve this. I wish things were different, but this is the easiest way."

Jean looked at her struggling daughter. Sophie had tears in her eyes. Much of Jean's anger at Sophie evaporated. She knew her daughter well. Jean could pass along the story Zach had shared with her, but Sophie wouldn't accept a secondhand account. She'd want to hear it from Zach himself. But she'd have to actually talk to him for that to happen, and thus far, obstinance had kept her from hearing the truth. Once Sophie heard Zach's explanation of what had actually transpired, maybe she'd understand that it was a series of mistakes started by her father.

But even George would not have gone through with this crazy scheme, had he known it would turn out this way.

"Sweetheart, I know you're doing what you feel is right." Jean reached out and rubbed Sophie's shoulder. "You want it all wrapped up neat and tidy and over with. But the easiest way isn't always the right way. Maybe you have more than the issue of the debt going on here. Is it being obligated to Zach that's bothering you? Would you behave differently if the lien-holder was a bank? Maybe you've let your emotions override common sense and turned a simple situation into one gigantic problem."

In Jean's opinion, Sophie had taken sole ownership of the mission to save their business—and with sole ownership came responsibility for any failures. She saw this as a failure, even though she had nothing to do with it. Plus, she wanted to wipe away any blemish, as she saw it, on her "perfect" dad's record. Thrown into the mix was an uneasiness about her feelings for Zach—feelings that might be making her more uncomfortable than the indebtedness to him. Sophie had always been independent, but often risk-averse. Opening her heart and giving into powerful feelings for another person was a risk she had never taken before.

"It's a gigantic problem, all right, but I don't want you to worry," Sophie said. "What's done is done."

Jean sighed. It wouldn't help the situation to berate Sophie any further for doing what she thought was right. "I'm not worried, sweetie, and I apologize for getting mad at you earlier and making things even more difficult for you. But things have a way of working out in the end."

"I hope you're right." Sophie placed her hand over her mother's, which still rubbed her shoulder. She squeezed it lightly. "I really hope you're right."

CHAPTER TWENTY-ONE

Sophie yawned and stretched her arms over her head. She'd like to lay her head down on the desk for a quick nap, but she had work to do. It was Saturday morning, and Sophie and June were in the office finishing up things left undone at Friday's close of business. June planned to spend the full day clearing Paper Mountain in hopes of sorting through all the remaining papers in the bookcase. Sophie was finishing up a draft for some new advertising that would update the ads that were currently running on social media.

Sophie took a swallow of her second cup of coffee, hoping to dislodge the cobwebs from her brain so she could think and write. She was hungover this morning—not from excessive partying, but from another restless night. Each time she closed her eyes last night, the image imprinted on her eyeballs was the back of a man who looked a lot like Zach. The man stood before the counter at the tax office with the deed in his hand, preparing to transfer one hundred acres of Cameron land into his name.

Once Sophie did manage to fall asleep, she couldn't escape the image of the man as strange dreams took over. In one dream, the clerk behind the counter seemed more interested in flirting with Zach than processing and recording the land transfer. Zach didn't rebuff the flirting but seemed pleased by the attention and flirted back. Sophie's cries of "No! Stop!" had awakened her. This morning, the dreams were all jumbled together, and she was almost certain that her cries of "Stop!" had been because of the deed and not because Zach was flirting with the clerk.

In truth, Sophie wasn't certain about much of anything this morning. No, that wasn't completely true. She was certain and pleased that so far, the business of Cameron Stables was performing well—better than she had anticipated at this point. The amenities she'd added and the marketing strategy she'd implemented had been correct decisions. The steady number of reservations was promising, and they had just booked their first wedding for a full week in October—a couple from Chicago. If things continued this way, the income generated by the property might be adequate to sustain the business within a couple months and require minimal help from Sophie's personal funds.

But despite the fact that the business was on an upward trajectory, Sophie couldn't shake her sadness over what she had done—deeded away part of her ancestral lands to Zach. Maybe, as her mother said, she had let her anger drive her to act too hastily. No, she had been over the situation many times and was still unable to come up with an alternative plan.

Friday had been the last business day on which Zach could record the deed this week. Sophie had checked the county taxing authority website immediately after she got to the office this morning. There hadn't been any change in the land's description. The records still showed that she and her mother still owned the full acreage. But there was nothing unusual about that. The county government wouldn't have updated the records by today with a transaction that had only been finalized yesterday. But why did she keep checking? She had drawn up the papers herself. It was done. And Zach had probably handed it off to Cal to take care of.

As Sophie worked throughout the day, she kept glancing at her phone. By midafternoon, Zach still hadn't called. He hadn't called yesterday, either. Her plan—hoping he would call so she could ignore him—was a failure. Constantly monitoring her phone while Zach didn't call was turning out to be more punishment for her than for him.

Sophie needed to get out and get some air. She left the office to make the rounds and visit with the staff. She no longer considered Zach's Squad new hires. Beau and Chandler were natural horsemen, and Chandler helped Ben with trail rides and riding lessons. Beau assisted Pete with horse training. Johnny and Troy kept busy with duties around the barn and anything else Tank asked them to do. On her last visit with them, Johnny had asked her how to enroll for online classes this fall at the local community college. He was interested in business administration and finance. Sophie couldn't hide her pleased smile as she instructed him on the process and offered any future assistance he might need.

Sophie spent a few minutes with Tank, then left the barn and stable area and walked to the entrance gate to visit Maggie. Maybe the operation couldn't be characterized as a "well-oiled machine" yet, but everyone was doing their part to keep things running smoothly.

The fresh air had revived Sophie somewhat, but the sadness that had weighed her down all day still hung over her. She had to keep reminding herself that Cameron Stables was no longer indebted to Whittaker & Co. or needed to fear foreclosure—and that was a good thing.

It was almost quitting time for June when Sophie reentered the office. June was sitting on the floor, leafing through a stack of papers on her lap. When June was finished with the day's sorting, only a small portion would remain in the bookcase. Sophie's dad's filing system would soon be history. Looking through the tubs and deciding what to keep and what to shred was a chore Sophie was not looking forward to—and a job for a rainy day when nothing else was happening.

June pitched a paper into the tub marked "Financial," then leaned over and pulled it back out. She turned the sheet of paper over, pressed the folds out with her hand, and read it again.

"Sophie, I think you need to look at this," June said. "It's about your dad's loan with Mr. Whittaker." June placed her unsorted stack on the floor, stood up, and brought the document to Sophie.

"What do we have here?" Sophie asked as she took the paper from June and began to read its contents.

The document was on Whittaker & Co. letterhead, but it was an informal letter from Zach to her father. Sophie's face blanched as she read. Zach advised her father against setting up the interest-only mortgage with a balloon payment due in two years. George's plan to deduct the interest payments from his taxes would not be cost-effective—more trouble than beneficial. Zach strongly advised George not to listen to Bill McClain, his barber, for financial advice, but to find a reputable advisor who could guide him through this rough patch and strengthen the business's finances instead. Zach ended the letter by saying that the money was a gift as thanks for all that George and Jean had done for him.

"Oh God," Sophie moaned. She squinched her eyes tightly together and fell back hard against her chair. "What have I done? Mom warned me. She told me to talk to Zach."

"What? What's wrong?" June asked, coming around the desk to stand beside Sophie.

"I just deeded away part of our land because of some tax scheme cooked up by my father and his buddy Bill. Why would he do such a crazy thing? Why would Zach go along with it? He of all people should have known better."

"Is there anything you can do?" June asked.

"No, not if Zach recorded the deed yesterday. That was the final step."

"You think Mr. Whittaker would record it?" June asked. "He seems like a very nice guy to me."

"I really don't know." Sophie rubbed both hands over her face. "I've been pretty adamant that I won't stop until I pay him back somehow. The deed is signed and is legal. I feel like a fool! He'll never forgive me for accusing him of taking advantage of my father when it was Dad's crazy idea from the start."

Would Zach file the deed? He might, just to shut her up and teach her a lesson. But Zach didn't seem to be vindictive or to go off half-cocked and let anger make him do something he'd regret—something like what she'd done. "I have to show this to my mother. That'll be the hardest part of this whole mess. She might never speak to me again. She told me to stop and think about what I was doing. I didn't listen and now I've made a huge mess of things."

First, she needed to call Zach before another minute went by. She called his number with an apology already forming in her mind. It rang several times before going to voicemail. Sophie hung up without leaving a message. This was something that would take more than a voicemail to fix. Her stomach clenched as she picked up the letter and went in search of her mother.

Sophie met Jean coming across the lawn toward the main house.

"You don't need to go to the entertainment pavilion. I just checked everything there, and it's all in order. Darlene should be coming soon to set up." Jean looked at Sophie's face. "What's wrong?"

"This," Sophie said as she handed the letter to her mother.

Jean took the letter and read it through. Sophie braced herself for the emotional dressing down she deserved, expecting her mother to explode with a barrage of angry accusations. Instead, Jean just shook her head sadly as she looked at Sophie. She didn't say anything. A tongue-lashing would make Sophie feel bad, but this stony silence was even worse.

"Go ahead and say it. You told me so," Sophie said. "I'm so sorry. I don't know how I can make this up to you. Why did Dad listen to Bill McClain?"

"I'm not going to say anything. It's just land. It's the accusation that Zach was trying to steal our property that you should worry about fixing."

"I know. God, I'm such an idiot." Sophie's voice quivered. "Zach was just humoring Dad so he would accept help." Sophie took the letter back from Jean and reread the first paragraph. "I feel awful! I really screwed up."

"You thought you were doing the right thing. George and Bill thought they were right, too. I frequently cautioned George about getting dragged into Bill's schemes, but he wouldn't listen. Not listening seems to run in the family. Did you call Zach?" Jean asked.

"I called, but he didn't pick up. And he hasn't called me since Wednesday."

"Maybe he got tired of calling and having you ignore him," Jean suggested bluntly. She started walking toward the house. Sophie followed. They reached the back porch and sat down.

"I'll apologize to him, Mom. I promise. I won't blame him if he never speaks to me again, much less accept may apology. But

I promise to try."

"I know you will. A lot of your problem is that you've been working too hard trying to save this place—and doing it all by yourself. You went off the deep end because you've stressed yourself out. It's hard to see things clearly when you're already tied into knots with worry. Your father made this mess, but he didn't mean to. And he certainly didn't mean to leave it for you to straighten out. He always had good intentions, even when he was wrong."

"I know, but *I* should have known better and talked to Zach, like you suggested," Sophie insisted, on the verge of tears. "I've completely failed you and the business. I've broken up land that's been in the Cameron family for generations, and I managed to do it in just over four months. What kind of stewardship of Dad's legacy is that?"

"You always did things quickly." Jean reached over and patted Sophie's arm. "'Haste makes waste' was never something you believed in."

"I thought you'd be angrier," Sophie said. "Yell at me! I ignored your advice and warnings."

"Anger at you won't accomplish anything other than make you feel worse. I believe that things usually work out for the best. Maybe something good will come of this." Jean's expression turned thoughtful. "Will you do something for me?"

"Of course. Just name it," Sophie replied. "Whatever you ask. It's the least I can do after what I've done."

"You need a break. Go to bed early this evening and get some rest. You've been working twelve-to-fourteen-hour days, sometimes even longer, for weeks now. You can't keep up this pace much longer. Tomorrow morning, take Rose for a ride up to Mystic Peak. Rachel and I can manage whatever comes up down here. The peak always helps you get your equilibrium back. You need that right now."

◆

A hazy fog swirled around the top of Mystic Hills as Sophie saddled Rose, mounted, and rode out of the stable yard. It was early, just before six a.m. The peaceful silence of the morning would soon be broken by the sounds of the staff arriving as they prepared for another day of completing their assignments around the property.

Sophie angled north, toward the trail leading into Mystic Hills. The trees at the back of the high meadow stood like toy soldiers lined up in formation against the lightening sky. Sophie veered farther west and skirted around the tents so as not to disturb the guests. There wasn't any visible activity in the vicinity of either tent as she passed. The guests were either still asleep or out taking an early-morning hike along the trails.

Sophie had taken Jean's advice and gone to bed early last night. As she sank into her bed, she forced all thoughts of financial statements, marketing strategies, debts, or land deeds from her mind. She soon relaxed, and exhaustion took care of the rest. Her mother was right. She was "worn to a nub," to use one of Grandma Cameron's expressions. She fell asleep shortly after she lay down.

She woke up refreshed, but by her first cup of coffee, memories from the previous day had returned. She needed to speak with Zach, but she dreaded that conversation and the recriminations he would rightly throw at her. Dreading it though she was, she had to apologize for doubting him. She also wanted to hear firsthand about the business deal he'd made with her father. Deal? No, it couldn't be called anything other than a *scheme* cooked up by her father and Bill McClain.

Sophie's mother was angry with her. Zach was angry with her. He might actually hate her for accusing him of tricking her father into losing the property. And worst of all, she was angry with herself for the way she had handled the whole affair. She had never considered herself to be a hothead, but somehow, getting a foreclosure notice from Zach while he knew how hard she was working to save the property had sent her off the edge of sanity.

White-hot fury had griped her when she received the foreclosure notice. She, Sophie Cameron, would show Zach Whittaker that he wasn't the only one who could make tough business decisions. And the thought that Zach would take her family's property after her father had given him a home when he was a homeless teen had infuriated her. On top of her fury was the hurt that Zach hadn't come to her before going forward with the lien on the property.

She could make tough business decisions? Ha! She'd let anger make her decisions, and that wasn't very businesslike at all. Despite knowing that the loan was her father's idea, she stood by the transfer of the one hundred acres to Zach. The deed was done, and she wasn't one to renege on a deal.

Sophie slowed Rose to a walk and entered the trail leading to the peak. The trees thinned as they neared the crest, and the rocky butte of Mystic Peak came into view. Sophie reined Rose to a halt, then sat looking out over the valley for a few minutes. So much had happened recently, it seemed like years since she last sat here.

The only visible change since her last visit was the surveyors' flags on the nearside of the meadow. The line of bright-red flags waved in the breeze, taunting her with a reminder that the fence line might soon be moved toward Mystic Peak. One hundred acres would be carved out and no longer be Cameron land. The visual evidence of what she had done made her stomach clench.

Sophie dismounted and tied Rose's reins to the limb of a nearby scrubby oak tree where Rose could graze on the mounds of green grass under the tree. Sophie found a large flat boulder with a view of the valley and sat down.

"Dad, I've made a colossal mess. Can you forgive me?" Sophie looked up at the blue sky, hoping for an answering sign from her father. Nothing. The only sound was the wind whistling through the tall pine trees. Sophie moaned. "I didn't think so. I can't forgive myself, either."

The other elephant in the room—or on the peak—that needed some thought and that might distract her from her failure as a businesswoman was her friendship with Zach—if their former status as friends could ever be salvaged. Were they only friends? Hadn't they frequently tiptoed around the edges of a romance? Shared kisses in a moonlit garden, a gentle hug here and there, and Zach's voluntary assistance in modernizing Cameron Stables all pointed to *something* between them.

Zach had been nothing but kind and helpful whenever she needed it. Was it like her mother said? Zach stirred feelings within her that she'd never experienced before, and that scared her. Was she afraid of giving someone that much control over her life and her emotions?

From the first day she saw Zach in the meadow, she'd felt more drawn to him than any other man she'd previously known. Her original assumption had been that what she felt was just a natural female reaction to a masculine, good-looking man. She never believed in love at first sight, despite the story her parents told of their first meeting. But she did believe in lust at first sight. And her reaction that day in the meadow was proof that she'd had a very bad case of "lust at first sight."

That she lusted after a good-looking man wasn't the most important issue at hand this morning, but *all* her issues involved that same man. She could handle lust—usually—but

deeding away her family's land to Zach, needlessly, was a different kind of issue. To paraphrase a popular song that played on
the local radio station, her whole life was just one big country
song. Except for the drinking and partying, her adult life pretty much fit the story the song told: fall in love, get your heart
broken, work all day and never get ahead, then make a mess of
your life. Sophie's recent actions demonstrated that she was an
expert when it came to making a mess of her life.

Yep, that song described her life as she saw it this morning.
But had she ever been heartbroken? Really heartbroken? Or in
love? The decision to divorce Robert had been difficult at first.
They were comfortable with each other, and severing ties—even
in a friendship, much less a marriage—was tough. But they
both agreed that divorce was the best option, worked it out like
adults, and ended the relationship as friends. It was all unemo-
tional and very clinical. Had she ever been in love with Robert?
Was true love that easy to get over?

When she'd agreed to marry Robert, she had apparently
confused familiarity—or maybe it was lust—with love. The
marriage made sense at the time because they had the same
career and spent most of their time together. But having careers
in common didn't make the marriage happy because they never
grew beyond that state. Something was always missing.

During their short marriage, Sophie often felt like their
marriage was a second job. She always felt as if she gave more
to the relationship than Robert did. She coddled, appeased, lied
to herself, and tried to squeeze bits of romance into their busy
work life and Robert's sports affixation. Even the familiarity—or
lust—between them wore thin after a while. She understood
that it took effort to keep a marriage strong, but was she selfish
to expect a reward for all her effort at some point?

Sophie psychoanalysis this morning of her failed marriage,
of love and lust, and of what made men and women click was

mostly a distraction from her real problems—Zach and the land deed and if there was anything she could do to fix the mess she'd created.

But seriously, how did one recognize the difference between lust and love? And how would she categorize her attraction to Zach? Was it just lust that would wear off quickly, or did it go deeper than that and was more lasting? Sophie picked a daisy from a clump that grew beside the rock she was sitting on. Idly turning it in her hands, she began a game she had played as a child. As she plucked the petals one by one, she added an adult twist. "Is it love?" One petal fell to the ground. "Is it lust?" Another petal joined the first. She continued repeating the phrases as she stripped more petals from the flower. "Is it love? Is it lust?"

"Great question," a voice said from behind her. "What's the answer?"

Startled, Sophie looked around as Zach slipped from Big Boy's saddle and looped the reins over a bush next to Rose. She had been so caught up in her thoughts and the daisy experiment that she hadn't heard him enter the clearing.

Sophie's stomach tightened with dread. The moment had arrived. She planned to apologize, but she needed more time to prepare her confession. "I was just playing a childhood game." Embarrassed at being caught, she looked away.

"Uh-huh," Zach replied. "That's not exactly the way I remember the game."

"It's the X-rated version." Sophie shrugged. "How did you know I was up here? Or did you not come looking for me?"

"I came looking for you." Zach nodded. "I asked a chipmunk where to find the most stubborn woman in the world, and he pointed me your way."

"Cute! I'm guessing it was my mother who actually told you I was up here."

"Maybe." Zach approached her with his easy, confident stride. He was dressed much the same way he had been the day they first met. The felt Stetson hat had been replaced by a summery Western-style straw hat, but he wore blue jeans, boots, and a similar chambray shirt, its sleeves rolled up on his forearms. Cowboy Zach in uniform! Definitely a lusty sight!

Sophie almost smiled at her thought, but Zach's serious scowl wiped the smile off her face. He wasn't wearing sunglasses, and his eyes glinted with suppressed anger.

She hadn't seen him since he rescued her from the ditch the night of the storm a week ago. The bruise on her forehead had turned a yellow and purplish hue, and her bones no longer hurt when she breathed or moved, but the memory of the muddy water swirling around her remained fresh in her mind, as did her gratitude for his rescue that night.

"What's the answer?" Zach asked again, nodding toward the daisy in her hand. He took off his hat and laid it down on the rock. He stretched out his long legs beside her.

"I didn't finish. I don't think it's very scientific." Sophie tossed the daisy aside, but Zach caught it in midair.

"Let's finish the game. Just a few more petals to go." Zach began pulling off the petals and repeating "Is it love? Is it lust?" until he reached the last petal. "Well, would you look at that? The petal is split right down the middle. We have a winner! It's both love *and* lust!" He twirled the daisy between his fingers, then tossed the yellow center into her lap.

"It's a tie. Yay!" Sophie looked over at him, then sobered. He still wasn't smiling. He wasn't going to make it easy for her to apologize. She didn't blame him. She might as well get it over with. "Zach, I… I want…"

"Why didn't you return my phone calls? Or talk to me?" Zach interrupted. He shifted his position to face her. His dark eyes bore into hers.

"I'm an idiot?" Sophie asked, still trying to lighten the mood. "But I'm smart enough to know I'm an idiot?" She hoped joking would soften the look on his face so they could have a "clear the air" discussion. And she didn't have a better explanation for avoiding him. But he dashed her hopes—he wasn't playing along.

"Hmph," Zach replied, still not smiling.

"I apologize for the mess I've created. I found your letter to my father yesterday—the one explaining the crazy deal he forced on you. But just to be clear, I stand by *my* deal. I made it, and I meant it. You can start moving the fence line whenever you're ready."

"Well, aren't you the gracious, magnanimous benefactress!" Zach's sarcastic comment was laced with anger. "My word that I didn't trick your father wasn't good enough? You think I want your land? Or need your land?"

"I got a foreclosure notice!" Sophie's anger sparked as she reminded him how the controversy started. "The notice informed me that you planned to take all of our land, not just a hundred acres."

"Point taken, but that was a mistake. I've tried to call you several times since Saturday night's storm. I wanted to find out how you were doing but also to explain how this situation got started. I was too busy trying to keep us from drowning on Saturday night to bring it up. And knowing how stubborn you are, you would have jumped out of the truck into a storm to avoid hearing my side."

"I… I'm not that stubborn!"

"You've done nothing over the last few days to prove otherwise," Zach pointed out.

"Well, I've recovered," Sophie assured him. "I got some badly needed rest after my baptism in the muddy ditch. That helped."

"I know. Jean told me you were okay when she brought the deed over." Zach pulled a blade of grass from a clump nearby and began stripping it down to the stem.

"You spoke with my mother? But she said you weren't there when she came over."

"I wasn't. But I returned before she left."

"Hmm. I wonder why she didn't mention that…" Sophie said. She didn't expect Zach to provide an answer, but she did want him to answer her next questions. "Did you file the deed she gave you?"

"I filed it," Zach answered shortly.

Sophie's heart fell, and her hands clenched. What did she expect? She had brought this all on herself. No going back. "I acted without knowing the full story, but since it's done, I accept that. The land is yours."

"Still trying to be the bigger person? Giving away your land because of a half-assed, one-sided deal you made with yourself? You *are* George Cameron's daughter. More stubborn pride than common sense!"

"My father had his faults, but he was an honest person and he took care of his debts." He hadn't taken care of this one, but had he lived, he would have found a way to handle it better than she had.

"He did, but he didn't owe this debt. The money was a gift! For all he had done for me! He was too stubborn to listen to me or accept my help without turning it into a huge complicated fiasco."

"He was stubborn and too proud for his own good," Sophie agreed.

"To answer your question, yes, I filed the deed. I filed it where it belonged: in the office trash bin. You really think so little of me? You think I would take your land? I didn't accept your first attempt—the cashier's check—and I don't want your land." Zach raised his voice, still angry with her. "Even if I intended to file the deed, I couldn't. It wasn't signed by all parties."

"It was. My mother and I are the only owners. She…" A light went on in Sophie's brain. "My mother didn't sign it, did she? Why would she not sign?"

"She forgot. At least, that's what she said when she called to offer to come over and take care of it. But unlike you, she believed me when I said I wasn't interested in taking any payment for anything. The bigger question right now is when are you going to give up this… this…" Zach sputtered as he searched for the words to describe what Sophie was doing. "This ridiculous… crazy… whatever it is you've got going on in your head?"

Sophie sat silently and sucked in a deep breath. She was ashamed that she had let her pride and stubbornness get the best of her. Relief was a mild description of how she felt, knowing he had not filed the deed. Her intentions had been noble, but the thought of how close she had come to breaking up the Cameron land made her feel sick. Zach had helped her dodge a disaster—a disaster of her own making.

"Don't push me off this cliff, but you've been acting like a crazy woman." Zach broke the silence. He nodded to the steep drop in front of them.

"I was furious with you and apparently lost all sense of reason. When I thought someone had the rights to Cameron Stables, I couldn't think of anything other than that I had to fix it. I kept thinking of my dad's name being forever linked to losing Cameron property. He didn't deserve that, and I wanted to do everything I could to prevent it from happening."

"I understand that, but you were breaking up the property anyway by deeding a part of it to me."

"Yeah, well… I did say I lost all reason. I didn't think that part through. My mother didn't sign the deed, so officially, it's as though the transaction never happened."

Zach placed both hands on Sophie's shoulders and turned her to face him. He shook her gently. "Listen to me." His hands were gentle, but his eyes shot black darts. "I wouldn't have filed the deed if every citizen in Kingsville had signed it and notarized it twice. George was like a father to me. Even though we didn't see each other after I left, we kept in touch. Aside from him accepting bad business advice from Bill the barber over my advice, we had a good relationship. He guided me through some very difficult years. Give this up, Sophie."

"I know. I apologize for everything." Sophie placed her hands over Zach's, which still rested on her shoulders. "I'm sorry for this whole mess. You've been extremely helpful to me with finding staff, creating the apps, and everything. I'm grateful for all you've done. I want to put this behind us and be good neighbors."

Zach grimaced. "The Petersons, who live on the east side of my property, are good neighbors. You don't see me hanging around their place, helping Mrs. Peterson staff their farm, do you?"

"Mrs. Peterson has a husband," Sophie pointed out. "He might object."

"Exactly. Which brings me to the next point we need to discuss. Unless I've read the situation wrong, we've been avoiding this issue since the day we met in the meadow down there," Zach said, pointing to the place where they had first met. "I felt something, even after you insulted me and called me 'Cowboy, the hired hand.'"

"Trust me, insulting you was not my intention."

"I know. I recognized where your mind was that day."

"No, I was…" Sophie started to deny his implication, but she was unable to refute it and gave up.

"Never mind. Back to my point. I'm talking about us. You and me."

"You and me? You mean us, as in boyfriend and girlfriend?" Sophie teased, even as her heart rate kicked up a notch.

"No," Zach said. "Not 'boyfriend and girlfriend,' though that was my original dream when I was seventeen and worked for your father. That's no longer my dream."

"Uh… you didn't even know me when you were seventeen," Sophie ventured. "Did you?"

"Not in the way I wanted to. I mooned over you from afar. In my mind, you were a brave, free-spirited girl. I've come to realize since that you were just stubborn, even back then." A slight smile touched Zach's lips before he went on. "I used to watch you race across the meadow like Annie Oakley, your long hair a fiery blaze whipping in the breeze. Many possibilities—some X-rated—came into my young mind. Why do you think this city kid from Chicago worked so hard to become a good rider? My teenage fantasy was to gallop alongside you."

"You did? We'd ride off into the sunset? Very romantic, Cowboy!" The picture Zach painted of a lovesick young man having romantic fantasies about her made Sophie wish she had known teenage Zach.

"I realize now that it was more a teenager's unrealistic dream amplified by raging hormones than romantic." Zach pushed a stray lock of Sophie's hair behind her ears. His fingers lingered on her cheek. Then, he dropped his hand and added with a smile, "At the time, I'd have ridden off into the sunset or gone wherever you wanted to go. But even I knew that wasn't going to happen, so maybe my dreams were merely a longing for the unattainable. Your father wasn't about to let me near you."

"I don't know what to say. I didn't even realize that he kept you away from me." Sophie had been too busy worrying about her grades and the drama of high school cliques to notice any of her father's hired help. Was she "the girl" he had mentioned, the one he still thought about over the years? "Why didn't you come back before now if I left such a huge impression on you?" That sounded conceited, even to her. She amended, "I mean, if you wanted to get to know me better?"

"Life got in the way. I started my business. I also learned to rein in my hormones and to have more realistic dreams. And then, George told me you had married Robert."

"Another rash decision of mine that I came to regret. I'm sure you had plenty of other women willing to help you *manage* your hormones over the years, though." The words slipped out before Sophie realized what she was really asking. She looked away, but not before she saw Zach's eyes crinkle with laughter.

"Is that your way of asking if I had any serious relationships over the past fifteen years?" Zach placed his fingers beneath her chin and turned her to face him. "I wasn't a recluse, if that's what you're asking. I had relationships, a few casual, a few semi-serious, but we always parted ways for one reason or another. None seemed exactly right."

"So, there's no one waiting for you in California now?" Sophie was still having a hard time believing that he wasn't seeing someone. Zach was a handsome man, rich and successful. He could have almost anyone he chose, and California was full of beautiful women. She also had a hard time believing that his infatuation with fourteen-year-old geeky Sophie still lingered after all these years.

"I broke off my last relationship over a year ago," Zach replied as he drew back, offended. "You assume I'd flirt with you while having someone waiting in California?" He then added, "But you're known for your assumptions, aren't you?"

"Very funny! So, you are flirting with me now?" Sophie asked, getting him back on topic. She stopped herself from adding, "Tell me more."

"Don't get so full of yourself. No, I'm not flirting with you."

"Oh!" Sophie's bubble burst like a balloon blown against a spike.

"I'm not flirting. I'm serious," Zach continued. "I'm talking about *us*, about seeing where this goes. I'm talking about commitment, building a life together, having a family, pledging to love each other forever. That kind of *us*."

"Oh! Is Cowboy using sweet talk to get my land?" The moment the words left her mouth, Sophie knew they were a mistake. Her attempt at a joke to hide the warm glow that washed over her at the meaning of Zach's words fell flat.

"Let's be clear!" Zach's voice rose again. He was becoming annoyed by her teasing and her not taking him seriously. "If I've misread what's been happening between us over the last few months and you want me to leave, forget this… us… then I will. I will walk away and never contact you again," Zach said as he pulled her close and bent down until his face was only inches from hers. His breath whispered across her cheeks.

"No, please! I was kidding. I don't want you to go." Sophie was horrified at the thought of never seeing him again. The last few days, during their disagreement, had been like torture to her. She leaned back so she could see his face clearly. She placed her hands on the sides of his face, no longer teasing him. "I'm sorry. And you haven't misread anything. What I want right now more than anything is for you to kiss me."

"I can do that," Zach whispered. "But this time, no kissing and running, remember?"

At Sophie's nod, Zach threaded his arms around her waist and pulled her against him. He kissed her gently at first, then with the passion that had been building between them since they first met. Sophie sank into Zach's kiss, returning his kiss with a passion that matched his own.

Zach's kiss and her melting response to it answered her question of whether she had ever been in love before. No, she hadn't—not the true "take your breath away" kind of love. No more wondering about her feelings for Zach. What may have been just attraction in the meadow, had built and grown deeper with each passing day as she had gotten to know him over the last few months. She was totally and deeply in love with Zach, and confident that he felt the same way about her. He was here, still declaring his love for her, even after her crazy actions over the last few days.

"See? Love *and* lust," Zach said when they broke apart. "The daisy game was right."

"A powerful combination. Love and lust—as mysterious as the fairy fire in the woods behind us," Sophie replied. Then, she bent her head and nestled it beneath his chin. She could hear his heartbeat against her ear. She sighed contentedly.

Sophie's route to this point where she could acknowledge her love for Zach was as circuitous as Zach's fifteen-year journey back to her, Mystic Hills, and Cameron Stables. The difference was that Zach always had a destination in mind, while she kept floundering around, searching for something, without really knowing what it was.

It had taken a bang on the head, almost drowning in a muddy ditch, coming close to deeding away a piece of her heritage, and pushing away someone who was extremely important to her to make her question what she wanted from the future. But the final wake-up call had been Zach's threat to walk away and leave her. Losing him was something she couldn't contemplate, much less accept.

The Cameron legacy and Mystic Hills were safe for now. Sophie would continue to work and improve on her father's dream by building a thriving, peaceful retreat for visitors. But her horizons had broadened now. She had a new goal: loving Zach with all her being and creating a new lasting legacy of their own—the Sophie and Zach Whittaker legacy.

And one thing she knew with certainty—loving Zach would never feel like a job.